Egotistical Puckboy

Also by Eden Finley and Saxon James

Puckboys

Egotistical Puckboy
Irresponsible Puckboy
Shameless Puckboy
Foolish Puckboy
Clueless Puckboy
Bromantic Puckboy
Forbidden Puckboy
Possessive Puckboy
Stubborn Puckboy

EGOTISTICAL PUCKBOY

EDEN FINLEY & SAXON JAMES

canelo

First published in the United Kingdom in 2022 by Absolute Books

This edition published in the United Kingdom in 2026 by

Canelo, an imprint of
Canelo Digital Publishing Limited,
20 Vauxhall Bridge Road,
London SW1V 2SA
United Kingdom

A Penguin Random House Company
The authorised representative in the EEA is Dorling Kindersley Verlag GmbH.
Arnulfstr. 124, 80636 Munich, Germany

Copyright © Eden Finley and Saxon James 2022

The moral right of Eden Finley and Saxon James to be identified as the creator of this work has been asserted in accordance with the Copyright, Designs and Patents Act, 1988.
All rights reserved. No part of this publication may be reproduced or transmitted in any form or by any means, electronic or mechanical, including photocopy, recording, or any information storage and retrieval system, without permission in writing from the publisher.
No part of this book may be used or reproduced in any manner for the purpose of training artificial intelligence technologies or systems. In accordance with Article 4(3) of the DSM Directive 2019/790, Canelo expressly reserves this work from the text and data mining exception.

A CIP catalogue record for this book is available from the British Library.

ISBN 978 1 83598 485 7

This book is a work of fiction. Names, characters, businesses, organizations, places and events are either the product of the author's imagination or are used fictitiously. Any resemblance to actual persons, living or dead, events or locales is entirely coincidental.

Printed and bound in Great Britain by Clays Ltd, Elcograf S.p.A.

Look for more great books at
www.canelo.co | www.dk.com

This series is about the PR Nightmares of the NHL. These characters are flawed on purpose. Please don't expect perfection because it does not exist here. They're hockey players. The only guarantee is missing teeth.

The use of the NHL and any of its teams is a work of fiction. It in no way reflects the policies or opinions of the actual organization.

Names, characters, businesses, places, events, and incidents are either the products of the authors' imaginations or used in a fictitious manner. Any resemblance to actual persons, living or dead, or actual events is purely coincidental.

CHAPTER ONE

EZRA

Your lifelong dream disappearing in front of your eyes isn't supposed to happen so quickly. Three twenty-minute periods have never felt so short.

It's game seven of what has been the longest series in history, because we've gone into overtime in every single game. Except this one. Because in the last few minutes of the third, there is absolutely no coming back from this disaster.

Philly might have the home advantage, but there's no excuse for this shitshow. 6-1. *Six* to *one*. This is what it looks like when a team crumbles under pressure and loses their chance at even trying for the Cup.

Literal blood and sweat have been put into this season, and I'm about to add tears as well. Because as I watch Anton Hayes power toward me with a knowing *I win* smirk on his lips, it takes all my strength to only check him instead of doing what I really want to do, which is body slam him into the ice. What's a five-minute major penalty and a twenty-thousand-dollar fine in the big scheme of things?

But I don't. Because I'm professional and not a sore loser, and this game is already over.

Which is how we let another goal in before the final buzzer.

Fuckdamnit.

Okay, maybe I'm a bit of a sore loser.

Anton Hayes. What a walking douchecanoe.

I have no problem with ego. Hell, I probably rival every single guy for the crown of biggest ego in the NHL. But Hayes adds a whole new level of meaning to the word.

And coming from me, Mr. Egotistical Fuckboy, that says a lot.

Yet, people don't see him for the asshole he really is.

Like right now, while we do the ceremonial shaking of hands after the game and he gets to me, there's something condescending in the way he says "Good game." It's in his cocky smile, the one that calls me a "Loser" without him actually saying the word out loud.

I don't give him the satisfaction of a response. He's probably getting enough happiness from the smell of defeat that's hanging around our team. It smells a lot like old gym socks and jockstraps.

Also, there's no doubt in my mind that the cameras are on the two of us. Hayes and I have come head-to-head so many times on the ice I've lost count. Therefore, according to the media, we hate each other. People are told not to believe everything they read, but in this case, they should. Because it's absolutely true.

In the locker room, our coaches don't even bother with the "We'll get 'em next season" speech. It's the end of our year, and we're in mourning.

"You gonna shave that mess off your face now?" Diedrich nods toward my playoff beard, which is nowhere near as bad as some of the other players'.

"Dunno. Guys love it." I run my hand over the coarse hair on my chin, and it's all wet from perspiration. Yeah, I'm going to have to at least trim it. "They like it when it scrapes along their—"

Diedrich holds up his hand. "Got it."

The guys are cool with me being an out and proud player but get all weirded out when I go into details. Granted, I probably overshare way more than I should, but when I pointed out I had to listen to them talk about their hookups with puck bunnies, suddenly the entire team became stand-up dudes who speak respectfully about women in locker rooms.

Funny how that works.

Apparently, the cure to toxic masculinity is to show them how it feels to be talked about like a piece of meat.

You're welcome, ladies.

The team ends up going to a bar in South Philadelphia to drown our sorrows, but we're all so depressed it doesn't take long for us to split up. Some guys go to another bar, others make their way into the back where there are pool tables, but I choose to perch my ass on a barstool and order drink after drink until the loss doesn't sting anymore.

There might not be enough alcohol in the world to make that happen.

Two more series and the Cup would've been ours. So close yet so far.

Wagner, one of my teammates, slaps me on the shoulder. "We're heading out. You wanna come?"

I wave him off. "Insert innuendo about coming here."

"Damn, dude. How much have you had to drink? It has to be bad when you're getting lazy on the cum jokes."

"I'm not *that* drunk." I am that drunk.

"Hey, look at it this way. You're still a baby. For old fucks like me, we haven't got long left."

He says that like he's forty when he's a whopping thirty-four. That's what this career is like. You're considered old when regular people your age are in their prime.

I wouldn't consider myself a baby. At twenty-seven, I've been in the NHL for four seasons now. I grew up through the juniors and moved to the AHL after being drafted, so I've been playing my whole life, but the average career in hockey is five years. *Five*. Just ask my father—that's how long he lasted.

So this year, when he calls me tomorrow to tell me how much I fucked up on the ice tonight, my usual positive mantra of "There's always next year" will be even emptier than usual. Because what if there isn't a next year?

I need to drink more. Or less. One or the other. My thoughts are going to dark places.

"Need me to call you a ride back to the hotel?" Wagner asks.

"Nah. 'S'all good."

Maybe I should search gay bars in the area and go fuck all this depression out. Because drowning myself in sex is the mature and logical response.

I know I've been to a couple in this city before, but I can't remember them now. Or their names.

I half stand, half fall off my stool and throw some cash down on the bar for a tip. Then I move on wobbly legs and fumble my way out to the street.

The words on my phone are blurry as I type in *gay bar Philadelphia*, and when it turns up with weird-ass results, I blink into focus what I actually wrote.

Gay butt Philly cheese.

I'll bookmark that for later.

My second attempt works, and I find there's one only two blocks away. I could walk it. Uh, slowly. Because my feet don't want to cooperate.

If I'd known I'd have to walk past a sports bar, I would have Ubered somewhere else.

I'm too busy glaring up at all the orange and black that paints the building and listening to the rowdy celebratory crowd to watch where I'm going, when—

"*Oof.*"

Ouch, whatever wall I ran into hurts. Doesn't help I'm bruised from how many hits I took tonight. Okay, and gave.

Then I come face-to-face with said wall and find my worst nightmare. Philly fans.

Three of them. Tall as they are wide.

"No wonder you guys lost tonight when you hit like that, Palaszczuk."

Hey, it's not my fault his chest is twice the size of mine and I practically bounced off him. I ain't no delicate wallflower.

I have two options here. Keep walking or talk back.

My mind scoffs at me. Please, I'm Ezra-fucking-Palaszczuk. I don't know the meaning of walking away from a fight. "The other team was lucky."

"7-1 lucky?" one of his friends snickers.

"Boston sucks," the other one says.

"Fuck you." I try to push my way through them, but the bigger guy in front shoves me.

I'm drunk as shit and stumble, almost falling to the ground. I manage to right myself and charge toward this asshole to show him what it's like to take a hit from a professional hockey player.

My fist connects with his jaw with a satisfying crack, but then his two friends are on me, and all hell breaks loose.

I'm trying to wrench myself away when I'm jerked backward and a body moves in front of me, blocking me from getting my head punched in. Or worse, my pretty face. I swear I'm one broken nose away from being … unattractive. That would be a travesty for all gaykind.

Turns out I was wrong. Philly fans are not my worst nightmare. Being protected from them by Anton Hayes is.

"Hey, guys, back up a bit, okay? Palaszczuk is drunk and doesn't know what he's doing. It's not much different to when he's sober, really, but it's plain mean to pick on him when he's like this. It would be like stealing a kid's ice cream and then shoving it in their face."

Suddenly, they're all wide eyes and sweet smiles. Oh, and laughing. Can't forget the laughing.

"Anton Hayes? Is this really happening?" This big bear of a man turns into a puddle of fanboying.

"Here, let me sign your jersey," Hayes says.

"Oh, please," I mutter behind his back.

He looks over his shoulder at me, and I don't like the smug expression.

For a hockey player, he has the straightest teeth of anyone in the league. His dark hair is styled with gel, parted on the side like a preacher boy, and it looks nothing like it does on the ice when he takes his helmet off. It usually falls in his face and around his neck in wet strands.

If there's anything I hate more than Anton Hayes, it's how good-looking he is.

He signs each of their jerseys with a pen he pulls from God knows where—not even I'm egotistical enough to carry a Sharpie—and then Anton tells them there's a few more guys from the team inside and gets the bouncer's attention to let in his new friends.

"Let them know I sent you to annoy them. They'll love it."

With them thoroughly distracted, I make my escape. Or, I try to.

Anton catches up with me. "Where are you rushing off to? Another bar fight on the schedule?"

I shove my hands into my pockets and keep walking. "Is it really a bar fight when it was outside the bar?"

"What happened anyway?" His low voice always sounds so cocky and patronizing. "I only caught the tail end. You know, where you clocked one of them."

"Nothin'."

"Was it the gay thing?"

I gasp. "Yes. Because anytime I get into a fight, it's because my masculinity is threatened by homophobic twatfaces."

"Then what was it? The game? You let fans get to you over a goddamn game?"

"If you'd lost tonight, how would you take it?"

"Grow up, man. We've all lost games before. We've all been kicked out of the playoffs. Well, you know, except Buffalo, who haven't seen the playoffs in over a decade."

I laugh and then hate myself for it.

"Where are you going?" Hayes asks.

"Gay bar. Because of all my gayness that's gay, and that's all I'm known for. Apparently."

"Really? So because I assumed guys were attacking you over your orientation, you think that's my only impression of you?"

"If the skate fits."

Anton stops walking. "Seriously, Ezra. Why are you always such an asshole?"

I spin to face him. "Why are *you* always such an asshole?"

"You know, when most people save someone from getting their ass kicked, they get a thank-you."

"That's why you hate me? Because of my manners? Well, thank you, Mr. Straight, for stepping in to save my gay honor when I didn't ask you to."

Anton takes two steps back. "Wait, you think I'm straight?"

I blink. Then blink again. How drunk am I? Did I hear him right, or is my mind playing tricks on me? "Y-you're not? How did I not know this, and why haven't we had sex yet if that's the case?"

He stares at me like he's trying to figure out if I'm serious. "Holy shit, you really are that conceited. Maybe we haven't had sex because I don't want my sexuality splashed all over the tabloids. Unlike some people, my focus is and always has been hockey."

"Oh, so you're closeted. But why? It's not like we're the only ones anymore. Ollie Strömberg, Westly Dalton, Tripp Mitchell, Foster Grant, Oskar—"

"You think I haven't seen what you guys go through? The comments. The online hate. If people are going to hate me, I'd rather it be for my playing than who I have sex with. And I'm not closeted ... not exactly. My team knows. My family. The important people. But I don't want toxic people like those assholes back there to think they have a right to attack me for who I am."

I take it back. The third worst thing is being cornered by Philly fans. Second worst thing is being saved by someone I hate. But the worst thing by far is realizing that for years I've thought the tension between Anton and me came from a place of resentment. It turns out it's because I want to fuck Anton Hayes.

I did not see that coming.

CHAPTER TWO

ANTON

I consider myself to be a levelheaded guy. I'm a fair player, I work my heart out, I'd do anything for my family ... but there's something about Ezra Palaszczuk that digs under my skin and sets all rational thought on fire.

That confrontation could have been so much worse than it was. If it had turned into a fight, you can bet it would have been hot news by morning. Like I told Ezra, my focus is hockey, and that's all I want to be known for.

But I stepped in to help him without a thought.

Ezra sways, looking from one side of the street to the other. Those piercing blue eyes are heavy-lidded and unfocused. "Which way was I going?"

"Why?"

"Because I need to get my gay on." He stumbles a few steps, changes his mind, and then swings in the other direction. Only he overshoots and somehow ends up walking into me.

How the hell is this guy one of the kings of hockey?

I help right him, but he presses harder against me.

"We should fuck."

"I'm going to remind you of those words every chance I get." I pry him off me. "You're a mess. In what world would I be interested in someone who smells like a brewery and has the coordination of a two-year-old?"

"Of course. You're perfect Anton Hayes, you have *standards*, and playoffs, and a hockey stick rammed right up your—"

"You know, I have *no idea* why those men wanted to hit you."

"Jus po direct da cay blub."

"Was that English or Polish?"

"Cay Glub. Club Gay. Gay. Which way?" He flexes his jaw. "Why won't my mouth work right?"

This is what I get for interfering. An Ezra so far past drunk that even *my* conscience won't let me leave him here.

Sighing, I grab his arm and yank him toward the road just in time to flag down a taxi.

"Ohh, someone wants to bow chicka wow wow."

"Always, but not with you." I shove him in the back of the cab as soon as the door is open. "And your beard looks ridiculous, by the way."

He drops his head back and closes his eyes. "You're such a fuckface."

"Uh-huh."

"And you have two left skates. Goddamn pigeon."

"The hat trick I got tonight says otherwise," I say. "What score did Boston end up on again?"

"Fuck off."

"That's what I thought." I give the driver my address, and he pulls into traffic. "You play the role of a petulant child so well."

"And you play the peten-pretentious asshole. That's you." He hiccups. "Take me to the hotel."

"I'm not going anywhere near your team. I have a spare room. You can sleep off the alcohol and leave in the morning."

On the way home, I ask the driver to take us through the drive-thru to get Ezra food and water to help soak up the alcohol. He swears at me some more before tearing into his burger like he hasn't eaten in weeks.

I'd say it's the alcohol making Ezra act this way, but I'm pretty sure it's just him. We don't see each other often—thank fuck—but whenever we do, it reinforces why I choose to keep things private. Ezra makes it his mission to be as loud and obnoxious as possible, making sure everyone remembers he sleeps around with men, runs his mouth, and happens to have talent on the ice that is completely overshadowed by how annoying he is.

Every time he opens his mouth, I want to forcefully close it again. Zip his lips shut, or … the image of Ezra gagged and on his knees flashes through my mind, and I hate how much I like it.

If I was into that kind of thing, I'd almost consider taking Ezra up on his offer.

Almost.

Even gagged he'd still be … *him*. Entitled, eccentric, and egotistical. The three *E*s that make Ezra who he is.

We pull up to my condo in Rittenhouse Square, and I help Ezra from the car. It's in an older building, right on the park, but the whole penthouse has been redesigned. I fell in love as soon as I saw the space.

Thankfully Ezra's less sloppy, but I still try not to draw attention to us as we pass security. Chester, the concierge, congratulates me on a good game, and I thank him before stuffing Ezra into my private elevator.

"This is fancy," he taunts.

"You can talk. I've seen photos of your place. Anyone would think you're compensating for something."

"Screw you. I have a massive dick."

"Funny your thoughts went there when I was talking about your hockey skill." The thing is, Ezra actually *is* a great player. He's focused and talented, and whenever we go up against Boston, I know it's going to be a good game—well, except for tonight. But Ezra's behavior off the ice ruins every good thing he does on it.

He's wasting time drawing attention to his personal life, and seeing him splashed all over trashy sites online always grates on my nerves.

A therapist would say that I'm projecting all my internalized homophobia at the out and proud poster boy for gay pride, but it's not that.

It's that he makes it a point to be so … out. I might be gay, but that's not my whole identity. I don't want to let it overshadow the other things that make me *me*. I'm a hockey player, son … I give back to the community. I use my privilege to help others.

I don't want to come out to the world and be reduced to Anton Hayes, gay hockey player. And when I look at Ezra, that's all I see. He's perpetuating the image I want to avoid.

It's infuriating. And a little intimidating.

The elevator opens into my foyer, which leads to the vast living area. The skyline is brightly lit through the wall of glass overlooking the park, and I direct Ezra to the couch while I go in hunt of more water and some painkillers. When I return, he's slumped down in an armchair, jacket off, tie loose, and staring at the wood-paneled ceiling. He clearly hasn't touched his light brown hair since his shower tonight because it's all fluffy on top of his head.

"Here." I hand over the glass and pills.

"Why are you being nice to me?" he asks as he reluctantly swallows the drugs.

"This isn't nice. It's responsible."

His laugh is hollow. "Responsible. Right. Of course. What a fun quality to have."

"Better than being all fun and no substance." I should have dumped him outside his hotel, but I had no guarantees he'd make his way inside, and the last thing I want is for someone to see me going into his hotel room. Wherever he goes, gossip follows, and it'd be my luck that someone would see us together and assume we were sleeping together.

I eye Ezra, from his unfortunately gorgeous face half hidden behind that messy beard to his long, muscled legs. It's easy to see why he gets so much dick. I'm guessing there's not much conversation during his hookups because the moment he opens his mouth, it's an instant boner killer.

Ezra glances around the room. "Tell me again how you don't have a stick up your ass."

Just like that.

"How is it possible you're even more annoying off the ice?" I ask.

"Pure talent." He stretches his arms high over his head, and my attention immediately goes to his biceps. "Now you're done playing savior, want to show me where I'm sleeping?"

"It kills you, doesn't it? That I was the one to step in."

Ezra doesn't even try to deny it. "You wouldn't have been my first choice, that's for sure."

"Maybe if you had actual friends in the league, you would have had more choices."

"Fuck you." There's no venom behind his words. "I have plenty of friends."

"Teammates don't count. And since West disappeared, you're on your own a lot."

I know I'm poking at a sore spot. Ezra loves to give the illusion he's a party animal, but since Westly Dalton retired, he's lost his partner in crime.

"I don't need West."

"No, Ezra Palaszczuk doesn't need anyone."

"Whatever you're trying to say, just say it. You're a whole lot less amusing now I'm sobering up."

"Believe it or not, I'm not here for your amusement."

He pushes suddenly to his feet. "Why are you here, then? I didn't ask for it."

"What would have happened if I wasn't there tonight?"

"A punch to the face, then I would have ended up at the club I was headed to so I could get my dick wet."

"Is that all you care about?"

"Yes." He pretends to look me over. "Maybe if you did it more often, you wouldn't be so uptight."

A growl starts to build in my chest. "Just because I don't jump everything that moves, doesn't mean I'm uptight."

"You need to get laid."

"Unlike you, I can think with more than my dick."

"So can I, but my dick happens to be incredibly convincing." He cups his groin. "We haven't had a disagreement yet."

"Except for when you rubbed it up against me earlier."

"And still not even then. I'd totally sleep with a cocky asshole like you."

That throws me. I'd fully expected Ezra to deny it happened, not confirm that he'd go there. Given his track record, it shouldn't be a surprise considering he doesn't seem to care who he's with as long as he makes some stupid sports tabloid. "Let's be clear here. You're saying you'd let me fuck you."

"Why do you get to do the fucking?"

"Because there's no way in hell I'd bend over for you."

Ezra shrugs like he doesn't have a single shit to give. "You're literally my only option here."

"Actually, your other option is to go to bed and not sleep with anyone."

"So you're saying it *is* an option? Bullshit. There's no way you would." He steps closer, eyes issuing a challenge. "I'm not up to your standards."

"At least we both know it." I want to deny it. I want to tell Ezra to go to bed and be gone in the morning before I wake up. But it *has* been a while since I hooked up. That has to be the only reason I'm considering this. Sure, Ezra is hot, but I've turned down hotter guys who had terrible personalities.

"You'd never slum it with someone like me," he says.

"Never."

"I bet you're all missionary, aren't you?" He pitches his voice high. "Oh, excuse me, sir, would you mind if I used your buttocks to put my penis inside—"

"I've never said the word *buttocks* in my life—"

"Until now. I'm a great influence. A great lay too."

"I'll have to take your word for it."

"Just as well." He turns and heads for the hall. I'm assuming he thinks he's headed toward the bedrooms. He isn't. "You wouldn't be able to keep up with me."

"Like I couldn't on the ice tonight?" My feet follow him. "Oh, that's right, I kicked your ass."

"This ass?" He grabs it.

My gaze drops immediately, taking in the way the tight suit pants hug his perky cheeks. My cock twitches. Damn Ezra for having a sexy butt.

Still, I'm not ready to admit it. "You have more than one?"

"You're staring at it, aren't you?"

"Glaring. In the general vicinity of your back."

"I bet it's turning you on."

My cock agrees with him. "Impossible. You're still talking."

"I can stop if you like. Keep quiet and bend over ..." He tilts his head like he's thinking about it, which of course makes *me* think about it. "I've changed my mind. I can imagine you getting me into bed and emulating a dying fish. Flopping around all uncoordinated ..."

Pounding into him ...

"That's why you don't hook up, isn't it? You're embarrassed."

My fingers twisting through his rumpled hair ...

"I bet you're a ten-second man."

Making him groan ...

"Don't worry, it's *totally* normal. There are drugs for—*oomph*!"

I shove him into the wall and crowd up behind him. "Keep talking. I dare you."

He shivers at my voice in his ear but doesn't stay quiet. "That sounds like a challenge."

"No challenge. You've *never* been a challenge." One of my hands twists through his hair to yank his head back, while the other reaches for his belt. "Do you really want me to fuck you?"

Ezra pushes back with his hips. "Yes. Hell yes."

"Even knowing that every time I see you, I'll remind you of this? That it was me who tore you apart and made you come. I won't say a word …" As soon as his belt is free, I yank down his zipper and push his pants to his thighs. Then I reach into his briefs and pull out his cock. "I'll *look* at you and you'll know."

"I don't care. Just do it already."

I start to stroke him, and Ezra lets out a strangled gasp. His cock is one thick handful, and I almost regret not getting to suck him off, but I know what I want. I'm going to fuck Ezra stupid and shut him up once and for all.

"Hands on the wall."

"Make me." He grinds his ass back into my cock, making it throb.

With a grunt, I let him go and shove his chest flat into the wall. I press up against him as I reach for my wallet and retrieve the lube and condom I have stashed in there. I undo my pants, quickly tear the condom open and roll it down my aching shaft, and then open the lube and dribble it into his crack.

My fingers follow the lube until I'm rubbing his hole. "Beg for my cock."

"Never."

I push the tip of my forefinger inside him. "Beg me."

"Fuck off." He shudders as I work the rest of my finger inside him, and it doesn't take long until he's grinding back to meet each stroke.

I'm deliberately slow and shallow, even when I add another finger, and I can tell by the way Ezra pushes back that he's getting frustrated.

"I can give you what you want," I say into his ear. I'm about a breath away from taking him anyway. "All you have to do is either beg me or put your hands on the goddamn wall."

Even on the ice, I've never seen him move so fast. His hands hit the wall above his head, curving his back and making his ass stick out deliciously. Once I'm sure he's stretched enough, I pull back to look at him.

He glances back over his shoulder, and his stare immediately drops to my covered dick. "I'm on PrEP. You don't need a condom—"

My chuckle is low and deep. "Yeah, that's never going to happen. I don't go bare with hookups." I step closer and grab my dick, running it down between his ass cheeks. "Last chance to chicken out."

"You wish."

He's barely got the words out before I'm pushing inside. God, he's so tight and hot, and I watch every second it takes me to slide in and bottom out.

I take a moment to control myself, because I'm going to follow through. I'm going to make him come first.

"What was it you called me? A ten-second man?" I pull back and slam inside him.

Ezra groans. "Still haven't proved me wrong yet, have you?"

That's what he wants? Then that's what he'll get.

I grab his hips and then pull back until I'm almost the whole way out before pounding back into him. The first thrust almost sends him face-first into the wall, and he scrambles to adjust his hold before it happens again.

I'm not careful. I don't give him time to catch his breath.

I start fucking him with purpose, using him, taking years' worth of anger out on his ass. Ezra has always rubbed me the wrong way, and now, for the first time ever, he's finally rubbing me exactly the way I need.

"Listen to you," I gasp as I pound into him. "You love it, don't you?"

"Being fucked? Who doesn't?"

I almost laugh. "Wait until tomorrow. When your cock has settled down and you remember it was me. When the realization sets in that you were owned by Anton Hayes." *Nrg*. That makes me so hot, I'm closer to the edge than I realized.

"What about you?" He's breathless, pushing back to meet me. "When you remember how easily you gave in. How easily I played you."

His gravelly voice goes straight to my balls. I want him to both shut up and keep talking, but I'm determined not to let him have the last word.

I bite his ear until he cries out. "I want this moment burned into your brain. And when I lift that Stanley Cup into the air this year, *this* will be the moment it reminds you of."

Then I straighten, press his face to the wall, grab his cock with the other hand, and let loose. Every thrust forces his cock to slide through my fist. Forces my balls to smack against his ass. I'm grunting, sweaty. The sounds coming from him are filthy and sexy, and the raw smell of sex is turning me on, pushing me higher.

I watch as my dick slides in and out, disappearing and reappearing so quickly it's almost a blur. Either that or my vision is already going wonky. My hand tightens in his hair. Holding him in place. Keeping him at my mercy.

Ezra.

Pinned.

Controlled.

By me.

Fuck, I'm close.

So close.

I jerk him faster than I'd be able to if I wasn't determined to send him over the edge first.

Just a bit more …

A bit more …

Ezra gasps, and his ass clenches tight. The second his cum hits my hand, I let go. My orgasm crashes over me, and I fuck him through it, unable to stop if I tried. By the time I finally slow, finally start to get blood pumping back to my brain, I'm breathing hard and Ezra is slumped against the wall. I want to drop down against him and catch my breath, but instead, I force myself to pull out.

We're both gasping hard, and when he turns to lean back against the wall, I avoid his gaze.

I quickly tuck myself away, condom and all, as the awkwardness starts to kick in.

"The spare rooms are over there." I point. "Clean up before bed. I don't want cum in my sheets."

Then I stalk away to my bedroom. As soon as I have the door closed between me and Ezra, I turn and slump against it.

Reality kicks in way too soon.

I wait for the regret to follow, but oddly, it doesn't come.

All I can focus on is remembering the sound of Ezra's deep moans, the muscles in his ass, the way the shadows played over the side of his face, parted lips visible behind that filthy beard.

A smile starts to build as I realize I beat his ass twice tonight.

CHAPTER THREE

EZRA

There are a couple of things I'm grateful for when waking with the world's worst hangover. One, Anton doesn't wake when I slip out of bed and sneak out of his penthouse with an ache in my ass. Two, my fight with some random Philly fans wasn't secretly filmed and leaked to the press—thank the hockey gods for that. But thirdly, and this is probably the thing I'm most grateful for, I can blame being drunk off my tits for having the impression that sex with Anton Hayes is the best dicking out I've ever had in my life.

The alcohol made it good. It has nothing to do with his skill or magnificent cock.

To try to forget my indiscretions, and with the season being over, I deal with the usual end-of-season crap with the team and then run away to Vermont to hang out with my best friend for a while.

Westly Dalton used to be in the NHL. Used to be my ride or die. *Used to* be being the key word. We're still tight, but after he retired, we see less and less of each other.

Once I wear out my welcome there with him and his huge family of five kids, I go on vacation with some of the guys, and I finish off my summer visiting family in Poland with Dad. My father goes back to Poland regularly, but

I only make the trip maybe once every couple of years when he guilts me into going to see his mom and sisters and all my relatives who speak to me in Polish even though I can barely understand them.

I speak a little, but I'm nowhere near fluent enough to hold a deep conversation. I have some cousins who are pretty cool, so it's not complete torture.

This time though, I had to pick the year to go when my team was knocked out of the playoffs so close to the end.

"That last game was an embarrassment to watch," Dad says. We're barely at thirty thousand feet when he starts in on me.

"I agree," I say, hoping that will be the end of it.

It's not.

My father is what a lot of people will call distinguished. He once had dark hair but is now graying. Who knows where I got my caramel-colored hair from considering my mom is platinum blonde. Maybe their DNA mixed light with dark and got … me.

He has that overweight athlete's body where he's still fit but carrying a few extra pounds. And he's the epitome of a closed-off Polish man when it comes to expressing himself. He can't muster up a "Good job" but can tell me when I'm an embarrassment to his name.

The whole flight, I listen to Dad telling me how he would've played that last game better and giving me unsolicited advice on how to up my skills.

Never once does he praise me for helping to get my team that far. We didn't win the Cup, so we are losers. Obviously.

The only consolation to that is Anton didn't win it either. Philly was knocked out the next round, and I watched on with a huge smile on my face.

Still, a billion hours on a flight with someone who hates his own son, even the thought of Anton losing doesn't cheer me up.

When my dad played for the NHL, he'd come to the States after playing in Europe for a few years. He met my mom and had a quickie wedding and even quicker divorce. I like to tell myself that my mother wasn't a puck bunny, but I've seen the photos.

Got the mental scars to prove it.

The only reason they got married was because of me. That's not a secret.

Sometimes I wonder why I bother to make an effort with either of my parents, but as Dad likes to remind me, I'm where I am today because of him. He got me top coaching, made me practice six days a week, bought me all the equipment I needed and a lot that I didn't.

I'm his protégé. His pride and joy … but only if I win.

After a trip to my dad's motherland, I come home to my own paradise in Boston, and the last few weeks of summer are spent playing poker with the guys—because I do have friends in the league fuckyouverymuch, Anton Hayes—grilling on the terrace, hanging out and drinking beer and eating all the food we can't during the season.

My man-cave of an apartment is my own slice of heaven right across from TD Garden. The location is convenient for game days, not so much for practice, which is in Brighton.

Anton's right when he says my place is as insane as his, but there's one big difference. They may be in the same price range—I had to look it up because, you know, it's important to note the extra three hundred and fifty grand I dropped on my place means it's superior to his—but where his place is put together and an uppity kind of rich, mine is laid-back.

His apartment is filled with art and strategically placed furniture. Mine's got a beer fridge bigger than my actual fridge.

The overall theme of my place is dark wood and bright walls. It has *character.* Unlike Anton's.

During my whole off-season, I didn't think of him once. Not once. Definitely not every day for months. I didn't pay attention to the social media photos of him dressed up at charity events or in casual clothes while he was out with friends. And I definitely didn't wake up with his name on my lips and my hand wrapped around my cock.

Nope, nope, nope.

This is my denial, and I am happily living in it.

Summer passes so fast that training camp springs upon me in the blink of an eye.

A few rookies show promise, and leading up to preseason, I get a sense that we're going to have a good season this year. I don't say that out loud though. Never out loud.

That would be like walking under a ladder inside with an open umbrella and carrying a black cat kind of bad juju.

We endure a charity showcase, a dinner for the team and important people with money—all routine stuff. I haven't even *had* to think about Hayes until now.

As if the universe has decided to fuck with me, our first preseason game is against Philadelphia.

And okay, I will admit that one time I did contemplate contacting him and trying to see him over the break. Not for a repeat, no matter how much my ass wants it, but to come to some sort of agreement that we never speak of what happened again.

We haven't had the chance to have that conversation. The only reason I didn't seek him out is because I realized I don't need to face him to pretend nothing happened.

He didn't turn me inside out. He didn't fuck me so hard I felt him for days.

He wanted me to beg, and screw that. Ezra Palaszczuk doesn't beg. Ever. Even with guys he actually likes. I will never ask him to fuck me again. And I won't say please.

I've never wanted to voluntarily put myself on the IR list before. *I'm coming down with a sudden case of food poisoning and can't play. I accidentally threw myself off my terrace, and every bone in my body is broken.*

Damn it. I should not be letting Anton Hayes get in my head like this.

Fuck him. Or better yet, don't fuck him. Again. Because what the hell was I thinking? He sucks away all my awesomeness and leaves me a neurotic mess.

I am not this guy. I'm the fun-loving man-slut who doesn't get worked up over anybody. One hookup, and I turn into this?

I stare out my window at TD Garden across the street, where I need to be in fifteen minutes to suit up for the game, yet I can't bring myself to leave the apartment. We had a warm-up skate this afternoon and then got sent for downtime, but like my summer, it went too fast.

Anton would be there already. Suited up, styled hair, smug expression in place.

With my remaining moments, I take out my phone and hover over my best friend's name. He has a lot going on since he left the NHL, but I need his advice.

He used to be a fuckboy like me, but now he's all ... responsible. *Settling down* even. I shudder and hit Dial.

"Punch another fan?" West says by way of greeting.

I visited West and his five kids—all his younger siblings who found themselves without parents after a fateful car crash over a year ago—during the off-season. His time in the NHL was cut way too short, but he needed to be home.

I can't pretend to understand it, being the only child of a bitter divorced couple with a lot of younger half siblings I'm not close to, but West was always close with his family.

And now that West has settled down with his boyfriend, playing happy families, I *really* don't understand it. I'm not the type of guy who people want to settle down with, and I never thought West was either, so it was ... odd. I felt like an outsider the whole time I was sleeping on his couch, and I had to get out of there before I caught the monogamy.

NHL and happy families or not, we're still best friends, so I told him what I'd done—all the mistakes I'd made. Namely, getting drunk and all the events following that led to being railed up against a wall by Anton Hayes.

When I don't answer West right away, he says, "Oh no, *did* you punch another fan? I was joking."

I huff. "No. I didn't. But ... The game is against Philly tonight."

"Ah. Is it the first time you've seen Hayes since—"

"Yep. I'm not sure how to play it."

"Leave it off the ice," West says, like the answer should be obvious. "Pretend it didn't happen."

"You really think Anton would let me get away with that?"

"Anton Hayes is actually not a terrible guy."

"Lies. There's only one part of him that's not terrible, and—"

"Don't need to know. Thank you."

A muffled voice yells behind him, something about an Xbox controller.

"Ez, I have to go."

"No! You can't. I called for advice. Tell your kids to sit quietly for two minutes."

West bursts out laughing. "You should know that doesn't work with them."

True.

"Wesssst," I whine.

"You're worse than the kids. Just don't do it again. I know this is hard for you to believe, but you don't have to fall on every available dick. Gotta go."

He ends the call before I can thank him for not helping.

I take a deep breath. Though West's advice was not sound, his message is. Don't have sex with Anton again.

Easy.

I can't let one guy ruin hockey. Hockey is my life. Anton Hayes can't take that away from me.

—

Focus on that puck. Don't pay attention to jersey numbers. Don't look Anton in the eye.

That's been my mantra since we hit the ice, and the funny thing is, it's working. It's working so well that I've intercepted more passes in one period than in entire games last season.

I've stripped the puck and given our forwards so many shots on goal I'm disappointed they've only sunk two of them. That happens to be the same number of goals Anton has scored on his own.

I may be doing well, but so is he.

Damn him.

He looks completely unaffected by my presence, and I feel like an idiot for stressing about this game when it's obvious he cares even less than me.

I expected … something. A snarky comment, a dismissive look, but no, he's ignoring me as much as I'm ignoring him. And our playing is better because of it.

Who knew the key to success was ignoring your own biases? If I hadn't focused so hard on hating Hayes, maybe last season's playoff series would have ended differently and I never would've had sex with him.

Is this what growing up is? It feels like there's a life lesson in this situation somewhere.

Philly's offense comes flying toward us, passing back and forth between them. My gaze is laser trained on the puck, and I see the play before I make it. O'Ryan tries to pass to Hayes, but I'm faster. I extend my arm, and the puck finds my blade instead.

Then there we are, face-to-face, charging toward each other. Just Anton and me. It's the first time all night I lock eyes with him. There's no way I can get around him, so I quickly pass to Wagner at the other side of the rink, who crosses the blue line and then passes to Diedrich, who's gaining on the net. He shoots, and we take the lead 3-2. Our game only gets better from there.

One of Philly's rookies, Moreau, makes some stupid mistakes, which is understandable considering it's his first time in an NHL game. Even if it is only preseason and doesn't count for standing.

From this side, I can see he has talent, but he's so green. It costs Philly the game.

We walk away with the win, and I can't help but think, "Suck it." It's my turn to condescendingly tell Anton, "Good game," as I shake his hand, but when my palm lands in his, my mouth doesn't work. It opens, but nothing comes out.

The asshole smirks.

Then he's gone and we're all heading for the locker rooms.

"I told O'Ryan we'd take their team out for drinks before, you know, they become the real enemy when the season starts," Diedrich says.

The truth is, a lot of us are friends. Whether they play for your team or not, those guys out there on the ice are your brothers. There's a handful of queer guys from different teams who get together whenever we can and joke it's the NHL queer convention. We call ourselves the Collective, and it's not nerdy at all.

Nope. Not even a little bit.

Going out for drinks with guys from another team is common. Win or lose. However, if we'd lost tonight, there's no way I'd take Diedrich up on his offer, but winning? It gives me something to hold over Anton's head.

I turn to Diedrich with a smile. "I'm in."

CHAPTER FOUR

ANTON

If this were any other night, my response to Boston's invite to go out would have been a solid no, but I didn't have anywhere near enough time to taunt Ezra on the ice.

I hate that his team won, but neither of us has played a game like that before.

It felt amazing.

Just as amazing as seeing the fire in his eyes. The way he was trying to cover that he was remembering every detail. Because he was. I was too. But I have a better poker face than him.

And all through the press conference, I'm smiling more than I should be for someone on the losing team, but I'm too busy wondering how many drinks it'll take for me to work my way under Ezra's skin. I know there's exactly zero chance of having sex with him again when he'll have more than enough offers to hook up, but I want to remind him that no matter what, I've had him.

He needs to live with the fact he was owned by Anton Hayes.

It's that memory that has me puffing out my chest as we enter the karaoke bar Diedrich sent us the address to.

It's always odd playing in Boston. I grew up here but moved away for college. Even back then, Ezra and I were in the same hockey circles—not that he'd know it. Our paths rarely crossed, and I was the quiet kid who was third line and not very good in the beginning. Ezra ... well, he hasn't changed. He has his head so far up his own ass that he doesn't notice the people around him. I noticed him though. Maybe too much.

O'Ryan breaks off to buy the first round of drinks, and the rest of us head for where the Boston team is making their presence known. Only five of my team came with me, the others, mostly newbies, headed back to the hotel to mourn the loss.

When you've played as many games as I have, you understand the old philosophy of "you win some, you lose some." Except in the playoffs. Then losing is the equivalent of the end of the world.

The bar is already busy, but Boston has picked an area on the high side of the room to take over. I climb the two stairs to get to them and immediately look around.

I'd like to say I'm not searching for Ezra, but that would be horseshit.

It doesn't take long to spot the back of his head, light brown hair rumpled and sexy, reminding me of how it looked after I had it gripped between my fingers. He's leaning over the barrier, talking to some guy who might as well have hearts in his eyes.

It's not surprising to see Ezra flirting with someone. It *is* surprising how fiercely I hate it this time. I usually despise it because he's comfortable enough to do it so freely and out in the open, but I can't deny that voice in the back of my head telling me this is different.

I head toward Wagner like he was my sole target all along. He's close enough that Ezra should hear me the second I say anything, and I plan to take full advantage of that.

"Good game tonight."

Wagner turns to me. "It was from one of us." He laughs and pats my shoulder. "You were playing for the wrong team, Hayes."

"Stop trying to steal my winger," O'Ryan says as he approaches and hands me a drink.

"Yeah, imagine him and Ez on a team?" Wagner and O'Ryan chuckle at the thought that makes my stomach clench. A few of the guys saw our coaches in the bar together last night after the team flew in, and there have been rumors about a trade circling ever since. I'm praying my name is kept out of it, but I suspect it's all speculation.

As someone who was always unnoticed on my teams until I clawed my way into the spotlight in college, the thought of being traded stings. Logically, I know it's part of the game and that it doesn't mean you're a terrible player, but it's the feeling of being so easily replaceable that screws with my head.

I'm an egotistical bastard on purpose these days, because there's still that voice constantly reminding me I have to fight to be good enough, and I've worked out that if I fake confidence, I begin to feel it. I wear my ego like a mask, covering up that somewhere deep down, I still believe that being who I truly am won't cut it in professional sports.

I remind myself our coaches were having drinks, and that doesn't mean anything. Just like right now. Me having drinks in the same vicinity as Ezra.

Besides, anyone who would put Ezra and me on the same team should not be responsible for decision making.

"I don't see how it would make any difference which team I was on," I say. "Except if I was on yours, I'd be showing him up from the same side of the ice."

I swear I can feel his stare. Knowing I've succeeded in getting his attention lights me up. All I need now is for him to bite.

"He dominated tonight," Wagner says, loyal to a fault.

"Well, we all get lucky sometimes."

A scoff comes from behind me. Bingo.

"Getting lucky? Like you'd know anything about that," Ezra says.

"Changing the topic to sex, how unusual for you."

"Are you slut-shaming me?"

"Just pointing out you have a one-track mind. I'm not shaming you for being a slut but for being you."

"And yet, that's my most sought-after quality." Ezra looks me over. "Haven't had a complaint yet."

"Oh, don't worry, I'm sure there's one coming."

"You two really don't like each other, do you?" O'Ryan asks.

Ezra says, "No," at the same time I respond, "I don't think about him enough to not like him."

Normally, that would have been the truth. The only times I really think about Ezra are when I'm facing him on the ice or scowling at yet more ridiculous antics that have him splashed all over the tabloids. For the last few months though, I've thought about him far more than I'd admit.

The guy can fuck.

I might have been the one topping him, but I wasn't doing all the work.

"You realize that only makes *you* sound like an asshole, right?" Ezra's tone is light, but I can tell I've pissed him off. He's too easy to read.

"For being the one person on earth who doesn't give you attention? If that's the case, I can live with being an asshole." I tip back my drink and finish it in one mouthful. "Anyone else need a refill?"

I glance at Ezra, daring him to ask, but he wisely stays quiet. Wagner and O'Ryan are still going with theirs, so I leave for the bar solo.

It's pretty obvious why Diedrich chose this place. It's dark and moody, with the main lights coming from the stage, drowning those daring to do karaoke in a multi-colored wash of lights. When I was younger and grew up here, it was called something else. It reminds me of a large cigar lounge, one that's been updated to still look old but cater to a younger audience.

There's no dry humping on the dance floor here.

Pity.

I'm buzzing with the need to hook up tonight.

As I'm waiting for my turn to order, I glance back to find Ezra talking to that same man again and narrow my eyes in their direction.

I grab my drink, but as I get back to the table, the emcee's voice cuts through the room.

"Next up, we have Anton Hayes and Ezra Palaszczuk!"

I glare at the guys. "Which one of you did that?"

They all try to look innocent.

Ezra jumps the small balcony, and my pulse rate spikes as he heads for the stage. He takes a microphone, stands in the spotlight, and then his ice-blue eyes zero in on his target: me.

I'm determined not to look away, so I see the moment his smile starts. "Coming, Hayes? Or are you too scared to go head-to-head off the ice?"

The crowd bursts into "Oohs" and taunts.

I put down my drink. "Bring it." Even if karaoke isn't my thing, I'm a mediocre-to-average singer, so at least I won't embarrass myself up there. There's no way Ezra's deep, scratchy voice could carry a note.

I amble my way to the stage and take my own mic. "Queen okay?"

"Only if it's 'Don't Stop Me Now.'" He came up with that way too quickly.

"Fine. Deal." Who doesn't know the words to that one?

I channel some of the confidence I hide behind on the ice and pretend like this is an average night for me.

There're a few whoops from the direction of our teams, and someone catcalls, but up here the lights are too bright to make out exactly who it's coming from. It doesn't matter. They're traitors. All of them.

Ezra smirks at me—nothing new there—but for some reason, that one look cuts through some of my faux confidence.

Then the music starts, Ezra lifts the microphone to his mouth ... and from the first note of "*tonight*," I immediately regret all life decisions leading to this moment.

Ezra. Is. Incredible.

He nails the opening lines, with all the ease of Freddie Mercury himself, and as soon as the beat kicks up, he lets loose. I watch Ezra own the stage, completely stunned and barely remembering to sing along. How didn't I know this about him? How didn't I know that he had a voice like sex and the moves to back it up?

He hits the high notes, all high energy, and I shift to ease some of the pressure behind my fly as my dick starts to perk up again. I hate Ezra, but my cock likes this side of him.

He's so … free. So in the moment. Every decision I make comes with a list of pros and cons attached, even now. I lean into the performance, but not *too* much. Not enough to draw any kind of speculation that Ezra and I are anything more than rivals on the ice. Ezra doesn't look like he has a concern in the world.

The next chorus, he catches my eye and starts to strut across the stage toward me. The lights, his messy hair, the unbuttoned shirt, and that sexy fucking strut … I'm close to giving in and watching him, but like hell am I going to let Ezra beat me at anything.

So when Ezra turns and presses his back to my chest, arm thrown back around my neck, and starts grinding up against me, I grab his hip and reposition the microphone so my lips graze his ear as I sing. His ass fits perfectly up against my cock, and there's no way he can't feel my erection rubbing against him. The only thing stopping me from pulling away is the complete confidence that he'll be hard too.

I'd wanted to show him up, but when he lets go of me to take center stage again, the filthy look he throws back at me makes it obvious I failed to do anything other than stroke his ego.

By the end of the song, all eyes are on him as he builds and builds, nailing every note, thrusting his hips to the beat in a way that keeps drawing my attention to his ass. The music finally slows, and Ezra makes his way back toward me, singing through those last few notes, until we're face-to-face, noses almost brushing as we finish the song.

He holds my gaze like he's waiting for me to back down, and even with a voice that incredible, I refuse. He already looks cockier than I've ever seen him before.

Which is saying something.

But after that, he has a reason to be.

The bar goes nuts with applause, and when he turns to take a bow, I pretend to good-naturedly applaud him along with everyone else before exiting the stage.

I catch Ezra's eye and make sure he sees me duck down the hall leading toward the bathrooms, because after *that* I don't trust myself to face him in front of our teams.

I'm vaguely worried he'll find the guy from before and ignore me, but Ezra rarely gives up a chance to gloat, and after that, he's going to be preening like a goddamn peacock.

The sane reaction would be to put distance between us, but there's this need building in my gut to take all that energy he had on display and redirect it toward myself. After that performance, I wouldn't be surprised if everyone in this bar wants him. Which makes me more desperate for him to follow me.

Sure enough, barely two minutes later, he rounds the corner, huge grin stretched across his smug face.

"I thought that was supposed to be a duet?" he asks, feigning innocence.

"Yet as usual, you couldn't pass up the opportunity to be a complete show-off."

"Tell me I was great."

"I will never say those words. Ever."

"Lucky I don't need your validation, then. Too bad for you the slapped-monkey look on your face gave you away."

It's all I can do not to roll my eyes. "Humble as ever, Palaszczuk."

"Who needs humble when I can sing like that?" He advances on me, and when I step back, I hit the wall. "Admit you thought that was hot."

There's no way I can deny it. "Fine. That was sexy as fuck. My dick couldn't decide what it liked better: hearing you sing or the way you moan when you're impaled on it."

His tongue darts out to lick his lips. "You've been thinking about it, haven't you?"

"The way someone might remember a nightmare," I answer dryly.

Ezra laughs. Presses closer. If anyone needs to piss, it's going to be very hard to explain this away.

"We should do it again," he suggests.

"No."

"You hate that you find me so hot, don't you?" He leans in, presses his nose to the soft skin under my ear, and inhales. "Maybe I could do you this time."

I grab him and flip us so he's the one pressed up against the wall. "I'm gay, and you're hot. That doesn't necessarily mean I want you."

"Again," he taunts. "But you do, don't you?"

God I want to shut his mouth up. Instead of getting angry though, I meet him at his game. "I told you last time, Ez." I drop my voice. "If you want me to fuck you, you're going to have to beg."

"No way in hell that will happen."

I step back and shrug, acting like my cock isn't rock hard and weeping at my stubbornness. "Fine by me." I turn and walk away. "You know my terms."

I leave the hallway to the sound of him cursing.

CHAPTER FIVE

EZRA

Fuck, what time is it?

The buzzing of my phone can't be my alarm. I make sure to set that shit to *loud*.

The night comes back to me. I was on a high until Anton walked away and kept walking. The rest of the night is a blur of drinking and coming home alone.

My phone stops as I reach for it. I have a missed call from West and a text message.

It's a link to an article titled *Enemies to Bromance* with the thumbnail photo of me and Anton onstage singing.

I groan at West's message: *Let me guess. It happened again.*

I start to type out a reply, but my messenger app alerts me to an incoming video call. Only, it's not him. Well, not *only* him. It's the Collective group chat, and Tripp Mitchell, the goalie for Vegas, is the one calling.

When I answer, West is already on the call.

"Are you fucking Anton Hayes?" Tripp asks, his red hair a contrast against his pale skin and adorable freckles.

West bursts out laughing, and I want to wipe the smile off his damn face.

"No," I grumble. I don't know how out Hayes is. He said his team knows and his family. I told West because I trust him implicity, but he already knew.

"Ollie's asked him to join our group chat," Tripp says, "but he's still not entirely comfortable with being one hundred percent out to the public."

"Wait. Does everyone in the league know Anton is gay?" As I ask this, Ollie Strömberg himself appears on my screen and answers.

"I knew that. I thought our whole group did."

"So I'm the only one he didn't tell? Why?"

Three derisive looks are sent my way like the answer is obvious. Hey, just because I'm proudly out and don't care about being seen with men, that doesn't mean I don't understand others not being the same. I'm not *that* self-centered and tone-deaf.

"Why are we talking about Hayes?" Ollie asks.

"Ezra is sleeping with him and denying it," Tripp says.

"You're lucky you're across the other side of the country," I mumble.

Two more guys join the call. Caleb Sorensen and Oskar Voyjik. Soren has been retired for a few years now, before a lot of us were even playing, but he and Ollie were the first two out players in the league. They're the entire reason us other guys have careers while living our truth.

"How's my honorary nephew?" Ollie asks Soren.

"Running rampant." Soren looks exhausted. "He takes after my husband, and I've already been up for three hours. What's the emergency?"

"There's no emergency," I say. "There's a stupid article saying Anton and I are suddenly besties because we sang karaoke together."

"How did that happen?" Tripp asks.

"Diedrich and O'Ryan signed us up, and neither of us backs down from a challenge."

"Tell me again how you're not egotistical," West says.

"There's nothing going on."

Instead of reacting to me, everyone says, "West?" Like they're looking to him for confirmation.

"Ugh, I hate all of you," I say. "I'm not."

West coughs, poorly disguising the way he says, "Again."

I have no best friend. "You want to play that game, West? Really? What if I tell everyone you're in a serious relationship with a hottie mchottie professor, but you don't want to tell anyone because you're scared you'll jinx it and it will end, and then the kids will hate you because they already love him?"

"Duuuude," West says.

"You're seeing someone?" Tripp asks him. "Really? Mr. In Love With Ezra?"

West rolls his eyes. "You're one to talk about being in love with your best friend, Tripp. At least Ezra's gay. I had a shot. Dex is straighter than a blue line."

Tripp flips off the camera.

My awesome distraction has worked, even if it's brought up some past issues with West and me.

Once upon a time, we were more than best friends. But that ended when he retired, and I thought there were no hard feelings. I was wrong.

But that's all in the past now. We're both over it, and we're back to being there for each other like we always were. I'm happy he's found someone who can be there for him in a way I never would've been able to.

Tripp and West continue to bicker while I sit back in victory.

"I'm gonna let you guys talk this all out while I go back to sleep. All I have to do is hit the gym today."

"Prepare to lose tomorrow," Ollie says to me.

"You wish, Strömberg. Last night was the first of many wins we're going to take home this season."

A stream of "Boo" and "Whatever" gets thrown my way as I end the call on my side.

Then I do the worst possible thing I could do. I go back to the article and read the comments.

I've broken the golden rule, and now I can't unsee all the implications that Anton and I never hated each other and our rivalry is one big publicity grab.

Whether it's hate, lust, or the primal need to fuck and fight, whatever Anton and I have just got a whole lot more complicated.

-

Not only do we kick New York's ass the following day, we take out the next two preseason games too.

Four wins. Four. There's something in the vibe of the team that's clicking. There's a good chance we could head into the season undefeated. It's years like this I wish the preseason scoreboard counted.

The game is so unpredictable. A great preseason sometimes means it's all downhill from there. It sets up high expectations that could crumble under the slightest pressure.

Where we should be riding high, we're all scared shitless something is going to happen to bring us down, and we've still got two more games to play before the regular season kicks off.

We have a short practice today, and I arrive at the practice rink at the same time as Larsen. He approaches me like an excitable puppy with what he thinks is a great idea. "So I've been thinking. What if we don't change our socks for the entire season?"

We scan our security cards and enter the building, where Diedrich is just ahead of us. "Scaring off the other teams with smelly socks isn't the best offensive strategy."

Diedrich, hearing me, spins. "Well, whatever we do, let's not let Ezra grow out his beard again."

I rub my chin. "Whatever. My beard is a work of art."

The guys snicker, but I don't know why. My beard is awesome. Especially now it's trimmed and neat. I'm keeping it, damn it.

We have a game in two days against New Jersey, and I hope we can keep the streak going, but as we walk into the locker room, it's like walking into a funeral. There's an air of quiet mourning, and for a brief second, I think someone actually died.

Trades can happen anytime. Usually during preseason, it's a drafted rookie or someone who isn't doing well. We've all been playing great, so I don't understand what's going on.

That's when my eyes land on Wagner's cubby. Our equipment manager is clearing it out.

"No," I say. "When did that happen?"

"Last night," Kosik says. "Orlov too. They're going to announce it today."

"Who'd we get?"

As if waiting for their damn cue, in walk the trades.

Rookie Josh Moreau from Philly and—

Fucking fuck fuck.

No.

This is not happening.

I blink a few times, but Anton Hayes still stands there, bag over his shoulder, sullen look on his face.

Coach Stephenson walks into the room and shivers. "Wow. Cold reception in here. I can see you're all aware of what's going on. Before any of you complain"—he sends a pointed look my way—"you know how these things go."

I have to admit, the trade is decent for us. Trading our third-line center for a second-line winger is a smart move. I will never deny Anton has talent. But Wagner for a draft rookie? Wagner may be nearing retirement, but he's a solid player and a veteran. Trading that for someone green and unpredictable is a risk.

I bet Coach used Wagner as leverage to get Hayes in on the deal. *We'll trade you two solid players for an excellent one and a risky one.*

I understand it from the outside, but come on, our preseason was showing promise. All the unwashed socks in the world can't help this.

Hayes refuses to look at me, and I don't blame him.

"Get settled in," Coach says to Hayes and Moreau and then turns to me. "Palaszczuk, my office. Now."

I throw my head back like the petulant child I am and follow him into his office.

He closes the door behind him and tells me to take a seat. "I don't need to tell you to pull your head out of your ass on this, do I?"

"No, sir."

His lips flatten. "Why don't I believe you?"

"Philly is screwing with you. Why would they so willingly give up Hayes to us other than knowing our rivalry could undo this whole team?"

"What's with your rivalry, anyway? It's not like you've slept with his wife or girlfriends or ..." He trails off, probably putting two and two together. Anton doesn't do girlfriends, and he's never been married because—"Oh."

"We don't like each other. End of story. He grates on me, and I'm too awesome for him. It's the story of my life, Coach. You should feel sorry for me. No one likes me because of how jealous they are."

"I'm starting to see Hayes's point," Coach grumbles. "Just stay away from him, okay? You play on the left. He plays on the right. You should be able to manage that."

That may be true, but we're still teammates, and when we're on the ice together, we'll have to trust each other. Like that's possible.

I mock salute Coach anyway because there's no way to undo this. The decisions he and team management made might have screwed us all, but we're the ones who have to deal with it.

Coach stands. "Go get suited up, and I'll see you out there. This trade was supposed to be a steal. Don't make me regret it."

"Why's it automatically my fault if you do? Hayes hates me as much as I hate him."

He slaps my shoulder on the way past. "Because you're so awesome. So, so awesome."

"I don't appreciate the sarcasm, Coach," I call after him.

He whistles as he hits the corridor and heads toward the ice.

Okay. Professional time.

Keep my hands to myself, my dick in my pants, and pretend Anton Hayes is just another teammate.

This will not be the team's downfall. I won't allow it.

CHAPTER SIX

ANTON

It's a relief when Coach calls Ezra away and I can unload my things into my cubby in peace. I'm unsettled, maybe even resentful, but I know this is part of my job, and I need to suck it up.

Clearly being a good player means nothing when it comes to a trade. Besides, the person I should be feeling bad for is Wagner. He's only got a year or two left to play, and now he's having to uproot his whole family because of this deal.

All I left behind was an apartment that I loved.

To be back in Boston.

I have so many mixed feelings about the trade. The first one is feeling disposable. The second is being back here, knowing my childhood home has been sold to another family, and my parents are states away. The food bank I used to volunteer at is gone, and I haven't kept track of which friends from high school are still around and which have moved on.

I'm alone.

Which isn't something I've felt before, even when I moved away to college, then got drafted to my first team.

These guys are Ezra's, and fitting into that dynamic will take time.

Diedrich offered for Moreau and me to stay with him until we get settled, but I chose to go with the hotel option. Diedrich has a gaggle of children, and his family will have enough issues with one hockey player, let alone two. This will be Moreau's first time living out of home since he was lucky enough to be drafted to his home team in Philly. That guy is going to have a lot of adjusting to do.

Kosik joins me at my cubby. "Anton Hayes." His smile is huge. "You would have been my last guess."

"You and me both."

"How are you and Palaszczuk going to handle this?" I swear the locker room goes silent while they wait for my reply. I take it we're not avoiding the elephant in the room, then.

"There are twenty other people on this team. I'm not going to hold *one* bad egg against you." I throw them a wink.

There are some chuckles.

"You don't need to worry about me though. I'm a professional." Figure we should get a few things out while I have their attention. "I'm also gay for those of you who don't know, but I assume that won't be an issue."

They hurry to reassure me it's totally fine.

"Team rule though," Diedrich adds. "None of us talks about our sex lives, okay? You do you, but we don't need to hear about it. And you don't need to hear about what we get up to."

"Deal." That's more than okay with me. "Why do I get the feeling Palaszczuk was the reason for that rule?"

Diedrich rubs his neck. "Might have been, yeah."

Ezra enters the room at just the right moment and cuts in. "Because I showed you animals how awkward sex talk is when you're not into the things being talked about."

"Yep, that." Diedrich slaps my back. "Better suit up. I grabbed you some practice gear, and I have a feeling with you two joining, today is going to be an intense practice."

Of course it will. Coming into a new team always presents issues, but a team with Ezra?

I meant what I said. I'm professional, and I'm not going to let this be weird. We'll work together on the ice, and I'll ignore him off it. There *are* twenty other people on this team I can give time and attention to. Some of them I'm already friends with.

So why, when we're getting changed, does my gaze immediately travel across to Ezra. To his bare ass. And all I can think of is when he bent over for me.

So much for professional, Anton.

Even though Ezra and I have never gotten along, I didn't regret sleeping with him. Until now.

If I'd known we would end up here, I would have shown better control. At the time, I thought I'd see him for a few games, maybe All-Stars if we had a good season, and then that would be it.

This rivalry-turned-besties story the press is running with is ridiculous, and it's only going to get worse now we're on the same team.

Our bromance is going to be put under a microscope, which will put me front and center of tabloid drama—the exact thing I don't want.

Bromance. What a joke.

This narrative is easier to sell with us playing together though, and I wouldn't have put it past the B's PR to start that rumor in preparation for exactly this. I should have seen the trade coming days before I was told.

Nerves over being around Ezra add to the small seed of rejection from my old team, and the need to prove myself is all a bit too much. I'm known for being cocky. It's a defense mechanism I developed from years of being a mediocre player. Fake it until you make it was my mantra in high school, and by the time I hit college, that confidence came naturally on the ice. But I'm struggling to bring any of that attitude out today.

Just as Diedrich predicted, the coaches keep us on the ice for far longer than usual. I get next to no downtime as Coach Stephenson tries to get the new first line working together. I've graduated from second line to first with the trade, so I need to prove that I belong here. Not only with the team but as one of the guys who get the most ice time.

It's so different to Philly where we knew each other's plays and tells inside and out. It was instinctual. Here, I'm working a lot harder to read the ice.

I grit my teeth after sending the puck sailing toward where Larsen should be but isn't, and I try to hold back from letting my frustration show. These are usual teething issues that we unfortunately only have today and tomorrow to fix before our game against Jersey. This practice isn't going well, and when I slip and glance over at Ezra, his expression confirms as much.

He doesn't say anything, but the spark in his eyes is enough.

That, folks, is the great Anton Hayes … choking.

Nope. This is me. Still refusing to let him get to me.

Coach dismisses everyone except Larsen, Diedrich, and me. He makes us run drills for another half an hour before he's satisfied, and by the time I get to the gym, nearly everyone has finished their cooldown.

I grab a bike and try to ignore the mild stiffness in my thighs from prolonged time on the ice. Even though things are familiar—the rink, the gym, a team—it's completely foreign at the same time. Change is something all NHL players have to get good at, but it's always been a weakness of mine. I love the thrill of the lifestyle, but I work better with consistency, in my own environment. It's why I completely dominate at home games and have to work harder while we're away.

I need to find that consistency again, and considering I grew up here, that shouldn't be a huge issue. All I have to do is set up a routine, and I'll settle.

In Philly, sometimes after practice, I'd sneak away to a shelter to volunteer. It would center me, make me feel like I'm contributing to the world, but I'd do a lot of the behind-the-scenes tasks because I don't actually want anyone to know that I'm doing it. As soon as the media catch on to things like that, it cheapens the experience, and my parents always raised me to give to those less fortunate than myself. It was one of their conditions of paying for all my hockey shit. They'd see players like Ezra, who was born a prince of hockey because of his dad, so he had all the top-of-the-range equipment thrown at him. Me, I had to work for it. My parents could afford it, but their number one priority was teaching me humility.

The charity thing stuck with me because it reminds me of how privileged I am, so I continue to give back because it's important to do something good for other people other than throwing money at the problem—though I do that too. I may not act like it on the ice, but I can acknowledge the world doesn't revolve around me.

Unlike other people in my vicinity who think the sun shines out their ass.

I'm so lost in my thoughts that I don't notice Larsen and Diedrich leave and another person enter the room until I catch sight of him in the mirror.

Ezra is leaning up against a wall not far from me, arms crossed as he watches me work out like he has all the time in the world. His hair is still damp from his shower, and he's trimmed that ugly beard of his so that it's actually sexy. Or maybe since sticking my dick in him, I find any small thing about him sexy.

I slow down my pedaling on the bike and come to a stop. "Yes?"

"Coach sent me to see if you were done yet. He wants to run through game tape of New Jersey."

"And he sent you. Total coincidence, I'm sure."

"Coincidence. Right. Fifty bucks says the coaches throw us together at all opportunities to force us to get along."

"So you're saying I need to get used to your ugly mug?" I grab my towel and run it over my face and neck. "Let me shower, and I'll be out."

"Sure."

I'm halfway into the showers when I realize Ezra is still following me. "What are you doing?"

"Thought I'd come check you out like you were doing to me in the locker room earlier."

Apparently, I'm not as subtle as I thought. "There you go being conceited again."

"That's how you're going to play it? Would it really kill you to play nice with me?"

"I'm like ninety percent sure that would be detrimental to my health, yes."

"Hmm, only ninety. I'll get it out of you one day, then."

I give Ezra a chance to leave, but he settles against the tile. Fine. It's not like we aren't going to be showering together weekly in the future, so why not start now? I strip off and hit the showers, keeping my focus locked in front of me and not on whether he's checking me out.

Besides, there's only so much attention I can give him when it's taking all my restraint to keep my dick from getting hard.

"Anyway, we should probably try to at least get along. For the team."

"Sure."

"That was easy."

I turn on the tap and step under the warm water. "What did you expect me to say?"

"I thought for sure there'd be pushback or a smart-assed comment or *something*. I'm beginning to worry the articles were right. Is this the start of a bromance?"

I cringe at the thought but cover it by lathering up with soap. "It depends. Are you still a douche with a big mouth who likes attention and fucks anyone who'll have you?"

"Yes."

"Then my feelings haven't changed." I duck back under the water to rinse off. When I shake the water from my hair, Ezra's still there.

"Are *you* still an uptight asshole who expects people to live by your standards and not their own? You don't need to reply, by the way. I already know the answer."

I growl and turn off the shower before getting a towel and wrapping it around my waist. Being naked and close to Ezra is too much temptation.

When I advance on him, I swear there's interest in his icy-blue eyes, but I am one hundred percent not going to acknowledge it. That will only encourage him.

"I'm not here for your games, Palaszczuk. We have a job to do. You stay on your side of the ice, and I'll stay on mine. I got so close to winning the Cup last year, and I'm not going to let you stand in the way of me getting it this season."

"You think *I'm* going to stand in the way? I'm hungry to win that Cup, and with you on the team, everything we've worked hard on in preseason will go down the drain."

"Or with my help, you might make it to the championship game this year. But if that's how you want to play it, how about you don't worry about me, and I won't worry about you."

"Score for us the way you did for Philly and we'll be fine."

I let my gaze drop to run over his tight T-shirt. It really is a crime how hot he is. "We both know I can score. On and off the ice."

And as I'm about to stalk off with the final word, Ezra hooks a finger into the front of my towel, gives it a tug, and watches as it drops to the ground. My half-hard cock is left on full display.

"I'll stay out of your way, Hayes." Ezra backs up for the door. "Remind your dick that you want distance next time you're eye-fucking me."

I scowl at his retreating back as I scoop up the towel and quickly dry off.

Sure, Ezra and I will get along.

The day he gets a personality transplant.

CHAPTER SEVEN

EZRA

There's a morning press conference the day of the next game, the first since the trade, so up there on the podium are Moreau and Hayes next to Coach Stephenson and our GM.

I've snuck in the back, behind all the media, because I can't help myself. That and we have our morning skate right after this.

Anton looks too damn good in his suit, his black hair parted and styled in that perfect way he has it after games. His smiles are easy, and his answers are short. He's the walking definition of perfect PR.

Unlike me. Exhibit A: I'm attending this press conference in jeans and my B's jacket. Big no-no, but the plan is to go unnoticed. That lasts all of two minutes until someone asks about the rift between Hayes and me.

Then suddenly cameras are pointed in my direction and toward the front.

Anton smiles again, still unflustered, and says into the mic, "Ezra Palaszczuk and I have only ever come to blows on the ice."

Hey, I'd offer to blow him off the ice, but he's adamant about pretending he doesn't want me.

"We're actually great friends," he continues.

I bet that was difficult for him to get out without wanting to hurl.

"Now that we're on the same team, there's no reason to be fighting over plays. You might not know it to look at Ezra, but he has a big heart and has even volunteered to help me with my latest charity campaign at the local animal shelter, Boston Paws. We're having a volunteer day this weekend, and he'll be there with me."

I'm going to be where with who now?

His dark eyes lock on me, along with every camera in the damn room, and suddenly his smile isn't so easy. It's downright evil.

I wave it off, acting like a good sport.

He's going to pay for that.

As soon as the press conference is over, I approach him in the locker room. His jacket and tie have been discarded, his suit shirt is unbuttoned, but that's as far as he's gotten.

The other guys are only starting to arrive, so it's still practically empty when I shove past Anton and send him flying into his cubby.

Anton rights himself and advances on me, only stopping barely a foot away.

I pump my eyebrows. "You know, if you wanted to spend more time with me, all you had to do was ask. No need to steamroll me into going on a date with you."

Moreau steps behind his old Philly teammate, but Anton holds him back.

"I got this," Anton says.

Then his dark and broody stare is back on me. "If you think spending any time outside the rink with you was by choice, you're more egotistical than I ever thought."

"That's your problem. Always underestimating me."

Anton licks his lips. "I can't wait to see you on Sunday at the shelter. Rumor has it you have this weird fear of cats."

My eyes widen.

"Guess what I signed you up for?" he continues. "Cleaning out all the little kitty cages. You're welcome."

I turn to the few guys who are here. "Which one of you ratted me out?"

I might have an irrational *superstition* about cats—not fear. Which everyone knows about after a stray black cat was found outside the arena one day. Larsen had brought it in to find a box for it, and we lost the next game. And the one after that.

"If we lose the game against Philly on Monday, we know who to blame." I glare at Anton. "Will you be able to remember whose side you're on?"

"Worry about your own game." Anton turns his back to me and finishes getting undressed.

I stand here and watch because while he's still and always will be an asshole, his body is divine.

He does have a point though, because later that night when we play against New Jersey, I take more penalties, more hits, and let way too many shots on goal happen.

It's a shutout, and we leave the ice with our heads low.

"Should've gone with the dirty socks," Larsen says as we head down the chute.

"Should've never traded and messed with our team dynamics."

Anton, who's in front of me, takes his glove off and throws me the finger. "I was nowhere near the worst out there tonight."

"Oh, did I miss where you scored?"

"At least I didn't spend more time in the sin bin than on the ice."

"Cut the crap," Coach says behind me. "The media is watching."

A few reporters are hanging around outside the locker room waiting for sound bites and after-game interviews. Anton and I close our mouths like good little boys, but I bet Coach is already having regrets about the trade.

—

My alarm goes off at dark o'clock so I can get my ass to the fucking animal shelter to do this charity shit because fucking Anton Hayes is a fucking fuck fuck asshole fuck.

If it wasn't obvious before, it's crystal clear now. I am not a morning person.

Mornings should be illegal. Unless I'm climbing into bed instead of out of it.

I throw on the nearest pair of jeans I find crumpled on the floor and pull a B's shirt out of my closet.

Anton couldn't pick a shelter close by, could he? Nope. I have to schlep all the way out to Gloucester. I bet he did that on purpose.

I grab coffee on the way but am ready for another one when I pull into the parking lot. Hell, I'm ready for a vat of it. Or an IV drip. Caffeine, get in my veins.

Anton stands by the door, arms folded, scowl on his beautiful face. No, not beautiful. Damn it. "You're late."

"You're an asshole," I bite back.

"Original." He opens the door.

"I'm not caffeinated enough for originality."

"Let's get to work. We need all the cages clean before people turn up to look at adoption."

"Don't worry. I'm sure we can find someone who'd want to take you home. Maybe. Actually, no, it's a tall order."

He lowers his voice, letting out a sexy but teasing rasp. "That's not what you said a few months ago."

"I'm a temporary stop. I'm no one's forever home."

Anton's dark brows furrow at me, but it's the truth. I'm not the settling down type. I have nothing against the sanctity of marriage or monogamy—maybe one day the urge to settle will pull me down the aisle—but I can't see it happening. The idea of long-term makes me itchy. I've never had that need to claim someone as the person who belongs to me.

I'm not convinced the need exists. It certainly didn't for my parents.

We get to a set of doors, and Anton grabs a pair of rain boots and shoves them into my hands. "Put these on."

"Why couldn't we have turned up when the cameras and people were here so it looks like we did it?" I grumble as I switch out my shoes.

"That's probably the most Ezra-like thing I've ever heard you say." He pushes cleaning supplies at me next.

"Hey, I'm not against charity, but the schedule is so grueling during the season, I want to take advantage of every chance I get to sleep in."

"Of course you do."

We enter the cat area, which is a depressing room if I ever saw one.

All the cats are in individual cages, not like others I've seen where they're housed in a big area together outside with play equipment. There's one climbing tree in the corner, and I can't help getting a prison vibe from it all. Each of them gets one hour of rec time outside their cell.

I would feel sorry for them, but cats are evil bastards. Who knows? Maybe they're all doing time for murder and eating their owners' faces.

"You can put the supplies down here." He points to a table.

"Yes, sir," I mutter.

"You really are cranky in the mornings. I was warned about that by a few of your teammates. Apparently, you go through roommates on the road faster than you do hookups. Now that's impressive."

"Thank you."

"Not a compliment." He heads for the corner of the room, and I follow him.

I want to point out my teammates are now his teammates too, but I don't. "Maybe I wouldn't be complaining so much if you'd volunteered for me to visit an old people's home or a cancer ward. I can cheer up a whole room by walking into it. But animals?" Just as I say this, we walk past a cage, and a cat hisses at me. "Cats don't like me. Where are the dogs?"

Anton opens one of the cages and picks up a black kitten. He lifts it in front of his face and does a ridiculous voice. "Pwease, Ezwa. Loooove me! I'm a cute innocent kitten, but everyone hates me because of stupid superstition that black cats are bad wuck."

"Black cats *are* bad luck."

"Hooold me." Without missing a beat, he practically shoves the poor thing in my arms.

It scrambles to get away, and I almost drop it, but then I hold it close to me, and—

"Ouch. It bit me."

"Maybe if you weren't trying to smother it, it would play nice. You know, they say animals have a great sense of reading people. They know when they meet a shitty person and show it."

"I think that's dogs. Cats hate everyone."

Anton grunts. "Fine, I'll hold the cat. You do the cleaning." He takes the evil thing back, and the tiny fluff ball immediately settles in his big arms and starts purring.

"Maybe dogs can sense good humans and cats can sense people who are dead inside. Just like them."

"Hurry up and get to work."

I sigh and start the job of emptying out the cage, which is already sparse apart from one toy, one blanket, and the litter tray.

Anton takes the kitten over to the climbing tree and watches as it explores. He has a slight smile on his face and almost looks peaceful.

"How do you know your way around here already?" I ask. "You were traded a few days ago."

"I was on time. Plus, I grew up here. Used to volunteer here during school."

"What? No way. How did I not know you were from Boston?"

"Is it because I don't say things like 'I'm wicked smaht'?"

"Hey, I've never said wicked in my life, but I still have that Boston edge in my accent."

He cocks his head. "Maybe you didn't know because you're only interested in yourself."

"Oh, right. That. But also, how did we not cross paths before going pro?"

Anton snorts. "Because you had your head so far up your ass you never noticed me before?"

"Wait … we were in the same league?"

"We only had one season where we played against each other because I'm younger than you, but yeah. It's hard not to remember the guy who thought he was above it all, even back then. *The Ezra Palaszczuk* who didn't have to work at anything. Natural-born talent, all the newest equipment money could buy—"

"You're forgetting all the pressure Dad put on me to make it all the way."

Anton shrugs. "I saw a cocky kid who had it all. I … I was quiet back then, still figuring myself out, and I had to fight tooth and nail to become the best at hockey. I didn't really hit my stride until freshman year of college. By then, you were already drafted and in the AHL."

I try to think back to when I was a teenager, and fuck, I barely remember my teammates let alone anyone I played against. "So, what I'm hearing is, you've had a crush on me since high school."

Anton lets a laugh slip out. "Can you get back to cleaning, please?"

"Sure. But just know, when we lose every single game from here on out, it's because you made me hold a black cat."

"I'll take all the blame."

"Good."

By the time we've cleaned out all the cages and moved on to the dogs who have much bigger and better living quarters, I'm exhausted.

But then an adorable old golden retriever mix tackles me when I open his cage, and it gives me a burst of energy. "At least *someone* likes that I'm here."

"Mm, an affection-starved, homeless dog. I don't think his standards are high."

"From memory, he's not the only one in this space who has slobbered all over me."

"Yeah, well, my standards that night took a massive dive too." While his words are still as cutthroat as ever, I can't help noticing the conviction is missing. His tone is lighter, and when I look up from where I'm playing with the dog, not only is he smiling, but he's smiling at *me*. I get the impression he's trying to remind himself how much he hates me.

We get the rest of the cages clean with the help of other volunteers who arrive not long after we start on the dog area. Then for the actual PR part of the day.

Adopt an animal, meet a hockey player.

This is the kind of PR I like. Not because it makes me look good, but meeting fans, especially young kids who look up to me, is not only an ego stroke, but it feels like I'm actually doing something good. I like giving people hope in a world that has so much wrong with it.

And when a teen boy comes up to me, his eyes cast down, head held low, I can predict what he's about to say before he says it. He's not the first confused-looking kid to come out to me.

His brown hair falls in his eyes. He has to be around fifteen, but he's muscular for a teen. If it weren't for the acne and braces, I'd assume he was older from his physique.

He glances around and steps closer, speaking low. "Umm, I wanted to say thank you for, umm, you know … umm—"

"What's your name?"

"Tai."

I hold my hand out to shake his. "You can all me Ez."

His face lights up. "Really?"

"Of course. It's nice to meet you, Tai."

"Uh, well, yeah, umm, thank you. Again."

"I'm guessing you don't mean for volunteering here."

He wears a small smile. "No. I mean …" The next part comes out in a rush. "For-coming-out-and-playing-hockey."

"I'm not doing anything heroic. I'm just being myself. Everyone should be allowed to be themselves."

He finally meets my eyes. "That's heroic to me."

Beside me, I sense Anton listening in.

"I hope one day you're as supported as I feel in the league." Okay, so not everything is perfect in that sense, but I feel a hell of a lot safer than I ever could have imagined at Tai's age.

"C-can I get a selfie?" Tai asks.

"Of course."

The whole time, Anton keeps watching us, and when Tai walks away, I lean in closer.

"Careful. With how hard you're staring, someone might think you have a thing for me."

Anton shakes his head. "Just when I think you might actually be a decent human being underneath all your shit, you come out with … *that*."

"Hey, I can be a decent human being and be full of shit at the same time, thank you very much. It's called multitasking."

"If you say so."

I will never, ever, ever admit it, but today has actually been fun.

Minus the cats.

CHAPTER EIGHT

ANTON

Even as I'm shown through the third apartment I've viewed since coming home to Boston, I'm still not feeling it. The places are fine, but I don't get the same sense of *home* like I did back in Philly. It's a whole lot harder being back here than I thought it would be.

I don't know if it's my playing, the team, trying to be Ezra's teammate, or a combination of everything.

The game the other night was a mess. It's been so long since I've played a shutout match that I forgot how hard they hit you mentally. I have one job out there—to score—so if I don't score, I've failed.

Not my team. *Me*.

The final preseason game is tomorrow night in Philly, and Ezra's taunt of remembering who I play for keeps ringing in my ears. The only thing I'm using to keep my mood up is the thought of sleeping back in my old apartment. I know I'll need to get around to leasing it or selling it eventually, but for right now, I'm holding on to that place like a lifeline.

"How's this one?"

I cringe and turn to face Gerard. "I don't love it."

"Why aren't I surprised?"

When I got back to Boston and needed to find a place, he was the first one I called. We were hockey buddies in high school, and instead of aiming for the big time, he wanted to go into real estate like his mom.

"You NHL stars sure are high-maintenance," he says.

I flip him off, which only makes him laugh. "Show me an apartment worthy of an NHL star and we'll do business."

The thing is, he has been showing me great places. They meet the brief I've given him, but what they're missing is the inexplicable quality that grabs hold when you walk into a place and it refuses to let you forget about it.

"Still at that hotel?"

"Unfortunately. Though with the number of away games we have coming up, it's not like it's much different to how it normally is during the season. How's the family?"

"Great. Michelle has been asking when you're coming to visit. I think she has a crush."

"Can we blame her?"

"Fuck off, asshole. Your lifestyle has made you look old."

I rub my jaw. "Wow. Realtors in Boston are a hell of a lot less professional than I remember."

"Seriously though, when are you going to make time for us? We want you to meet the little one."

"You're not worried I'll steal your wife?"

He gives me a derisive eye roll because he knows that will never happen. Gerard is one of the first people I ever came out to. One of only a few from my high school days.

"If you get desperate for dates to all those charity benefits you hockey players go to, I'll let you borrow her. Then

I can brag to all my friends that my wife is still hot enough to bang an NHL player."

"I'll keep that in mind, thanks. Though, my no-date rule is working for me just fine."

"Don't you want to settle down? I can show you a few houses big enough for a husband and maybe some little Antons running around."

Gerard is living the kind of life I would have if I'd never made it in hockey professionally. Solid career, partner, new baby. All things I want eventually, though I'm still unsure about kids—that's future Anton's decision.

"Ooh, I was expecting you to cringe or flinch," Gerard says. "You're actually thinking about it."

"I was contemplating which would be worse, a screaming kid or nagging husband. I don't think I could handle both."

Gerard laughs. "Come and meet Mick. You'll see that not all kids are screamers."

"I'll visit in the off-season. With the trade, this is going to be my most intense year yet. I have something to prove."

He claps my shoulder. "I am so glad I didn't chase after that dream. It seems stressful."

"And being a Realtor isn't?"

"Not with the market the way it is. I'm raking in more than you in commission alone ... probably."

I snort. "You wish. But we'll catch up when I can. I'll text you when I can do dinner or something."

"In the meantime, I will continue to find you places you hate."

I thank him as he locks up and head back to the hotel, annoyed I still haven't found what I'm looking for.

It's not like I've never played for other teams or moved out of home, but the decision feels bigger this time around.

I blame Ezra.

Because I can.

Because he's always there.

Because out of all the other players in the league, he's the one guy I can't stand and yet the one person our team seems set on me getting along with. The photos from the charity day are everywhere, and the GM and PR department are eating up all the attention Ezra's and my "bromance" is getting.

If the press knew how much time we spent bickering as opposed to actually working at the shelter, they'd be printing different stories.

I have to admit Ezra did better than I was expecting. He complained, but he got the job done. And then with the public, and that kid ...

I saw a different side of him. A side I *admired*. I hold my orientation close to my chest because I don't want it to define me, but watching how grateful that teenager was to see representation in pro sports made me want to kick my own ass for staying out of the spotlight.

When I get back to my room, I drop back on my bed. Some of the team were heading out for a quiet dinner, but I turned down the invite. The sooner I get to know these guys, the better, but we have an early flight tomorrow, and I really need a good night's rest since I haven't had one since leaving Philly.

It's just started to get dark outside as I finally drift off, but I'm woken a moment later by my phone blaring through the room.

" 'Ello?" I answer groggily.

"Are you serious right now?" comes Ezra's incensed reply.

My lips curl into a smile, while my eyes stayed closed. "Ah. Always good to hear your voice."

"Get your ass to this team dinner. It's the least you could do since you got cat juju all over my game."

I chuckle. "You did *what* with a cat?"

"You know what I mean."

"Is there a point to this call?"

"Yeah. We did rock, paper, scissors over who would call you, and I'm the one who got screwed." There's noise in the background. "I have to make sure you're on your way."

"I'm not."

"Then get on your way."

I hum, pretending to think about it. "No."

Ezra curses in what sounds like Polish. "Moreau is here."

"Good."

"He came with Diedrich."

"Okay."

Ezra sighs. "Why aren't you coming?"

"I'm not turned on."

He swears again, this time because he really should have expected that answer. "Funny."

"Thank you."

"You're such a dick." Frustration bleeds into his voice, and the more annoyed he becomes, the more my cock starts to take notice. I almost want to suggest that if he begs me, I'll come—maybe in more than one way—but I really need to forget what happened between us.

We're on the same team now, and encouraging anything like that will make things messy. Maybe I shouldn't go back to my apartment tomorrow after all. All I could picture when I walked into that hallway was Ezra pushed up against the wall, no matter how many times I told myself to move on.

The one time I let my dick take control, and this is where I end up.

"Come on, Hayes. I thought you weren't going to let your opinion of me get in the way of winning the Cup?"

"I'm not, but I don't see how going out the night before a game is going to help with that."

"It's called team bonding."

"It's called a distraction." I finally open my eyes and look around the dark room. "You're good at those."

"Distractions?"

"Obviously."

His voice drops to a delicious level that my body agrees with. "See, it almost sounds like you're calling *me* a distraction."

"I'd have to notice you to find you distracting."

"You noticed me when you were dicking me out."

Of course he had to go there. "Are you going to bring that up every conversation we have?"

"Probably. You don't like it, so that makes it fun."

"For you ... Look, I know we don't like each other, so I'm going to say this once and never again. I'm pissed about the New Jersey game, and *yes* I feel like it was my fault. Now tomorrow, we're playing against my old team, and I have more on the line than any of you to make sure we win." I've fought too hard for my first line spot, and I'll do anything to hold on to it. "If I want to look you guys in the eye again, it needs to happen. I'm so sorry you lost the rock, paper, scissors thing, but I'm not coming. I'm going to bed, and I recommend you all do the same. O'Ryan is going to make sure Philly is ready to show Moreau and me what we're missing."

There's silence on the other end, and I wait, expecting Ezra to come back with a stupid, obnoxious comment. He doesn't.

"It's a team game, Hayes." He pauses. "You must think you're really important to assume *you're* the only reason we lost."

He hangs up, and while at surface level his words sound like an insult, I think ... did Ezra Palaszczuk just *reassure* me?

There goes any chance of sleeping tonight.

—

We're deep in the third with scores locked up at two apiece. I'd been right that O'Ryan would be on fire tonight, but Wagner is also playing the best game I've seen from him in a while.

If it wasn't for our goalie saving our asses, there's no way the score would look the way it does. My back is drenched with sweat, and the crowd is absolutely deafening. I'm not used to being on this side of the ice, playing with these guys, and having the home crowd here against me, but dammit if I'm going to let them get in my head.

We line up, ready for the faceoff with only a minute left on the clock.

Diedrich shoots to Larsen, who passes back to Ezra.

Ezra blows past everyone, skating circles around all of them like they're mere cones and he's running a drill instead of what they really are—two-hundred-pound men trying to hit him as hard as they can.

His eyes lock with mine across the ice, and they don't leave me as he passes me the puck. I flick a wrist shot at the goal and hold my breath.

The lamp lights up, and relief sweeps through me. I'm hit from all sides as my teammates converge, and we end up in a tangle of strangling hugs and back pats before we get back to it and run out the few seconds remaining on the clock.

It's one of the sweetest home-side upsets I've experienced yet, and when the buzzer finally sounds, the weight of all that expectation, of all the pressure I've piled on myself, finally shifts.

Thank fuck.

I can breathe again.

We line up to shake hands, and instead of the usual smug mask I wear in this situation, I take my time, wishing my old team a good game. Because it was. They had us right up until the end.

There's already music pumping in the locker room when I walk in, the guys in various stages of undress.

Kosik snaps his towel against my thigh as he passes, heading for the showers. "Finally showed up to play, eh, Hayes?"

"Just giving the rest of you time to catch up to my awesome."

"Awesome?" Ezra snickers. "That's one word for it."

Feeling better than I have all week, I steal the towel slung over his shoulder and snap it against his ass. Ezra jumps and throws a scowl at me. I loop the towel around my neck instead. "I need this more than you. After all, you only need to shower if you actually played."

"Who got the assist on that last goal, jackass?"

"I was too busy scoring to see." Normally I'm all about sharing the credit, team effort and all that, but the way Ezra's glaring at me …

I like it a bit too much.

"Hayes, Palaszczuk, post-game conference," Stewart Frankenhorn, the team's PR rep, says from the door.

Of course. Because what's some more attention on this bromance? We scored a goal together, so see, everyone? We really are friends.

I channel that line of thinking on the walk there.

We get the formalities out of the way, and then the questions start. They certainly don't hold back.

"You two worked like a team out there. Is it safe to say the rumors are true? Your feud is put behind you?"

I predict we'll be answering about ten different questions that are the exact same thing worded differently. We've already said repeatedly that we're friends now.

"There's no need to fight when we're on the same side," Ezra says.

"Your playing was fluid, though, like you've been playing together for years," the same reporter says.

I lean in closer to my mic. "We have been playing together for years. Just on opposite sides. I know how to read Ezra like a book. It's how I used to score on him so much."

The reporters burst into a round of laughs while I smile over at Ezra.

He cocks an eyebrow at me, and it's like I can read his mind.

You know exactly how to score on me.

Ugh, is it possible for someone to be so cocky that their replies manifest themselves in your brain?

Once the press circus is over with, and by the time we come back from that to hit the showers, we're the last ones in the locker room.

The whole time we shower, I stay firmly turned away from him. There's nothing more awkward than popping a boner in the showers, and I always get horny after a win. Seeing Ezra naked on top of that will be way too much to resist.

The best thing I can do is shower as fast as I can, dress, and get my ass home. Well, after the celebration that I better haul ass to tonight. I owe O'Ryan a drink after that.

I know a lot of the guys whine about having to wear a suit before and after games, but I like it. It makes me feel part of something bigger than me. Reminds me that this is my job, and I take it seriously.

If only the same could be said for everyone. My suit is navy and fitted. It looks great, but I made sure it wouldn't draw too much attention.

Ezra's? He has a whole collection of suits I wouldn't be caught dead in, and today's is a black and pale gray floral print. Pants *and* jacket.

"You look like my nanna's garden," I tell him on the way out of the locker room as he falls into step beside me.

"And you look like an usher. But I promise not to hold it against you."

"How generous."

"I can hold something else against you, if you like."

I quickly scan the corridor and make sure all the journalists have left. Then I glance over at Ezra as he pumps his eyebrows at me.

Goddamn. "Like a grudge? Because that's not new information."

"I was thinking something more physical. Don't make me spell it out for you, Hayes."

"I would if I thought for a moment you could actually spell."

Ezra steps close. He grabs my wrist, just two fingers, and it's nowhere near enough to hold me in place, but my feet stop moving anyway. "Come on, this is bullshit. We worked well together out there tonight, but we can't be in the same room without getting pissy at each other. I've seen you checking me out in the locker room—"

"I never—"

"We both know it. And the solution is, we fuck it out."

"There's no end to your ego, is there? I check you out, so what? Who says that means I want you?"

"Don't you?" His eyes are issuing a challenge, and his fingers flex that bit tighter.

"Fine. Yes. There's nothing I enjoyed more than making you desperate, and knowing that no matter how much you might hate me, I'm still the one who made you come."

"How do you know I wasn't thinking of someone else?"

I step forward, way too close than is safe in this hall where anyone could walk past. I drop my voice. "You think I missed the way you moaned my name? You loved it, didn't you? That's why you're always bringing it up?"

I did too. There's no denying that. Fucking him was hot as hell, and I can't stop picturing doing it again. I want to shove him to his knees and feed him my cock, to bend him over and rail him again, to jack him until he comes so hard he goes cross-eyed.

"You have a talented dick," he grudgingly concedes.

"Well, you know what you have to do, then, don't you?"

"There's no fucking way I'm going to beg you."

"Fine." I go to walk away when Ezra's grip on my wrist tightens.

He tugs me back. His gaze darts between my lips and my chest, clearly conflicted. Finally, so quiet I almost miss it, he whispers one word through clenched teeth.

"*Please.*"

CHAPTER NINE

EZRA

I told myself I wouldn't beg, and I hadn't planned to, but that *please* fell out of my mouth without permission. I'm sure Anton's going to use that one word against me for the rest of my life, and as much as I'd like to say using my manners doesn't equate to begging, I can't deny the desperate need in the way it came out.

Anton stares at me, and I hold my breath.

It's a torturous two seconds before he wets his bottom lip and mutters, "My place. One hour."

My lips curl, and I lower my voice. "Aww, you going to go home and get ready for me? Are we going to flip the other way this time?"

"Nope. I'm going out with O'Ryan for a drink. Maybe you should spend the next hour prepping that hole for me." Anton walks away, and I have to reach into my pants and adjust myself before following.

I catch up to him. "Where are we getting that drink?"

"You want to come hang with the enemy?"

"Not the enemy yet. Regular season starts next week. Besides, if I'm there, I'm hoping we won't make it an hour."

I see it—Anton trying to contain his smile. He sucks at it.

"You're going to be insufferable the whole night, aren't you?"

"I'm so hard it's uncomfortable."

Anton glances at my crotch and then sighs as he takes out his phone.

"What are you doing?" I look over his shoulder and see he's texting O'Ryan.

"Bailing on drinks."

I tell myself not to be a smug bastard because at this point, anything could make Anton change his mind. "Uber?"

"I have my car. I went and picked it up during our downtime. Coach gave me permission to drive it up to Boston tomorrow instead of flying back with the team." We head for the parking lot.

"You know, there are people you can pay to drive your car to Boston for you."

"I don't mind the drive. Besides, my Porsche is my baby." He hits a key fob, and the lights of a Porsche Cayenne flash.

Sleek black, all the extras … it might not be the sexiest Porsche out there, but it's still impressive.

I act unfazed. "Eh, my G-Wagon has more room. Your back seat doesn't look spacious enough to do sex acrobatics."

"We're not teenagers. We're not having sex in the back of a car."

I tsk him. "Live a little. Spice it up."

We drop our gear bags into the back seat, and they take up nearly the entire space.

"See? Not big enough." I slide into the passenger seat, while he gets behind the wheel.

He turns to me. "Okay, if we're doing this again, I think we need some rules."

"I'm not good at those."

"I've noticed."

"Hey, I only visited the sin bin once tonight, thank you very much."

Anton slow claps. "How many times was I in there? Oh wait, none."

"Of course Perfect Anton Hayes wouldn't ever be caught dead in a sin bin. Oh, the horror of breaking the rules!"

"Rule number one. No talking." He pulls out of the parking lot and heads for his apartment.

"At all? Or during sex? Because I can't not be vocal during sex, so that has to be vetoed."

Anton glares at me.

"Oh, so, like, *now*. Got it." I'm not used to rules—the lack of respect I had for my father meant I broke the few he tried to give me, until he didn't bother anymore. I should be telling Anton to go to hell with his bossing me around, but I think I like it.

I shut my mouth, but I don't do well with silence.

My fingers tap my leg, my cock strains behind my fly, and even though this car is a smooth ride and the leather seats are nice, I've never been more uncomfortable in my life.

I shift, trying to stop the ache between my legs.

Anton's eyes are lazily focused on the road, but I can't help noticing the tent in his suit pants too.

How is it possible to hate each other as much as we do, but the thought of getting naked with him is like a direct hit of electricity to my balls?

Anton's apartment isn't far from the arena, but it's still too long for me to deal with silence and not occupy myself with something else, so I lean closer to him and reach across to run my hand up his thigh.

His legs are so powerful and thick. They have to be for how fast he is on the ice.

"What are you doing?" He doesn't take his eyes off the road.

I mime locking my lips.

"Fucking smartass." But despite his words, he widens his thighs.

I inch my hand higher and rub over the bulge in his pants.

He lets out a heavy breath. "Are you trying to make us crash?"

"Apparently the only time I can talk is if we're having sex, so I figure if I jerk you off, I can say anything while my hand is on your dick." I go for his fly, but my seat belt holds me back, so I unclick it and then have better access to undo Anton's pants.

Anton catches my hand. "Seriously?"

"Come on, break the road rules with me. Live on the dark side. Step outside the box and have mind-blowing sex outside of the bedroom for once. Who knew you were so vanilla?"

He side-eyes me quickly before focusing back on the road. "If I remember correctly, we had some damn hot sex up against a wall not that long ago."

"Whoa, wild child, settle down. Ten feet outside the bedroom is too crazy."

"I'm starting to think the no-talking rule should be a constant thing." He releases my hand so he can put on the turn signal, and I don't waste time in taking his cock out.

I'm surprised when he lets me.

"Do you want my hand or my mouth?"

"Jesus." His grip tightens on the steering wheel until his knuckles turn white.

"I don't think I can get Jesus for you, but I do get the impression you want my mouth. You just don't want to ask for it."

Anton's lips purse.

"Oh, how the tables have turned. You wanted me to beg, and now you need to." I stroke his cock from tip to base, and he shudders. "Tell me to suck you off."

A strained noise comes from the back of his throat, and then he reaches to cup my face and run his thumb over my bearded cheek. "I want to fuck this mouth." His thumb moves across my lips. "Give me what I want."

The urge to refuse is strong for no other reason than to leave him hanging and to be an asshole, but the way I let down a tiny bit of my guard by saying please, he's doing the same right now.

His dark gaze flicks to mine again for a brief moment, and the suspicion and dash of vulnerability has me giving him exactly what he wants.

I lower my head and lick along his slit while I still work him over with my hand. His cock is the most amazing dick I've ever seen, but no way in hell will I tell him that. The head is swollen and red, and there's one thick vein running down the underside.

As I suck him into my mouth and ease down his long length, I move my hand into his pants and grip his balls.

I get lost in his scent, his sharp breaths, and the faint salty taste of precum. The choked noises he lets out, the strangled gasps of shock, like he was under the impression I didn't have skills until now, only spurs me on to give him the best damn blowjob of his life. Even if it is awkward as hell in a moving car.

"Shit, red light." Anton hits the brakes, and the sudden stop forces his cock into the back of my throat.

I choke and splutter until the car stops, then yank off him, hitting my head on the steering wheel and setting off the horn.

"You're so right," Anton says dryly. "This is so much better than sex in a bed."

I laugh. "At least it's not boring."

"Mm, concussions are known to be fun. How's your head?"

"Never had any complaints," I quip. I sit up, moving back onto my side, and rub the back of my skull.

"My place is literally around the corner," Anton says.

When he pulls into his parking spot in the underground garage, he turns the car off and then tucks himself away. His cock has deflated since the red light incident.

I stare at him, at the slight hesitance on his face, and in the low light, with his dark hair unstyled and falling across his forehead, he looks like a billboard model for expensive vodka. Or clothes.

"Changing your mind?" I taunt. "You can still kick me out."

"Somehow, I don't think getting rid of you is as easy as that."

"Sure, keep telling yourself I'm that pushy." I lean back in my seat and rub my cock through my pants. "It has nothing to do with wanting this. Nothing to do with wanting to make me come again."

Anton's gaze doesn't leave my crotch as he says, "Nothing at all." He clears his throat. "Get upstairs. Now."

I grab my bag from the back. Anton leaves his, and I have to hurry to catch up to him. "In a rush?"

"Yes."

The elevator is empty when we step in.

"Perfect," I purr and try to pull him close.

He shoves me off him and says, "Cameras."

Damn.

I keep my distance until he unlocks his door and steps aside to let me in.

Everything is the same as it was when I was here last. Nothing is packed, and everything is in its place.

"You do know you live in Boston now, right? Aren't you bringing all this stuff with you?"

"Do you want to talk about my furniture or do you want me to fuck you?"

"Why can't we do both?"

"Why do you care?"

"Mm, growly Anton really gets me hot."

He gives me a blank look.

"Frustrated Anton is even hotter."

Anton grabs my wrist with his big hand and pulls me down a hallway. "Get in there." He opens a door to his master bedroom.

"Ooh, yay, sex in a bed. Did we learn nothing from the car ride here?"

Anton ignores me. "Strip."

I turn to find him scrambling out of his suit, so I take my time, loving the way he glares at me when he's completely naked and I still have my pants on.

Instead of complaining, he dips his fingers into my waistband and pulls me against him.

Chest to chest, skin to skin, the prickle of anticipation rushes through me. My lips tingle as I expect him to close the gap and kiss me, but then that makes me realize we didn't kiss the last time we hooked up.

My stomach flips as he leans in. Closer. Almost there.

Then his head drops, and he stares as he pushes my pants and underwear down, freeing my cock.

"Go over to the window," he orders.

"You going to push me out of it?"

"Mm, that fantasy actually turns me on more than the thought of taking your tight ass again."

"What about fucking me and then throwing me out the window?"

Anton laughs. "*Nrg*, I think I might come."

I go stand by the wide ceiling-to-floor window. He has a small balcony off his bedroom, so at least I know if he gives in to his fantasy, I won't fall twenty-something stories to my death.

Maybe I should be concerned I'm willing to have sex with someone I'm only ten percent sure won't turn homicidal on me, but I'm not.

Anton rummages around in a drawer behind me, but I can't take my gaze off the city. Even when Anton steps up behind me and presses his hard cock against my ass cheek.

"Going to do me like this again?" I ask.

His forehead lands on the back of my neck. "When I can't see your face, it's easy to believe you're someone else."

"You say the sweetest things."

"Let's get one thing straight. This isn't about being sweet. Nothing about this is romantic."

"Insults are pretty romantic to me."

"Of course they are. It's how you cavemen communicate." His lubed finger slips into my ass crack, and his breath lands in my ear. "Let me in."

I bend and put my forearm on the glass pane in front of me. "Are you sure this window will hold us both? I really don't want to explain to Coach how we both fell through a window naked and need to go on the IR list."

Without warning, Anton's arm tightens around my waist as he spins us and pushes me toward the bed. I catch myself, my hands gripping his comforter, my chest flat against the mattress, and my ass sticking out.

"The no-talking rule is back in play," he says.

"But—"

"Ez, if you want my dick"—he rubs his cock down my crack—"you'll shut the fuck up."

Sex with Anton goes against everything I believe in. Like shutting up. And begging. *Saying please.*

Yet, I do as he says because the second he has me prepped and his cock breaches my hole, he turns me out like nobody ever has.

He gives only a few seconds to adjust to his fat cock before he lets loose. With each thrust, each sting, my body hums.

I don't know how he does it or why it's so good with him. It just is.

Every time his cock pegs my prostate, my legs tremble.

I lower my head and rest it against the bed while the sounds and smell of sex fill the air. Anton grunts, and I moan. His balls slap against my ass every time he pushes in. My face burns, my gut heats, and I only want more. I crave it.

"Damn, Ez. You feel so good. Too good."

The snarky comeback sits on my tongue, but I swallow it down. I get the feeling he was testing me. I'm supposed to be silent.

Anton slams inside one more time and stills. At first, I think he's come, but then he leans over me, that raspy voice in my ear once again. "Tell me how much you like me fucking you."

"I do," I admit. "I want to take a mold of your perfect dick so I can make a dildo and fuck myself with it."

He grips my hair. "Or you could ask me to do it."

"You mean beg?"

A laugh hits my neck. "There might be some begging involved. You're so hot when you're needy."

I push back because I need him to keep moving inside me. "Fuck me, then." My cock drags along the comforter, teasing me with that tiny bit of friction I need.

Anton stands still while I fuck myself on his dick, but it's not enough. I need him to meet me thrust for thrust. I need him to tear me in two.

"Please," I find myself saying ... again. It falls out way too easily.

Anton Hayes is a sadist. This is practically torture for me.

"That's better." He pulls out of me and then slams back in, and I cry out.

I reach between me and the bed to stroke my cock.

"You going to come?"

"So close. So—"

He gives one more hard push inside, and it sends me over the edge. I tense and come all over my hand and his comforter. Anton quickly pulls out of me, snaps off the condom, and then jerks himself against my back. The slick sounds and heavy breathing let me know he's close, and it only takes a few seconds for the spurt of warm cum to hit my skin.

We tumble into a pile of limbs and breathe hard. I'm turned to jelly, my eyes are heavy, and he must sense it.

"Stay if you want. Or go back to the hotel. Up to you. I'm going to shower and go to sleep."

I don't push my luck and ask if showering is an invitation. So while he disappears, I use his comforter to clean myself off. He's already going to have to wash it anyway. I swipe my underwear off the ground and pull them on. Anton takes the shortest shower in history and is back out before I find my shirt.

He throws a towel at me. "Shower's all yours if you want it."

As much as I'm mostly clean, I figure I'll get it out of the way now, but I underestimate the power of Anton's six showerheads. The water comes at you from two angles and feels like heaven on my tired muscles.

I stay in there so long that Anton's snoring when I get back out.

He did say I could stay, but the thought of climbing into bed with him feels too … intimate.

I get back into my suit and check my phone, noticing an email from my agent. It's a YouTube link to the cologne ad I shot during the off-season.

Anton's smart TV catches my eye.

I might not be comfortable with staying in his bed, but if he wants me here, I'll give it to him.

I grab the remote and flick through to YouTube on his TV. Then find my ad and put it on a loop. I only wish I could be here to see his face when he wakes up to my presence.

CHAPTER TEN

ANTON

When I wake up to the sound of Ezra's voice and his face swimming in my hazy vision, I assume I'm in some sort of fever dream ... or nightmare. I squint around the bright light coming through my bedroom window and focus on the TV. On Ezra. In a commercial?

I watch in horror as Ezra smolders at the camera, shots of his face interspersed with shots of a cologne, and his voiceover of random words mixing with the wannabe rock music. The whole thing is terrible.

But damn.

He looks sexy.

I palm my morning wood, too lazy to do anything about it. If Ezra had stayed last night, I could have put his mouth to good use again. I've never had road head before and probably won't again, because the number of times I almost crashed was concerning. It felt way too good.

And is yet another example of me letting Ezra wreck my brain.

I'd never normally do something like that because it doesn't take much for the car beside you to work out what's happening and snap a picture, but that voice of reason disappeared at approximately the same second Ezra's lips wrapped around my dick.

It's no wonder he's always getting himself into trouble.

Fifteen minutes later, and I'm still in bed watching the screen. Idiot.

I kick off my covers and strip the bed, then toss the sheets in the wash. I've got a long drive ahead of me today, and then tomorrow we're right back into practice.

The thought of driving all that way only to have a hotel room waiting for me on the other side is depressing. I really need to find a place to live.

When I walk out of my apartment, I do so knowing it's the last time.

Most of my clothes are already in Boston, and the remainder of my crap will be boxed up and shipped with a moving company. When I sell, the furniture will be included.

Sure, I might love my apartment and my car, but the smaller material things aren't something I get attached to.

Unfortunately for me, five hours in a car and then meeting Boston traffic leaves me with way too much time to *think*.

And no matter how many times I go over plays and team dynamics, my thoughts keep circling back to Ezra.

There's no denying I'm attracted to him. His caramel-colored hair and ice-blue eyes combo makes him one of the most handsome men I've ever seen. At first I wasn't a fan of the beard, but the way it scraped my abs and thighs last night has effectively changed my mind, and if we're going to hook up again, he's sure as hell keeping it.

If we hook up again?

Urg. Nope.

I've slipped twice now, and while it's stupid to regret it, I also know it wasn't the most well-thought-out move I've ever made.

We have to work together. We have to find a way past our animosity to something almost civil in order to do the job we're being paid to do. Sure, fucking it out of our system helps, but that's a short-term solution. I can't imagine how hooking up with a teammate could ever end well.

If the rumors are true, Ezra's most likely done with me now. He never stays focused on one man for long. Well, except for whatever that thing was between him and Westly.

Apparently, they were dating, but not. Sleeping together, but not exclusive. I shake my head as I check my mirrors and overtake the car in front of me.

When I'm with a man, I'm far too possessive to share. Sure, I've had threesomes with one-night stands that were hot as hell, but they're always very discreet, and never with anyone I'd see again.

With a boyfriend or partner or someone I'm seeing regularly—even if he does happen to be a smartass with a big mouth—it's exclusive or nothing with me.

Which is reason number seven hundred and fifteen for why last night was just us working out our tension together.

But I know if he comes at me again, I'll find it very hard to say no.

There's something about being with Ezra that's addictive.

He doesn't put on a show; he doesn't hide how he feels even though he probably should when he's with me. He's uninhibited. I like it. I also like him clenched around my cock, but that's different.

Fuuuck.

My thoughts are on a constant loop of the same thing. Should I or shouldn't I? Pros and cons—and the fact the cons column outnumbers the pros by a lot should make the decision far easier than it is.

By the time I finally pull up at the hotel, I've made a decision. A decision that really shouldn't have taken me five hours to come up with:

I'll wait and see what happens.

I never claimed to be a genius.

Back at practice, nothing is overwhelmingly different, but there's a shift I can feel in the locker room. It's like the air between me and Ezra is electrified. I wish I could ignore it or go back to that place where I couldn't stand the guy.

His attitude overrides anything else, but then he'll make an awesome save on the ice, or I'll remember the way that kid thanked him or focus on that teeny-tiny sliver of vulnerability he showed when he was drunk that first night together.

But whatever conflicting thoughts I might have, my one certainty is that we need to get along for the team's sake. And maybe because I *want* to get along in general.

So when I approach him on the way off the ice after practice, I drop the usual hostility we have with each other. "You skated well today." The words taste like chalk in my mouth. Complimenting Ezra goes against every natural instinct I have.

He glances over at me. "Is this you lulling me into a false sense of security before you stab me with a skate?"

"Come on, Ez …" I slap him on the back. "Our skates are nowhere near sharp enough to make it through your thick skull."

"Seriously. What do you want?"

To go back in time and never start this conversation?

"You wanna be a dickhead, fine. Don't worry about it." I go to stalk off, but Ezra grabs my practice jersey and pulls me to a stop.

"Can you really blame me for being suspicious? All you do is remind me that I'm a fuckboy who doesn't take hockey seriously and is a subpar player."

I grin. "But you *are* those things."

He flips me off, and I don't blame him. "Yet you slept with this fuckboy anyway."

Ezra doesn't bother to keep his voice down, and I quickly glance around to make sure our team is well out of earshot, but it looks like they've all disappeared into the locker rooms.

"Would you keep your voice down?"

"Why? Embarrassed? Everyone here knows you're gay."

It's on the tip of my tongue to say yes, but then we'll end up circling back on the same bickering we always do. This is supposed to be moving on from that.

And what a surprise that Ezra is making it difficult.

Nothing to do with me at all.

I shove a hand through my sweaty hair. "I'm not embarrassed."

"I know you better than to believe that."

"I'm *private*. There's a difference. And I don't think our team needs to know that things are more complicated between us than straight-up animosity."

"There's nothing complicated here. You're overthinking it. We don't like each other, but we got each other off. It doesn't have to mean any more than that."

"Right. Nothing more." I huff out a frustrated breath because I don't completely believe it.

I catch his eyes and try to work out his expression. There's something that happens when his gaze sharpens on me that speaks to me on a primal level. My gaze dips to where a wet curl of hair is stuck to his neck, and I can't help wondering if his sweat smells as intoxicating after a grueling practice as he does when I have him bent over and working for it. I lick my lips completely unconsciously, and Ezra's eyes snag on the movement.

"The way you're eye-fucking me makes me think you want it to happen again."

I let my stare roam down his face and to his wide chest, picturing myself stripping him out of his gear. "No idea what you mean."

"Problem, boys?"

I straighten quickly at Coach's voice and find him peering around the doorway of the locker room. "Nope, we're good here."

Which is actually not that far from the truth. Fuck, pigs really do fly.

I hold my head high as I stalk away, wanting to make sure Ezra is left with no doubt that he hasn't been able to ruffle me. I'm used to masking signs of weakness, and that skill is going to come in handy when dealing with him.

Ezra wears his emotions up front, and no amount of snark or cockiness can completely hide the way he's feeling at any one time. Especially because I get the feeling he never actually wants to.

The idea of letting people be privy to your every thought is so foreign to me I find it difficult to understand.

Good thing there are no feelings in hockey. Hockey is the one thing I can do in my sleep.

And when we enter the rink at TD Garden the next day for our first regular-season game against New York, I'm confident.

I feel good. Pumped. The energy is high, and the crowds are loud.

Diedrich, Larsen, and I have started to find a rhythm that works. We still mess up, and it's not smooth yet, but when we make a flawless play, I'm hit with that rush of adrenaline I don't get from anything else.

I'm slowly starting to find my place here, becoming more comfortable with the team. I almost feel like the old me again. The guy who has his shit together.

I've also managed to keep a professional distance since Philadelphia, and Ezra's been doing the same, but every now and then he'll catch my eye, and I can't stop myself from giving him a smirk. It's too easy. Too fun.

I don't want or expect it to get me anywhere other than under his skin.

The minute I hit the ice, I can feel it. The win. Normally I don't like to get ahead of myself, but there's something that feels so right, and it's like the rest of the team feels it too. Right from the puck drop, we win possession, and then it's like we can do no wrong.

Diedrich, Larsen, and I work together seamlessly, and even though New York is on their game, they're no match for us. We manage a goal each before we enter the last period.

Other than one goal Ollie Strömberg gets past us in the middle of the second, our defense is equally tight. Ezra's game is clean, and he doesn't get sent off once.

At the next face-off, Diedrich takes control of the puck and sends it sailing into my blade. I fly up the open ice, and all that's standing between me and my next goal is

New York's goalie. I can almost taste the next point, can *feel* the crowd's cheers. It's one and one as I cross the blue line, draw up close, and—

I'm clipped from behind. My skates fly out from under me, and I smack into the ice. My momentum almost sends me into the boards, but I pull up short, afraid to move for one second as I test out the damage.

Thankfully, everything seems to be working.

Kosik reaches me first. "You good, Hayes?"

"Yup." I push myself back upright and shake out the arm I landed on. He slaps me on the shoulder, and we skate back to where Poulsen is being sent off the ice.

"Power play!" Ezra shouts as he skates past.

We're already leading by two, but one more point will pull us far enough ahead that there'll be no coming back for New York. We have a one-man advantage—we need to use this.

We take our line, and I face Ollie Strömberg, waiting on the puck drop. He's a legend in the game for being one of the first out players in the NHL. I admire him.

But not today.

Today, he's in my way.

Play starts, and the second Diedrich takes possession, I'm off. He passes to Kosik, back to Diedrich, to Larsen, who shoots a snapshot my way. I deke past Ollie, and as I'm about to line up my shot, Johansson blocks me. We fight for possession when I catch Ezra out of the corner of my eye.

I pass backward to him, and like he was expecting it the whole time, the second the puck hits his blade, he shoots. It sails straight past the goalie and hits the net.

The lamp lights up, and the crowd is almost deafening in response.

It's all over for New York.

We're unstoppable.

And as the clock finally runs down and we come out on top, I'm still riding the high.

When we leave the team box and head down the chute, I linger for the fans hanging merch over the side. Larsen and I sign a few things and pose for photos.

"Anton!" a teen girl shouts. "You're my favorite."

"Thanks, darlin'."

Her face goes red. "This is for you." She drops a furry stuffed cat over the side, which I catch and hold in the air, using it to wave to her as we leave for the locker rooms.

Larsen sniggers. "Don't let Ez see that thing."

I glance down at the cat. It's black and fluffy with a red heart ribbon around its neck. "It's a toy. He's not *that* superstitious, is he?"

"Yup. He makes the rest of us look levelheaded."

A slow smile creeps over my face as I tug the ribbon off. "Don't worry. I'll be sure to hide it the second we get back."

Right in Ezra's locker.

And luck is with me because when we reach the locker room, he and Diedrich have been called away for the press conference, so it's all clear.

I put the kitty right in the center of his cubby so there's no missing it.

Then I strip off my pads down to my base layer shirt and pants and start to whistle as I jump on a bike to cool down. My muscles are extra tight tonight, so I need to make sure they're stretched out enough that they don't seize up tomorrow.

We're about to hit the road for eight days to play Dallas, Arizona, Vegas, and Colorado.

And when a string of Polish curses hits my ears as Ezra finds his present, I have to laugh into my sweaty shirt so he doesn't know it was me.

Though I guess it's a given because he storms into the workout room and throws it at my head.

"What? Stuffed animals are bad luck too?"

He glares one more time before stomping out again.

CHAPTER ELEVEN

EZRA

We lose to Dallas 3-2, and I know exactly who to blame. We hit the locker room with the same air of defeat that always lurks when we lose, but on the bright side, I played so badly, there's no way the PR team will want me for interviews.

"Still think your present was funny?" I ask Anton as we strip out of our pads.

"Come on, Ez. It was a gift from a fan. It has nothing to do with why you fell on your face more times tonight than your entire season last year. That was all you and your talent."

I want to wipe the cocky expression off his face. "You do know which team you play for now, don't you? We're supposed to be getting into the other team's head, not our own."

"All of this because of a stuffed toy? Superstitions aren't real."

Half the team gasps.

Finding a hockey player who doesn't have at least one superstition is like finding a unicorn in your backyard.

"Even if you don't believe in them, you have to believe in routine. Anything that throws that off has the potential to hurt our game."

Anton purses his lips. "Fair point."

"Now I need to go fuck all this bad juju out."

Larsen, who's next to me, shudders. "We promised no talking about our sex lives. I don't even want to know what juju means in the gay world."

"It means exactly what it sounds like," I say. "Lots and lots of cu—"

Larsen covers his ears. "La, la, la, la, la."

I turn back to my cubby, but Anton's closer to me now.

He steps into my space and lowers his voice so the others can't hear. "And who are you planning on fucking this out with?"

I slap his shoulder. "Don't worry. I wasn't planning on begging tonight. I need to mix it up. Dallas has one of my all-time favorite gay bars. Nothing like fucking a little sin out of some pent-up, sexually frustrated religious type."

I don't let him respond before I head for the showers.

If I was honest back there, I would've said I planned to do it with him, but it's true I don't want to beg tonight. My ego took enough hits on the ice. I want to be the one in control, and there's no way Anton will give that to me.

He still doesn't trust me, let alone like me enough to go there.

Plus, I'm starting to … I don't know. The thought of leaving here with him is *too* easy, and I'm not falling into that trap.

That's what happened with West, and then before I knew it, he had feelings for me, and I unknowingly hurt him. I don't want to hurt Anton—no, I don't want to hurt *anyone* like that. My sex-life works for me because feelings never get involved.

Some of the guys are heading out for a late dinner, some are going to bed, but as soon as I drop my gear back to my hotel room and grab a condom and lube packet from my luggage, I'm out the door and calling a cab.

It's a short drive to the Circle, but as soon as I walk in and catch sight of all the thirsty-ass guys in here, something's ... off.

There's no other way to describe the ick feeling in my gut telling me I shouldn't be here. I push through it and go to the bar to order a drink. Or six.

As I sip my bourbon, I spin on my stool and lean back against the counter so I can scout for potential hookups.

I like this place because the lighting is low, and the atmosphere is laid-back and not as hyper as a pure hookup bar. The dance floor isn't a bump-and-grind kind of space but has actual line dancing, but if I do want to bump and grind against someone, there's a room out the back where you can go to get your rocks off. Names don't even have to be exchanged if you don't want to.

A few guys walk past me, eyeing me from head to toe. I lean back, stretching my long torso for them to get a proper look.

Being a famous athlete, I should be careful about who I spend my nights with. Many times I've ended up on trashy sites looking messy with a cute guy in a club. It's not ideal when that happens because while the league frowns upon it when it comes to straight guys being photographed in different states of undress with women, they really hate it when it's photos of two guys being splashed all over the internet.

Double standard, yes, which is why I don't cover my face by wearing a baseball cap—my own little act of rebellion against the flawed system—but at the same time, I try to make sure whoever I hook up with won't exploit me for it.

I turn and order another drink, but when it's placed in front of me, the bartender's hand lingers, and our fingers brush against each other.

He's new, or at least, I don't remember him from any of the times I've been here. I would've remembered the mane of curly blond hair and bright blue eyes.

"You look familiar," he says, "but I know I haven't seen you in here before."

I eye him in the cocky way I always do when I flirt. "Sports fan?"

He screws up his face. "Hell no."

I laugh. That's one trait I look for in a hookup. If they're a fan, they're more likely to document their experience.

"Maybe you just *want* to recognize me, then." I wink.

He looks at his coworker who's busy at the end of the bar and then leans in closer to me. "I'm not supposed to hit on customers, but my break is in twenty, and you're gorgeous."

I lick my lips as a prickle of doubt shoots down my spine.

On paper, he's the perfect candidate. Needs to be secretive because he's not supposed to fuck customers. Doesn't know who I am. Hot. He's definitely hot.

Then why don't I want to jump his bones?

"Thanks, but I'm—" A hard presence presses against my back.

I know who it is without having to turn around, and I light up from the inside.

The bartender retreats. "Ah. Got it. No problem." He nods down at my drink. "That one's on me."

I try to school my face before I turn around, but Anton's large hand grips my hip.

His breath hits my ear as he leans in and says, "The bar is mirrored, dumbass. You can stop looking so smug now."

I meet his eyes in the reflective glass, and he is the type of famous athlete to hide his face with a cap. The dark scruff on his jaw makes it appear more square than usual, and I want to feel the roughness on my skin.

That *ick* feeling disappears.

"I told you. I'm not in the mood for begging."

"Then don't beg." Anton takes my hand and pulls me toward the back of the club where that dark and private room is. He moves like he's on a mission, and that's when I realize something.

"You've been here before," I say over the noise of the club.

"Duh. It's discreet. Unlike certain bartenders."

"Careful. That sounds a hell of a lot like jealousy, but that can't be right."

There are some other guys in the room when we get there, but it's practically pitch-black, so it's hard to see anything.

Anton pushes me against a wall and presses his hard cock against mine. "Let's get one thing straight. This has nothing to do with jealousy and everything to do with not wanting to get an STD panel done every time we hook up."

An unwelcome gasp parts my lips. "Are you saying you want to regularly fuck me? I think you might like me, Hayes."

"See, I think I might be starting to, and then you open your mouth. But yes. I want this to happen again. I want to keep doing it until I no longer have the urge to shut you up by sticking my dick in you. However long that will take."

My smile is almost painful. "I dunno. I am *really* annoying."

"I've noticed." Anton reaches between us and pops the button on my suit pants.

I ditched my jacket back at the hotel and rolled my sleeves up on my shirt so my biceps bulge. Those babies have gotten me more hookups than I can count, so I always try to show them off. But Anton's muscles are just as impressive, and I can't help gripping his arms while he works open my fly.

When he gets it undone to the point he can take me out and wrap his fingers around me, my whole body thrums in anticipation, but his touch doesn't come.

"I only have one stipulation …"

The word *anything* almost falls from my mouth, but I hold it back.

"I'm not going to be your side toy like Westly Dalton was. I don't share."

I knew I wasn't going to like it. "Now, that sounds like commitment, and—"

"You can fuck whoever you want once I'm done with you. This isn't about being together. It's about being able to enjoy each other without worrying about where you've been. That guy out there looked like a walking petri dish."

"There's a difference between playing it safe—which I encourage—and sex-shaming. I told you I'm on PrEP."

"This is my only stipulation. Take it or leave it."

I've never been good at focusing on one person, and I've never seen a reason to, but we both know this is only temporary. I'm sure I can keep my wandering hands in my pockets until Anton and I have this out.

"No more begging?" I ask.

"Not unless you want to."

Fat chance. "You going to fuck me here, then?"

"I had another idea." Anton drops to his knees and flips his hat so it's on backward, and my legs buckle.

Anton Hayes is about to suck my dick. I'd be lying if I said I haven't thought about this because I have. A lot. I've been wanting to find out if Anton's mouth is as talented as his cock.

Some guys are teases, drawing out blowjobs like they have all the time in the world to taste, suck, and slurp all over your dick. They try to make it into a work of art. And sure, that can be hot as hell, but sometimes you really need them to get to business.

It shouldn't surprise me that Anton is the other type—the type who can go straight to deep-throating you while tugging on your balls to the point you're on the brink of coming after ten seconds.

"Holy fuck." My head falls back and makes a thud against the wall, but I don't care.

He takes all of me to the root, his nose buried in my groin while his throat works around the head of my dick, and when I pull out halfway so I can thrust back inside, he takes it easily.

Had I known how good he was at fucking and sucking, I might have made the effort to put aside our differences a long time ago.

I keep going with shallow thrusts, enjoying the buildup while cautious of how much he can take, but like me, Anton must get impatient with blowjobs because he stops playing with my balls and reaches around to grip my ass. He sets the pace and depth, and *damn* it's an impressive depth. I briefly worry about breaking his nose with my pelvis, but that thought disappears when his hand dips into the crease of my ass.

The second the pad of his finger presses against my hole, I unleash inside his mouth.

I try to hold back the moans I usually let go of while I come because I'm conscious of others in this space, but holding out means the sounds that come out of me are desperate and strained.

When I'm spent, I tap Anton's shoulder and sag against the wall. He stands, looking as smug as ever, and then he grips my shoulder tight to push me down.

"Need to … Breath … can't catch," I say.

"Trust me. This will be fast. Open up."

I lazily open my mouth and let him inside, but unlike him, I'm too blissed-out and recovering from that monster of an orgasm to really put in any effort.

Anton doesn't seem to care. He doesn't force it on me either. He pushes about a quarter of the way inside, and I manage to swirl my tongue around the tip. Then he keeps his thrusts small and shallow while he takes his hand and strokes himself.

I'm on the floor, cock still hanging out of my pants, while he uses my mouth to get himself off.

He leans forward, putting his hand on the wall to hold himself up while he takes his own pleasure from me.

This might be even hotter than doing it myself.

"Will you swallow?" he grits out, and I give a small nod.

When he does come, his thick thighs quake, and I grip them tight as if that can help hold him up.

I regret our road head incident not ending like this, with my mouth full of his cum, but I can say it was worth the wait. I swallow him down, drinking him in, and then a second later, his cock slips from my mouth, and Anton slinks to the ground next to me.

I lean over and wipe my mouth on his shoulder, and he laughs and shoves me off him.

"This probably isn't the most sanitary place to sit," I point out.

"True." He puts himself away, and I do the same. Then he stands and holds out his hand. "Let's get back to the hotel."

The warm Texas air hits us, but we're silent as we wait for a cab. I almost don't want to ruin this with words. *Almost.*

I go to open my mouth, but Anton covers it.

"Shh. I didn't think this was possible."

"What?"

He removes his palm. "You. Being quiet for more than two minutes. It's … peaceful."

"I guess you know what you have to do to shut me up from now on."

"Deal."

We lock eyes, and for the first time, he doesn't seem to be looking at me in annoyance or lust.

"Think you're going to be able to keep up with me?" I ask. "If I'm not allowed to hook up with anyone else, you have to take care of my every whim."

"I'm sure I can manage."

Hmm, we'll see about that.

When we get back to the hotel, we enter at the same time but are far enough away that it looks like we arrived separately.

He holds the elevator door open for me, but I turn in the direction of the reception desk.

"You go on up. I need to ask for extra towels. Kosik is a towel stealer."

Anton smiles. "I never did trust that guy. Now I know why." The doors close, and I beeline to the desk, where there's a pretty receptionist.

"Can I help you, sir?" She overtly checks me over, and that's how I know she has no idea who I am. She probably knows I'm with the team, but that's it. Any hockey fan knows I'm gay.

I bring out my flirt A game. "Hey, I'm Anton Hayes. I'm here with the B's? I was hoping you could do me a favor."

"Anything, Mr. Hayes."

"I want to wake up early to get in a workout before we leave for the next game in Arizona. It's a grueling schedule."

She nods sympathetically. "I bet it is. What time would you like a wake-up call? I can put it in the system."

I pretend to think. "Four? Yeah, four a.m. sounds good to me."

"Done. Four a.m. is a lot of dedication."

"Thanks." I give her a flirty wink as I walk away.

Just because Anton and I have decided to fuck on a regular basis, that doesn't mean I don't still owe him payback from that stupid cursed cat he left in my locker.

Happy morning wake-up call, jackass.

CHAPTER TWELVE

ANTON

I'm jolted awake at way too early o'clock by the sound of the hotel phone.

"Wha's happening?" Moreau says in his sleep, and I quickly roll over to answer.

" 'Lo?"

"Good morning, Mr. Hayes. This is the wake-up call you ordered."

I blink into the pitch-darkness of the room and catch sight of the glowing numbers on the clock. "Four a.m.?" My voice is gritty with sleep.

"That *is* the time you requested," the bubbly voice says. "Enjoy your workout."

She's gone before I can question her further. I hang up the phone, completely confused.

Clearly, it wasn't the wrong number if they knew my name and ... workout? What's going ...

Fucking Ezra.

Extra towels. Sure. Right.

Asshole.

Moreau starts to snore again, but now my brain has clicked in, no attempts to fall back asleep work. I have a very good guess this is to get me back for the cat incident, but where that was all in good fun, this is cruel. He's lucky the game is tomorrow, but we've got our practice skate at Gila River Arena later today. That isn't going to be fun after a late night and an early morning.

Oh yeah, he's going to pay for this.

An hour later, I'm still fighting sleep, so I figure I might as well do what she suggested and head down to the gym. It's quiet, with only two other people there, one who clearly recognizes me by the way he trips over his feet on the treadmill.

I jump on a bike and put my AirPods in, hoping I won't be distracted.

And even though it's early, I'm humming with satisfaction.

Orgasms have a way of balancing out lack of sleep, and jerking off into Ezra's mouth was one hell of a high.

My only regret from last night is shaming him about sleeping around. Random hookups are a fun time, but what else was I meant to say? That I'm a possessive motherfucker? I already told him I don't share, which was close enough to the truth, but one of the main reasons I try to avoid anything serious is because it turns me into a spoiled brat of epic proportions.

My toys are mine.

I can only imagine the media shitstorm with them using my being gay as an excuse for my borderline possessive and unhealthy behavior. Sure, things are better for queer athletes now there're a few of us in the NHL, but we're still expected to toe that line of being gay while playing into het stereotypes.

It's why Ezra gets so much attention for his antics.

We can be gay, but we need to either be in a committed relationship like Ollie Strömberg, or be a sweet, fun guy like Tripp Mitchell, or keep things out of sight and out of mind like me.

We're *not* supposed to have a different guy in our beds every night.

We're not supposed to be … *toxic* isn't the right word. If he wanted out, I'd let him. But if I caught him with someone else while we were together, things would be *unpleasant*.

Westly Dalton might have been content to be Ezra's side hustle, but there's no way in hell that's happening with me.

It's not even really about the jealousy either. Once we end things, I'd be more than fine watching Ezra in a full-blown orgy without feeling a thing, but when I'm with a guy, I want to be the only one he's thinking about.

And when things are cooling off, I'm the one who ends things.

My fear of rejection is way too strong to let anything else happen. It's one of the reasons being traded stings so badly.

And maybe that's part of why I don't want to come out. Because no matter how much support is in the world, there will always be rejection as well. People will say cruel and hurtful things, and there's no way around that.

By the time I'm back in the hotel room, I have a text waiting for me from Ezra, asking if I had a good sleep.

I chuckle, because game on, Ez. Is a wake-up call really the worst he can do?

It's hot as balls in Texas, and Arizona is going to be no better, so after showering, I pull on a pair of sports shorts with the team logo and a T-shirt. Moreau is wearing the same.

"Damn, that game last night was a mess," he says as we stuff all our things into our bags and leave. "Did you see Philly won five nothing?"

"I did. And I'm happy for them."

"That could have been us."

I understand what he means, and it's a total rookie way of thinking. "But it wasn't. I know it's hard, the rejection sucks, and it's even worse when the new team can't get their shit together, but that's our problem now. Trades happen, and we need to be able to adjust quickly, otherwise we'll be replaced for good. You want to make a name for yourself? Focus. Forget about Philly, and show these guys you're worth the money they're paying you. There are worse jobs we could have."

He chuckles. "That's true. I feel like I'm doing so well, then I hit these roadblocks in my mind and can't find a way around them."

"All normal. No matter what level you're at, they'll still happen. You'll just find better ways of figuring them out." We get into the elevator, and I hit the button for the lobby.

"How do you?" he asks.

I picture Ezra on his knees again. Okay, so my ways of managing might not be exactly healthy, so that's probably not advice I can give. "I remind myself of how lucky I am. I'll buy something stupid because I can, I'll find a way to give back—charity-type things but on the down low and not because I've been scheduled to do it—and when neither of those things work, I hook up. There's nothing good sex can't fix."

The elevator opens into the foyer as those words leave my mouth, and it's clear some of the team have overheard me when Larsen says, "I hooked up last night, and I already feel better about the game. Kind of."

I refuse to look at Ezra, but I can feel him smirking in my direction.

Whatever. He already knows he's a good lay ... The blissed-out look on his face flashes through my mind again, and okay, maybe he's better than *good*.

I'm determined not to show how tired I am as we head to the airport. When we finally step aboard the plane, I figure two hours is a good amount of time to sneak in a nap.

Until Ezra takes the seat next to me.

"You look like you could use some beauty sleep."

I link my hands behind my head and turn to him. "I'm good, actually. Incredibly well rested. Best sleep I ever had." I don't even try to be believable because if Ezra calls me on it, he'll give himself away.

We watch each other, both clearly trying not to smile and hoping the other person breaks first. But there's only so long I can stare into Ezra's pale blue eyes before my blood starts to heat. I cave first and avert my eyes.

Most of our team have spread out across the plane, some of them settling in to take naps, others playing on their phones, and most of them wearing AirPods to try and get out of their heads for a bit. Games like the one last night can stick with you if you let them, so like I said to Moreau, we need to learn how to bounce back fast. Arizona won their last game, so they're going to be looking to exploit any weakness they can.

The only thing I can hear is low murmurs of conversation and our coaches discussing the game plan for tomorrow.

When I glance back at Ezra, he's still watching me, only his gaze has dropped now. He's taking in my long torso and spread thighs. I let them fall open wider to mess with him, but I can't deny loving the way he looks at me.

I pull out my phone and type out a text to him one-handed.

> You look like you're going to come in your pants.

He snickers as he reads the message. Then pointedly looks at where the outline of my cock is clearly starting to chub up.

> Hey, you promised last night you'd take care of these needs. Wanna join the Mile High club?

> No chance. You need to learn to be patient.

> Going back on your promise already? That's cool, I know of a great gay bar in Arizona …

The growl that leaves me is completely unintentional. And Ezra looks delighted. His tongue swipes over his lips as he types out another message.

> I'll never forget the monster dick I got there last time.

I pluck his phone from his hand. "And that's enough from you," I whisper to make sure we're not overheard. The row in front of us is clear, and Diedrich looks like he's nodding off behind us.

Ezra swoons dramatically. "The way he held me down and made me choke …"

"If you think I'm going to get jealous, you're going to have to try a bit harder than that." The last time Ezra was in Arizona, we weren't hooking up, so I don't really care what he got up to then.

"I thought about him last night while I was on my knees for—"

"*Don't.*" The word comes out louder and harsher than I meant, and Kosik tilts his head from up the aisle toward us. I smile at him until he turns around again.

"Not jealous." Ezra winks. "Got it."

"You sure think a lot of yourself," I say, voice pitched low again.

"I mean …" He shrugs. "If you were this awesome, you'd understand."

"It really is a surprise your skates can hold up the weight of your head."

"Which one?"

I laugh despite myself. "You're really … something."

"That's almost a compliment, coming from you."

"You know, I think it might be."

This time when we lock eyes, some of the smug cockiness has melted away, and I get a glimpse of the real Ezra underneath. Not that cocky isn't Ezra—it's not really an act with him—but there's something more there too.

"Can I ask you something?" he says.

"Can't guarantee I'll answer, but shoot."

"Why did you sleep with me that first time back in Philly?"

"Don't make me give you more compliments. I'll never survive it." The truth is, he's hot. I've always found him hot. That's part of the reason why I notice all the dumb shit he does. And then when he was in my apartment, goading me to have sex with him ... what was I meant to do when I had Ezra Palaszczuk at my mercy?

"Fine, then. Do you regret it?"

It's on the tip of my tongue to say yes. Just one word. So easy to get out, but for some reason. It won't come. Instead, I give him something like the truth. "Not as much as I should."

He hums. "Yeah. Me neither."

A moment of comfortable silence falls between us, which quickly turns uncomfortable. I'm not used to anything other than tension between us, so this ... whatever it is, doesn't sit right.

"Though I guess that's easy to say when I blew my load less than twelve hours ago," I say to fill the stifling quiet.

Ezra groans. "Twelve hours is forever."

"Well, I hate to point out that you're going to be waiting longer than that. We're at the arena this afternoon, and Coach won't let us out the night before a game."

"Fuck." Ezra relaxes back into his chair. "Why couldn't they have roomed us together?"

"Probably a good thing. I don't imagine our team would appreciate losing games because we've been up all night."

"Oooh, as soon as we're back home, we're trying that."

"Hmm, maybe." I don't have an apartment yet, and I'm not so sure I want to go to Ezra's. It's a good thing I don't need to worry about that for a while because after Arizona, we still have Vegas and then Colorado to go.

"I wasn't lying when I said I'll be difficult to keep satisfied. You might as well move in with me now."

"Can I ask *you* something?" I throw back at him.

"Umm. You know what, I take my question back. Let's pretend like that never happened."

"Ezra …"

"Fine. Same answer as you though. If I don't like it, I'm not answering."

"Fair." I tap my foot as I try to think of how to say this. "Why do you do it? Not the sleeping around part—that's whatever. But why do you draw so much attention to it?"

He opens his mouth, closes it, then opens again. I really didn't think it was going to be that hard for him to answer, especially because he could throw out something Ezra-like and claim to be *that* awesome.

Eventually, he shakes his head. "Yep, I don't like it, next!"

"Come on, I gave you something, at least."

"Barely."

Well, I can't make him answer. But where I thought Ezra did it because he likes the attention, I'm starting to suspect I was wrong about that.

He folds his arms, sliding down farther in his seat. "It's not on purpose."

"What?"

He lets his eyes fall closed. "The first time pictures of me went up, they were a total shock. I hate it, but there's not a whole lot I can do at this stage. It's out there, so whatever. I try to be careful, but there's no way to actually know if you can trust someone you've met seconds before."

"Is that why you and West …"

"Yup. It was convenient for both of us, especially since we roomed together. He was—and is—the only person I trust."

"And he was okay with you hooking up with other people?"

"Yeah, we're not talking about this."

"I'll take that as a no."

Ezra huffs. "You're almost as annoying as I am."

"Gotta keep you on your toes somehow."

"There are far more fun ways to manage that." I think the conversation is over when he turns away, but I catch him whispering, "He never told me he wanted more."

I have to tread carefully here, but I need to know. "I have another question, and this one you have to answer."

"I agreed to keep this thing only between us. I don't owe you anything else."

"You do, because the answer will determine whether I end it now or not."

He's clearly confused when he turns back to me. "*You* end it? Why are you the one who gets to call the shots?"

"Are you in love with West?"

He gapes at me. "Fuck off, Hayes."

"Simple yes or no."

"No. He wanted me, I didn't know that, so I did some really shitty things not realizing I was hurting him. That's why I'm no one's forever—because I can never tell when I screw things up. I'm not in love with him, but I feel guilty for the way I treated him. Happy now?"

I shouldn't be, but I am. "Very."

"Whatever. I'm tired."

"Like *you're* the one who was woken up at four a.m." I hadn't meant to tell him that, but when his mood shifts back to the Ezra I'm familiar with, I'm glad I did.

"So much for that awesome amazing perfectly great sleep," he says.

"You're an idiot if you think I'm not going to get you back for that."

Ezra's grinning as his eyes fall closed again. "What are you going to do? Spank me? Too bad I'd like that."

Well, I'm pocketing that knowledge for later. "You'll see."

—

Our game against Arizona is a tight one, but we pull off the win right before the buzzer, preventing the game from going into overtime. The end score was only 2-1, and we had to fight for every minute. I know the crowds love high-scoring games, but there's nothing like taking out the win you truly fight for.

It would be even better if I could drag Ezra away for some hot sex, but Coach is still pissed from the game in Texas, and none of us wants to go out to celebrate with such a tight win and another game so close. Which means unless we find a stroke of luck, it'll be almost a week until we can hook up again.

Diedrich and Ezra are called away for the press conference again, which means they're entering the workout room as most of us leave it. The team strips off and heads for the showers, and as soon as they disappear, I have an idea.

Left alone in the empty locker room, I gather up a pile of sweaty clothes and stuff them into my bag. Then after the showers, I throw a couple of wet towels in there for good measure.

We're heading out for a late dinner at the hotel when we get back, and as everyone enters the restaurant, I grab Kosik and pull him to the side. "You're rooming with Ez, right?"

He narrows his eyes. "Why?"

"Can you keep a secret?"

"I could be persuaded to."

"Okay, I'll pay for your drinks *and* dinner if you accidentally drop your room key."

"I'm not going to walk in on you guys fucking, am I?"

I stifle a laugh. "Fuck no. You know I can't stand him."

"Then …"

"It's for a prank." When he doesn't look convinced, I add, "Harmless, I swear."

"Okay, but you have to promise not to touch my stuff."

"Hand on heart. Which bed is yours?"

"The farthest from the door. Ezra said something about windows? I don't know. He has too many superstitions to keep up with."

"Your stuff is safe."

That gets him on board. "Better be a good prank." He takes out his wallet, grabs the room key, and pretends to drop it as he walks inside.

I'm quick to swipe it off the floor and leave. Back in my room, I grab my bag, sneak down the hall, and swipe into Ezra's room. His Nike bag is right beside the closest bed, and when I drop mine onto the mattress and unzip it, I have to hold back a gag.

Sweaty hockey players are disgusting.

I pull back the covers and dump the contents onto the sheets. Jerseys and undershirts, a pair of pads, and … oh shit, someone's jockstrap. I use my foot to kick it toward the pillows then lay out the damp towels over it all.

The whole thing is going to smell ripe by the time we're done with dinner.

Perfect.

On my way back down, my phone vibrates with a text.

> Should I be worried about where you are?

> Just taking a dump.

> Now there's an image I can jerk off to later 😳

I chuckle as I tuck my phone away and stretch my arms over my head. I have a feeling that jerking off will be the last thing on Ezra's mind by the time he gets back to his room.

CHAPTER THIRTEEN

EZRA

All throughout dinner, Anton shoots me these looks I can't decipher. Probably because he's actually smiling at me. And not at something I'm saying or doing, but, like, just in my direction.

I think he's broken.

When he gets up halfway through and heads for the restrooms, I count to sixty and then follow him as subtly as I can, but in the men's room, he's actually pissing, and so is Diedrich.

I didn't even see Diedrich leave the table.

Damn, no hookup, then?

I don't need to take a leak, but Diedrich is looking at me as he washes his hands with a confused expression, so I take the place next to Anton and think of waterfalls and running water.

Diedrich leaves, and I turn to Anton.

"I thought that was an invitation. You've been staring at me all night."

"You think everything is an invitation. Someone breathes near you, and you try to hump them."

"In my defense, nine times out of ten, I'm right."

He slaps my shoulder. "Not this time." He crosses the bathroom to wash his hands, and I do the same.

"Then when are we going to fuck again, and when can I get a turn at your ass?"

Kosik walks in, and fine, I get it, a bathroom hookup in the restaurant our entire team is eating at is not a good idea.

Anton starts in the direction of the door, and I follow him out. "Patience," he says. "When we get the chance, we'll take it, but after that game, I'm exhausted. I'm going to go back to the hotel and sleep in my big, comfy bed. I suggest you do the same. Big game against Vegas in two days."

Anton gives me that weird smile again as he walks away, but it's not until we get back to the hotel room that I'm able to decode it.

Kosik comes back when I do because he says he lost his room key, and as soon as I open the door, the stench of a thousand men assaults my nostrils.

Now, the smell of one or two sweaty men in a bed is hot. Especially when mixed with the scent of sex. But this?

I have limits.

"What the fuck did he do?" Kosik asks and lifts his shirt over his nose.

"Who? Wait, let me guess. Anton fucking Hayes."

Everything looks in its place, except my blanket is less perfect than Kosik's.

We approach the bed cautiously, and I almost gag as I pull back the covers to find wet towels and half the team's base layer clothing everywhere.

"That smell ain't coming out," Kosik says.

"You're the one who let him in here. You should give me your bed."

"He said it wouldn't affect me."

"Didn't think that one through, did ya, genius?" I pull off all the bedding and wrap the offending garments in the sheets and then chuck it all in the bathroom and close the door.

"I don't think that worked," Kosik says, still holding his nose.

I grab some deodorant from my luggage and spray that shit everywhere, while Kosik strips down and gets into his bed.

If either he or Anton thinks they're getting off so easy, they're sorely mistaken.

I get down to my boxer briefs and climb in next to Kosik.

He nudges me. "Sleep on your bed."

"There're no sheets. Also, hold still." I curl around him and then lift my phone to take a selfie.

"That better not show up on any puck bunny websites," he warns. "Unlike some people, I actually like getting pussy, thank you very much."

"Don't worry. It's for a special someone."

"Eww. Are you going to jerk off to a photo of me? I love you like a brother, dude, but I don't want you plundering my booty."

I have to laugh. "Are you calling me a butt pirate? Offensive much?"

"Fuck off."

"Nah. You owe me. I can't believe you sold me out to Hayes."

"If I let you sleep in my bed, will you shut up about it?"

"Yes."

He grumbles under his breath. "Fine. Just go to sleep already."

"I have to do one thing first."

I attach the pic and send it to Anton with the caption: *I really don't have any complaints about the outcome of this prank. Hope having your big, comfy, nice-smelling bed to yourself was worth it.*

—

The next morning when we emerge in the lobby, I don't have to make eye contact with Anton to know he's glaring at me.

It makes me insanely happy to be the focus of his attention.

"Anyone else get the best sleep ever?" I ask.

"Someone got laid," Diedrich taunts.

I open my mouth to draw this out, but Kosik beats me and ruins my fun.

"No, he did not."

"You liked me spooning you all night, big guy. Don't lie." I blow him a kiss.

"Who wants a new roommate on the road?" Kosik asks.

"Uh, why were you two … spooning?" Larsen asks.

"Yeah, Hayes? Why did I spend the night curled up next to Kosik?"

"I have no idea what you're talking about." The fucker smirks, and I'm so pissed Kosik couldn't let me pretend we had sex. Just for long enough to make Anton crazy.

One thing's for sure: payback is going to be bigger and better.

And it starts as soon as we get on the bus to the airport.

He sits down the front, and I'm toward the back with Larsen.

My phone vibrates in my pocket.

> Book a hotel room on the Strip somewhere for tonight.

Tempting, but I'm not going to bite.

> Sorry, can't. I'm catching up with Tripp. You know, bros before hoes.

> Tripp Mitchell? As in the goalie for Vegas? Gay Tripp Mitchell?

> The one and only. Want to mess with my bed again tonight so I have an excuse to stay at his place?

> The only excuse you need to fuck anyone else is that you're done with me, so go for it. Just know your actions have consequences.

Damn him.

Tripp isn't my type. He's too nice. But I did promise I'd catch up with him. If you were part of the queer collective with us, you'd be bound by law to do the same.

Law? Really?

Yep. Another law is you have to have fucked at least one of the others in the group. I'm your ticket in.

And who exactly did Strömberg and Sorensen fuck considering they were in relationships with other people when they came out?

It's a new rule. It was unanimously decided that I would take one for the team and hook up with you. You're welcome.

You're so full of shit.

We both know I'm full of cum.

You will be.

> Promise?

> Tomorrow. After the game. We'll find a way.

—

As soon as we're checked into the hotel and I warn Kosik not to "lose" his room key again, I order an Uber to meet Tripp at the D on Fremont St.

It's where we always go whenever part or all of the NHL queer collective is in town for obvious reasons—the name alone.

I walk into our favorite steak house and find Tripp already there with, unsurprisingly, Dex Mitchale. They're sitting on one side of a high-walled booth, so I slide in opposite them.

"You brought an outsider?" I pretend to be outraged.

"It's only Dex."

"What if I want to talk about a guy I hooked up with who has a weird-shaped dick?"

As the words fall from my mouth, the waiter appears. "Uh, umm … I'll give you a few minutes."

Tripp smiles. "You're going to scar the waitstaff for life."

"Please, like he doesn't like the D," I mutter.

"Really?" Dex asks. "How can you tell?" Dex leans over Tripp to try to see the waiter's retreating back. "Tripp, you should ask for his number."

"Yeah, Tripp," I taunt. "Ask for his number."

"I'm good. Thanks." Tripp buries his head in the menu.

Then Dex turns to me. "So, guy with a weird dick. Was the tip cut at the end to make it look like a snake tongue?"

I … have no words.

"I'm proving I can be one of you guys. Talk all the dicks you want. I own one. I'm not scared."

Tripp holds up his hand. "Please don't."

"All good. I'll need the Mitchell brothers to help me out with something later anyway," I say.

Tripp kicks me under the table because he hates, hates, *hates* it when he and Dex are referred to as the Mitchell brothers. Same last name, spelled differently.

And they couldn't look more opposite.

Dex is tall and lanky with dark blond hair. He's hot as fuck but dumb as bricks, and that's okay, because he's a loveable bastard. Not a bad hockey player either. Tripp is shorter and wider, with the reddest hair you'll ever see. His skin is flawless and covered in adorable freckles.

"What do you need help with?" Dex asks.

"Getting back at Anton Hayes."

Tripp groans. "Not getting involved."

"I'll do it," Dex says.

"It's official, Trippy. Dex takes your place in our group."

"Woohoo!" Dex fist-bumps me. "So what are we gonna do?"

"An oldie but a goodie. We're going to take all the furniture out of Hayes's room and put it in the hallway. I need you two to help me move it all. Oh, and to get the room key from the front desk."

Dex turns to Tripp with his big puppy dog brown eyes.

Tripp throws up his hands. "Fine. Let's stoop to Ezra's level."

Dex puts his arm around Tripp's shoulder and pulls him close. "This is going to be fun."

CHAPTER FOURTEEN

ANTON

I stumble out of the elevator with the rest of the guys I went out with, pleasantly tipsy and ready for a good, deep sleep before the game tomorrow. I would have preferred to fuck myself into a coma, but Ezra wanted to play games, and now we're both going to be unsatisfied.

Or at least, he better be.

Sniggers come from behind me a second before Moreau says, "What the fuck?"

I dismiss thoughts of Ezra and focus on the obstruction right in the middle of the hallway.

It's ... beds and chairs and desks ...

"What am I looking at?" I ask, circling it, even as what I'm seeing starts to register.

"I think you're looking at payback." Kosik sounds way too happy about that.

My head drops back on a laugh. Ezra. I could kill him.

"Payback?" Moreau echoes, swiping into our room and confirming my suspicions. The whole thing is empty. "What did *I* do?"

"Collateral damage," Kosik says. "I've been there, brother."

"Help us get this crap back inside." Unsurprisingly, my buzz is starting to wear off.

"Yeah, no way," Diedrich says, sidestepping it all and continuing to his room. "You guys are on your own."

"Larsen?"

"Nope."

A muscle in my jaw twitches, and I grab Kosik's shirt before he can walk away. "I'll make this easy for you. Either help us, or Moreau and I are coming to your room and tonight you'll be spooning two guys."

He groans. "Why do I keep being punished?"

Moreau grumbles something under his breath as I grab a lamp off the pile and use it to prop the door open.

"What was that?" I ask him.

"I said we should make Ezra fix this."

"There's no way anyone can make Ezra do anything." I drag a mattress up onto its side and nod at Kosik to grab the other end.

Instead of being irritated like I'd expect, I'm hit with unwelcome amusement. Damn Ezra is messing with my head. I should be annoyed, but if I know Ezra, and I think I'm starting to, there was nothing malicious about this.

It's supposed to be a fun prank, so that's how I'll take it.

And how fucked in the head am I to be happy that this proves he spared me at least one thought while he was out with Tripp?

It takes us almost an hour to get everything inside and the room put back together properly. It's late, and while I'm not pissed about the prank, I am worried about how a shitty sleep before a game is going to affect me.

Then again, I wasn't so worried about that when I was making suggestions for getting another hotel room.

I tug off my tie, toss my suit jacket over a chair, and fall face-first onto the bed. I only mean to be there for a minute, but the next thing I know, I'm jolted awake by my alarm going off.

I'm still half-asleep when I silence it, then blink groggily at the bazillion notifications filling my screen.

What the ...

I sit up as I swipe open my phone, trying to get my eyes to focus. It's ... a video?

I click on it, and Ezra's social media opens.

The video is captioned: *Welcome to the team. Total bromance.*

I hit Play, and there's me and Moreau outside our room, staring perplexed at the pile of furniture in the center of the hallway.

From the angle of the phone, Ezra's clearly around the corner filming, and damn I wish I'd seen him there last night. All I can be thankful for is that I laughed instead of swearing up a storm.

The rest of the team joins him, and all I can hear are chuckles and hushed voices as Moreau, Kosik, and I start putting everything back.

The news sites are having a field day with it. Some of them saying this reaffirms the apparent bromance we have, and others say it seems like we're trying too hard to be convincing and the rivalry is still going strong.

I close out of it all and text Ezra.

> You're a dick.

I immediately regret sending that when his reply bubble pops up, and I know exactly what he's going to say.

> What's that? You're obsessed with my dick?

> You are so predictable.

> Says the guy whose first reaction was to insult me. What a surprise.

I close out of my messages because he's right, but I don't want to admit that. Insulting Ezra is easier than complimenting him, and I catch myself going to do that alarmingly frequently.

Instead, I do a search for last-minute reservations and book a room in the hotel two down from us for tonight. No matter how the game turns out, I'll be making use of that bed.

Preferably all night.

Which isn't something we've done before, but it's been a while since I had a good sex marathon, and if anyone is going to keep up with me, it's Ezra.

The thing is, I know he's going to ask to top me again, and I'm not sure how I feel about that. It's not like I don't bottom when I'm in the mood, but when it comes to Ezra, the thought of giving up control to him makes me hesitate. Not because I don't *want* to give it to him ... but I'm scared of what will happen when I do. I'm barely holding him at arm's length as it is.

And I have no doubts he's going to want control one of these days, no matter which position he's in. I've got Ezra playing by my rules for now, but that dynamic won't work forever.

Especially because I sort of like it when he pushes back. That photo in bed with Kosik, his teasing about Tripp. It both makes me angry and turns me on.

Ezra knows who he is.

I thought I did too, but I'm starting to doubt.

When we make it to the arena that afternoon, we head out for a practice skate, then change into our suits early.

Coach has organized for some fans to come through for a meet and greet before the game, which is one of my favorite ways to get motivated and boost my high before I hit the ice.

There are some superfans out there, and being so far from home, getting to meet people who look up to you, is a great feeling.

The fans are waiting behind a sectioned-off area as we approach, and I beeline straight for the two people wearing my Philly jersey. I'm assuming it's a dad and son who would probably look similar if the son wasn't wearing a face full of makeup. He could only be … twelve? It's hard to tell, but they both beam as soon as they spot me.

"Anton Hayes," the dad says. "This is so exciting."

"For both of us, trust me." I pull out my Sharpie. "Want me to sign that jersey?"

"Hell yeah." He immediately turns so I can sign the spot at the back above his left shoulder blade.

"You're the best player," the kid says. "I can't believe Philly traded you."

"Best player?" Ezra says, sliding up beside me. He's in a snakeskin-print suit that should look ridiculous. It really should. But damn if I don't want to devour him in it. "You must be talking about me."

The kid goes red. "E-Ez-Ezra …"

"Palaszczuk, nice to meet you. Not a fan of your fashion sense," he says, pointing to the jersey. "But your contouring is to die for."

"Thanks. I taught myself from YouTube."

"Incredible." He uncaps his Sharpie. "That's a nasty number on your back, but why don't we balance things out. This doofus"—he nods to me—"can sign one side, and I'll sign the other."

"Yeah? Can you?" He hurries to turn around, and I watch for a second as Ezra leans in and signs the jersey.

"You'll be the only person ever to have a Philly jersey signed by Ezra Palaszczuk," I point out. "He's normally allergic to anything that isn't Boston."

Ezra winks at the kid. "Some people are worth it."

The smile he gets in return is enormous, and I'm hit with that moment again, just like when I saw Ezra with the teen at the pet adoption, that despite everything, all the shortcomings I'm convinced he has, people respect him. Kids look up to him. Because he doesn't hide who he is. It unsettles me. Because it almost makes me want to look up to him as well.

His dad shifts, catching my attention. "Ah, sorry about this. You're our favorite player, but, ah, Todd's always looked up to Ezra, and some of the other, umm ... I'm not sure the right way to say it. But my son's gay, and seeing others like him play the game, it's one of the reasons we love hockey so much. It helped us bond."

I turn back to where Ezra and Todd are laughing over something I missed, and an uncomfortable truth starts to kick in. My life is hockey, my image is hockey, and I'm damn good at it.

But there are a lot of other players out there, ones who are as good, if not better, and I have teams of people waiting to fill my skates.

What happens when hockey is over for me?

Watching Ezra with Todd, it's clear that when Todd looks at him, he doesn't see a hockey player. He sees someone he can look up to, who proves he can do anything, time and again, and his sexuality isn't a factor in that.

He inspires people.

I want to do that too. I want to give kids inspiration, to echo the message that queer players are in the league and kicking ass. I want to be a role model, and I can't do that if I'm scared.

It's my bias holding me back, I know that. The deep-seated fear I have of never being good enough. But it's not just me who faces the impact of my choice to stay private, it's every closeted kid out there who doesn't think things can get better.

It's Todd and the ones like him who shouldn't have to pick between a handful of people to look up to. His options should be endless.

So I open my mouth and utter something I've never officially said out loud in public. "Being a queer player in the sport isn't always easy, but I think I speak for Ezra and myself when I say we've been lucky to have supportive teams. I'm happy that the inclusivity has brought you two together." I cuff Ezra on the shoulder. "Sometimes I don't give this guy enough credit."

Todd's dad gapes at me. "Wait, so you ... You are, ah, queer too? And you guys don't actually hate each other?"

I'm surprised when Ezra doesn't jump in with a smartass comment, so I do it for him. "Well, he's pretty annoying, but I manage to put up with him most of the time."

We say our goodbyes, and as we shift behind our teammates to wait to meet some others, Ezra leans in, hand on the small of my back and lips at my ear. "Careful, Hayes. You got close to complimenting me again."

"Damn. I must have been thinking of that *other* Ezra Palaszczuk."

"Uh-huh." He pulls back, knowing gleam in his light eyes. "Don't think I didn't hear what you said. *You* outed yourself. You played the Q card."

"People know I'm gay."

"No one outside your circle or people you've hooked up with. Did it feel good to say?"

"Actually, yeah."

"I'm happy for you." He sounds so sincere, but then he keeps talking. "And also, you're welcome, because it's clearly my influence and my magical dick. I'll let you thank me properly later."

There's the Ezra I was expecting. I laugh before I can stop myself and shove him toward the rest of our team. I'm not going to admit to anything that I'll regret later, but after meeting fans and owning up to something I really shouldn't be keeping hidden, I'm feeling pretty fucking good.

Until that night when we go head-to-head with Vegas and lose on a total shut-out. Four to nothing.

Ouch.

CHAPTER FIFTEEN

EZRA

My phone rings in my pocket as we leave the arena for the team bus to go to the hotel. I don't have to look at it to know it's my dad calling again. I ignored his call after we lost Dallas because he's been holding on to all the condescending ways he can tell me he *raised me to be a better hockey player than that* for the whole summer. He's probably bursting at the seams.

I step aside and answer, using the excuse I don't have much time. "Hey, Dad. We're about to get on the bus, so I can't talk for long."

"You allowed too many shots on goal tonight."

Yes, because the entire reason Vegas scored four times was my fault and hockey is not a team sport or anything.

"I know." My tone is complacent. I've learned over the years that if I agree with him, we get off the phone quicker. Getting into a heated argument never ends well, and telling him to back off makes him start on the whole "You don't take constructive criticism well" angle.

"What are you going to do about it? You need to ask your coaches to run defensive drills. For some reason, you forgot the number one rule in defense. Always be between the player with the puck and the goalie."

Coming from an ex-center forward, he really has no right to talk to me about defense. And maybe I'm bitter. Maybe he is trying to help. To bond with me. But why do I always hear from him when we lose? Can't he praise me for once in his life?

And yet he doesn't understand how I got the rage to be a better defenseman than forward. It's a real mystery.

"Yep," I say.

"Keep your eye on your opponent's chest. Not the puck. That has always been your downfall since you were in junior league. You'd think the NHL would've beaten that bad habit out of you by now."

I grit my teeth. "You'd think."

Anton walks by me to get on the bus but pauses with a frown on his face. It looks like he's about to ask if I'm okay, but I quickly turn my back on him.

"Dad, I really do have to go. Everyone's on the bus already."

"Do better. I didn't spend my life savings building you up to be one of the greats for nothing."

"Always good to hear from you, Dad," I say dryly.

He ends the call.

I force down a steadying breath, trying to channel the fuckboy I'm known for being, and when I almost have it under control, I turn to climb onto the bus ... and almost crash into Anton.

He doesn't say anything, just watches me for a moment. Then he reaches out and grips the back of my neck, steering me ahead of him. I think I've managed to avoid having to explain or talk about it when he leans in, warm breath in my ear, and says, "I'm sorry."

When he lets me go, I always want to ask him not to.

I climb on the bus and throw myself in the first available seat, but by the time we've reached the hotel, I've shaken off the cloud of negativity. Over the years, it's gotten faster and easier to block it out.

"I'm going to go sulk into a bottle of tequila," Larsen says when we reach the lobby.

"Don't write yourself off," Diedrich says. "We have the game against Colorado in two days."

"Sure thing, Cap."

I nudge Anton. "I'm hanging out with Tripp and Dex again if you want to join."

"What happened to your whole when the season's on, everyone else is the enemy?"

"Queer collective loophole. We have each other's backs no matter what."

"Wait, is Dex—"

"Ha, nope. He and Tripp are just joined at the hip. It's casual, not a queer collective thing tonight. There will be some rubbing it in our faces that they kicked our asses, but Tripp's one of my closest friends, so we take advantage of what little time we have to see each other. Our whole group is like that." If Anton is serious about coming out—he might not be. Telling one fan that he's queer doesn't mean he's ready to hold a press conference, but I want him to know that he has support.

"I'll come." Anton doesn't sound too confident, and I expect him to back out, but the offer's there.

"Meet back here in ten? I'm gonna head up to my room and change into something less formal. We're only hanging out at Tripp's place."

"What, no showboating around town? Do you feel okay?"

"Funny. But the last thing I want to do is show my face in public after that shitshow of a game." It's weird because our team has been all over the place, and I don't think it has anything to do with how our opponents are playing. Whenever we've lost, it hasn't been because the other team has been phenomenal, though I will say Tripp played the game of his life tonight. The only reason we didn't score was because of him. But our last few games, there's been a disconnect between the team when we've lost.

Like any time the score doesn't go our way, I overanalyze everything. It's hard not to because my competitive side makes me want to find a solution.

When I do the math though, I find a pattern.

We win on the nights after Anton and I hook up and lose on the games when we haven't.

Interesting …

When Anton and I meet back up in the lobby, it's on the tip of my tongue to tell him the only logical conclusion to our team problem is for us to have sex every single night, but that's taking superstition a little too far. Even for me.

It might be a good excuse to carry on what we're doing though. Minus the pranks. I didn't think last night's would blow up on social media like it did, though I should have known.

As we wait for our Uber to arrive in the Uber pickup bay, I feel Anton staring at me.

For some reason, nerves kick in.

I've gone totally casual in sweats and a hoodie unlike him, who's in jeans and a T-shirt, but I can't tell if he's checking me out or judging my fashion sense. "What?" I ask.

"You're quiet. It's ... unnerving."

"I thought you said you liked it when I'm quiet?"

"I take it back. It's too weird."

I gasp. "Are you saying you like my loudmouthed ways?"

"And now I'm confused which is worse."

I step closer, Anton actually laughing *with* me, not *at* me. "You okay with Dex figuring out you're gay? Because even though he's oblivious to most things, he'll clue in to that. Tripp knows already."

"Yeah. If they're friends of yours, I trust them too."

I'm not sure if he means to drop the *too* part, but it floods me with unexpected warmth. People don't trust me often. Trust me to have fun and say dumb crap? All the time. But outside of the Collective, people don't *trust* trust me. Especially not someone I'm hooking up with.

A car pulls up, and I check the details. "This is us."

"Where does Tripp live? Out near Summerlin like some of the other guys?"

"Nah, he's off the Strip, overlooking the Wynn golf course. You'll like it. It reminds me of your stuffy and uppity apartment back in Philly."

Anton groans.

"Oh, sorry, must not be mean to the apartment."

"No, you've reminded me I still have to find a place."

"Nowhere meet your standards of pretension?"

"Exactly," he says dryly.

We get to Tripp's building, where the concierge waves us through to the elevators, and when Dex opens Tripp's apartment door with a wide grin, I cut him off at the pass.

"Yeah, yeah, yeah, you won, we lost, wah, wah, wah. Dex Mitchale, you know Anton Hayes, right?"

"Only on the ice," Dex says. "Hey, man."

Anton lifts his chin.

"Where's Tripp?" I ask.

"Getting drinks," Tripp calls out from his bar area, and I follow his voice.

I round the corner and glare at him. "I only have one thing to say to you."

"What did I do?"

"What didn't you do? Seriously, how are you still single when you're so fucking flexible? It was like watching a contortionist on ice tonight."

Tripp preens. "I was on fire, wasn't I?"

"Put that in your Grindr profile. Fill up your photo reel of game shots."

"He doesn't have a Grindr profile," Dex says and then lowers his voice like he's letting out a big secret. "I'm starting to think Tripp's a virgin."

Tripp gives him the finger. "Fuck off. I'm just over the whole hookup scene."

"That's why you need a boyfriend," Dex says. "And to get a boyfriend, you have to use Grindr."

The rest of us crack up laughing.

"Yeah, that's not what Grindr's for," Anton says.

Tripp cocks his head at Dex. "Why would I want a relationship when I see what Jessica puts you through? Speaking of which, I'm surprised she even let you out tonight. Two nights in a row?" He mock gasps.

"Eh, that's chicks though," Dex says. "Guys all want the same thing. Sometimes I think it would be easier if I were gay."

Anton scoffs, Tripp throws back a shot of dark liquid, and I sigh. Dex really is a walking himbo.

"Gay relationships aren't much different to straight ones, dude." I shove him.

"What would you know?" Anton asks. "Have you ever had an actual relationship?"

"Don't go proving Dex's point, asshole."

"There it is," Tripp says. "I was beginning to think we were in an alternate universe. For a couple of seconds there, I thought you two might be friends, and what in the world is that craziness?"

"I think Ezra invited me here to induct me into your weird club because I came out to a fan tonight," Anton says. His voice stays steady, but I don't miss the nervous way he swallows. It makes me want to protect him or some shit, which is new.

"Really?" Tripp asks. "That's so awesome. I'm happy for you."

"I think I'm happy for me too? Though, now all I can picture is it getting out and the media jumping on it even faster than this ridiculous bromance story they've got going with Ezra and me."

"Oh, and the worst possible thing that could be said about you is that you're in any type of relationship with me," I say.

The three of them answer "Yes" at the same time. *Okay, rude.*

"Let's take this to the roof," Tripp says and hands out our drinks. "On second thought …" He grabs the bottle of whiskey and brings it with us.

We head up his stairs and out onto his terrace. He has the penthouse, and the lights from the Strip give the whole place ambiance.

Tripp has outdoor couches and one of those small, automatic gas fire pits to sit around.

Anton sits next to me on a couch, Tripp takes the opposite one, and Dex throws himself in one of the single chairs and places his feet near the fire.

"Your shoe will catch fire again," Tripp warns.

"Again?"

"He never learns," Tripp says.

We talk and joke around for a bit, trading the kind of relaxed conversation I have with these guys. The problem is, I'm not used to having Anton stretched out beside me, and my gaze keeps straying to his powerful thighs. His arm muscles when he takes a drink. The dark way he watches me every time I open my mouth.

We trade smiles a lot for two people who supposedly hate each other.

Dex sits up suddenly, and I look for a fire to put out, but instead, his gaze moves between Tripp and Anton. "You two should hook up. It would be perfect."

I almost choke on my drink. The way Tripp and Anton are avoiding eye contact is way too entertaining. It helps distract me from the way I want to point out Anton already has someone to hook up with.

"Can't," Anton says, turning his glass nervously in his hands. "I'm kinda seeing someone. Sort of."

Where the usual hatred of any indication of a relationship is absent, the notion still makes me uneasy. Especially when Tripp gives me a knowing look.

Oh well.

Tripp knows that I hooked up with Anton and that I'm probably the guy Anton is referring to, but Dex has no idea. It cements the kind of bond and support we have in our group. Tripp and Dex are the best of friends, but our experiences as queer athletes will always be put first. It's why I think Anton should be part of us.

"I actually had plans for him tonight," Anton says.

"You did?" I ask.

"Mhmm. Booked a hotel away from the team and everything. But ... he had other things to do."

Tripp watches us, clearly amused, and I make a mental note to tell Anton that he's not fooling anyone. Except Dex, which isn't hard to do.

"Maybe he could come see you after he's finished with his thing?"

"Depends on how long he's going to be," Anton complains.

I shift in my seat. "Check your phone. There could be a text telling you he's done already."

Anton takes out his phone, and of course there isn't one there because I'm sitting right here. "Says here he's ready to meet up."

I stand. "Sorry to cut this short. We'll see you guys when you're in our neck of the woods."

Dex fist-bumps me like he always does, and Tripp stands to give me the one-armed man hug.

"You guys are as subtle as a sledgehammer," he says so the others can't hear.

"I have no idea what you're talking about."

Tripp slaps the back of my head. "If you're going, I'm gonna go to bed."

"No," Dex says. "Don't make me go home."

"You know you're welcome to crash here anytime you want."

"You just wanna wake up next to me again."

Tripp closes his eyes briefly. "There's plenty of space, so I don't know why you always end up in my bed, but maybe you should think about why you don't want to go home."

"Because Jessica is there."

"And you don't think that's a red flag?"

I drag Anton away. "Let's go. They'll be arguing about Jessica for a while."

"What's Dex's deal?" Anton asks in the elevator.

"From what I can tell, he loves his girlfriend, but she's … high-maintenance. I think she wants a ring, and she wants it bad. Wants to be head of the WAGs for Vegas and fights puck bunnies off with a stick. I don't even know if she likes Dex or if she's with him for the status. Dex doesn't see her that way though. He doesn't see a lot of things."

"Like Tripp being totally in love with him?"

"Thank you. It's obvious, right?"

"Uh, yeah. Do you really think he doesn't know, or does he pretend not to?"

"Oh, he has no idea. I love Dex, I really do, but he's not the sharpest tool in the shed."

"The elevator doesn't go to the top floor?" Anton taps the side of his head.

I laugh. "Exactly."

I tap away on my phone. "There's an Uber three minutes away, but I need to know where I'm going. You said something about a different hotel?"

"I did."

Anton checks in while I wait at a slot machine and pretend to play. As soon as he heads for the elevator banks, I follow.

It all feels covert and over-the-top, but at the same time, the last thing either of us wants is for it to get out that we're fucking around.

Anton has a reputation and standards to uphold. I … well, the only thing sleeping with Anton would do to my reputation is uphold it for being a fuckboy.

We're silent on the elevator up to the room, and we both hang our heads as someone passes us in the hallway.

As soon as the hotel door closes behind us, I expect Anton to pounce on me, but he doesn't.

"Want a drink?" he asks.

"I didn't come here to drink, and neither did you."

"I might need another." He opens the minibar and takes out a baby bottle of Jack Daniels. He throws it back in one go.

"Need to be drunk to have sex with me now?"

"Nope. Just need a little liquid courage to ask you to top me."

This is … different. "Should I be scared? You telling Tripp and Dex you're seeing someone. Asking me to fuck you while being exclusive … This is—"

"Still an arrangement, you egotistical prick." His smile takes the bite out of his words.

"Good. Because I really didn't want to have to turn you down." The scary thing is, even if this was more, I'm not sure I'd actually reject him.

Anton approaches and takes my hands, putting them on his ass. "You really think you could turn this down?"

I lick my lips. "Fair point, but I'm trying to figure out why you're suddenly so open to giving it to me."

"I figure if we're going to keep hooking up, we should give each other what we want, and you've made it no secret you want my ass."

"As hot as topping you would be, I'm not into pressuring people," I say. "What do you want?"

"To keep doing what we're doing. I haven't had enough of you yet."

"I actually have a theory, if you want to hear it."

He steps back. "As long as you're getting naked while you ramble whatever ridiculous shit is going to come out your mouth."

"I did the math, and—"

"You know how to count?"

"So funny. You want to hear this or not?"

"Not, but you're going to keep talking anyway." Anton shucks off his shirt and then drops his jeans.

I do the same with my hoodie and sweats. "As I was saying, I did the math. Do you know we win games after we hook up?"

"What are you talking about?"

"I was joking before, but I think I seriously have a magical dick. Because we win. Think about it. Last night, we didn't hook up because you were too busy putting all your furniture back in your room." The memory still amuses me. "Seriously, that was so fun to watch."

"Your point?"

"We lost tonight. But we hooked up in Dallas and then won against Arizona. It's legit."

"So, you're saying that hockey has nothing to do with skill and everything to do with us. Just how much do you think the world revolves around your ass?"

We're naked now, and I pull him against me. "Tonight, everything will be about yours."

Anton tenses in my arms, and when he looks up into my eyes, there's hesitance there.

"Unless you actually don't want to," I say. "I'm not going to make you do anything you don't want to do."

He seems surprised by my answer, but he shouldn't be. I may push and tease and throw things out there that I want, but never do my needs exceed those of my partner's.

Even if he's Anton Hayes. This thing might have started out with deep-seated animosity, but I think we can't deny it's grown to something that's less like hate and a lot like … something softer. Harder to define.

He reaches between us and wraps his hand around my cock, stroking lightly.

I let out a shaky breath. Yep, don't hate a thing about this.

"I want this," he rasps. "But you need to go slow. It's been a while."

"Good thing we have all night then." I grip his ass cheeks and squeeze. "Get on the bed. Hands and knees."

He does as I say, and a thrill rushes through me at being the one in control tonight. I don't always need it—sometimes I don't even want it—but with Anton, it heightens everything. Probably because I know he's so against giving it up.

His hole is exposed for me, and I want to dive right in, but then I remember—

"Supplies? I didn't bring any considering you didn't tell me this was your plan."

"In my jeans." He smiles at me over his shoulder.

"If you'd told me before we went to Tripp's, I would've canceled on him."

Anton lifts up, still kneeling, but his long torso is upright. "You were right though. I appreciate you taking me to hang with Tripp because I do need more queer allies in the league. When it does eventually get out about me, I'll need that support."

"The guys will have your back no matter what."

"Does that include you?"

The question holds a lot more weight than the simplicity he's phrased it with.

"I'm hoping to have your back and front." I waggle my eyebrows.

"And afterward?"

After? Who knows.

CHAPTER SIXTEEN

ANTON

I'm not used to this. Needing reassurance. At times I think it's easier if I pretend Ezra is someone else, but then I look at him, and the confidence that flows through him so naturally encompasses me as well.

If he can find this easy, I'll fake like it's easy for me too.

All I know is tonight, I need to be held, and the only way I can think to ask for that is by getting Ezra to top me.

The orgasms are becoming normal for us; any form of emotion is not. The exclusivity, plus sex, plus making this into more than it is would be too close to a relationship for me, and that isn't something I'm interested in. I don't think it's something Ezra would *ever* be interested in, if past history is anything to go by.

"Cutting the shit?" he says, and it takes me a second to remember I asked him a question. "Even if we stop all this, even if I go back to wanting to crush you into the boards, I'll *still* have your back. Some things are bigger than holding a grudge."

"Like orgasms?" I play off my vulnerability, because that's not something I'm comfortable with.

"They are what got us into this mess." He steps up behind me and presses a kiss to my shoulder that I accidentally lean into. "Now, you're obscuring my view."

I laugh and plant my hands back on the bed. "Way to make this weird, Ez."

"Sure, because two teammates who now only kinda hate each other getting a Vegas hotel room to fuck each other's brains out isn't weird at all."

"Well, when you put it like—" My words cut off on a sharp breath as Ezra grabs my ass and spreads my cheeks.

"Nothing weird about this," he says before leaning in and licking along my crease. "I can honestly say that a few months ago, I had never contemplated seeing Anton Hayes's butthole."

"I'm full of surprises," I grit out, face flushed. "Would you get on with it?"

He hums, lips trailing down over my taint. The soft scratch of his beard sends warmth flooding through me. "I know this is hard for you, but I'm going to be calling the shots. And since we have the whole night, I'm not in a rush."

"Maybe you're not, but my cock is."

He reaches around and gives me a long, loose stroke that makes my arms shake. "Tonight, you'll find out what all the fuss is about."

I almost slip up and say I already know, but I refuse to give him that satisfaction. Letting him fuck me is already taking things a step further with Ezra than I thought I'd go, but when it comes to sex, I'm quickly learning that as much as I like to pretend to be in control, I'm not. All Ezra has to do is bat those baby blues at me and I'm hauling him into a dark corner somewhere. The man sure knows how to use his looks to his advantage—

Nrgh.

And his tongue apparently.

He laps at my balls as he fumbles with one of the packets of lube I brought. One of, because the optimist in me brought plenty.

And if seeing poor Tripp pining over Dex tonight was any motivation, I'm going to take what I want, when I want it, for as long as Ezra's willing to give it to me.

Slick fingers rub over my hole, and I let my eyes fall closed. I focus on breathing, on Ezra's mouth, on the anticipation of the first moment I'm breached just right. His touch is starting to wake up nerves that haven't seen action in a while.

"Ready?"

"Yeah, just—"

"I know." His soft laugh brushes my skin. "Relax and *try* to trust me."

Easier said than done, but as soon as Ezra feels the tension leave my body, he starts to work a finger inside.

"Mm, there we go." He nips my ass cheek before moving his mouth to join his fingers. "Once we've done this a few times, loosened you up, I'll be able to work you open with my mouth. I hate the taste of lube."

I tingle from my balls to my lips. "Sure, you're literally eating ass, but the lube is what you have issue with."

Ezra straightens, finger working deeper inside me as he blankets my back with his body. "I hate lube because I prefer to taste the man I'm with. It makes me so fucking hard."

I shudder as he presses his leaking cock against my ass cheek. "Next time, then."

"Next time." He presses a grin into my neck before kissing his way down to my shoulder. It's what I need. This closeness. His lips on me as he works a second finger inside. The intrusion is familiar and welcome, and the more I start to relax, the more the discomfort lessens, until Ezra is stretching me open with ease.

Then his mouth is gone.

I want to whine at the loss of contact, but I bite it off as his fingers brush my prostate. "I'm ready."

"Thank fuck." Ezra's fingers disappear, and his slick cock rubs against my hole.

I stiffen. "Condom."

"Relax, Hayes. I know your rules."

"Anton."

"What?"

I swallow hard. "You can at least use my first name if you're going to fuck me."

"I use your first name all the time."

"No, you use my first name when you're teasing me, otherwise it's always with my last name. Even tonight, when you introduced me to your friends. It was Anton Hayes. Not Anton."

I know Ezra's trying to smother it, but I hear his chuckle anyway.

"Fuck off." I go to shift away, but Ezra quickly grabs my hips and covers me again. Like that, I suddenly find it difficult to move a muscle.

"Want me to say your name?" His lips brush my ear, and his voice has lowered to a needy, sexy tone. "Mm, Anton. I can't wait to push inside your tight hole, *Anton*. I'm going to fuck you so good, *Anton*."

And even though it makes my dick throb, I can't help sigh. "What a surprise that your mouth is ruining things again."

"You weren't complaining about it a minute ago."

"Come on." I shove my ass back into him. "Get on with it."

"Whatever you say ... Anton."

"I'm regretting this already."

Ezra presses a kiss to the back of my neck. "Careful. It almost sounds like you want a connection. With me."

Of course he'd pick up on it and say something. I shift beneath him, and his fingers stroke gently over my skin. His nose runs along my hairline, soft moan barely audible, and after only a minute of his attention, I need more.

"I'm ready, Ez."

He straightens again, and I watch over my shoulder as he rolls on a condom. The sight of his long cock, swollen and dark purple, has me licking my lips.

He presses the blunt head to my opening, and a soft sound rumbles in his chest. Then he starts to push forward.

My fingers curl into the bedspread as I ease back, his cock splitting me open as he slides inside. It's been so long, and I've missed this. I don't like to bottom often, but when I do, with someone I trust, it feels out of this world incredible.

And as much as it unnerves me to recognize, I do trust Ezra. And not only when it comes to sex.

He bottoms out, and we both take a minute to breathe while I adjust and he probably tries not to come straight away. It's always the problem I have the first few moments after entering him. Everything is so hypersensitive.

Speaking of hypersensitive, my dick doesn't like this delay. "You can move."

"Damn, you *really* struggle to let go, don't you? What part of *I'm* in control did you not understand?"

"Then get on with—"

He pulls out and slams back inside, making my teeth knock.

Pleasure ripples through me. "Yesss, just like that."

"Don't worry, my magical dick's got you. Let's do it for the team."

I want to point out that his dick has nothing to do with whether we win or lose and his whole theory is idiotic at best, but then he starts to move, and the thought of arguing goes out the window. Each of his movements is slow and steady, and when I try to push back and speed things up, he takes my hips and holds me in place.

"Give it up, Anton."

"I will when you give me what I want."

"Shocking to hear, I'm sure, but not everything is about what you want."

Ouch, okay, that's true, but tell it to my poor dick. "I need you to fuck me."

"I am."

I press back onto him. "Harder."

"Anton."

"Ezra. Fuck. Come on."

His hands slide up my sides. "Let go."

"*Ezra.*"

"I said let go."

"Fuck …"

He waits, but I don't finish that sentence. Instead, I try to do what he says, I try to let go.

Ezra goes back to his measured thrusts. Slow stroke in, then out. It's driving me crazy. It's not enough. The pace and his distance from me isn't helping calm that neediness filling my chest.

"Damn, you've got some booty," he says, pressing in deep and holding himself there. "You should see it like this." He pulls back and slams inside. "The jiggle is addictive."

And even when Ezra starts to pick up the pace, it's still not enough to fill that spot inside me. The neediness. The longing for a connection deeper than cheap sex. Just this once.

It's different from what this is supposed to be. New and foreign, and I don't hate it, but it scares me.

"Ez ..." Hold me, touch me ... *kiss* me. Fuck. I don't know how to ask for it. How to make him give me what I want.

I pull off him and flip over.

His hand immediately moves to cup my balls. "What are you—"

"*Please.*"

One needy, uncertain word and we catch eyes. He holds my stare for a second, then two.

Ezra's mouth hitches with a smile. "Careful, almost sounds like you're the one doing the begging."

"If it gets me what I want, I'm not above it."

"And what do you want?"

"You."

His lips part, a range of emotions crossing his face. "You've got me."

Ezra grabs my thighs and pushes them up before kneeling between my legs. He holds one thigh and plants the other hand on the bed before pushing back inside me. He looks down, watching as he slowly pulls out and eases back inside again, giving me that delicious friction but still not the connection I'm craving.

"Come here," I say.

"Being bossy again?"

"Can you *please* come here?"

"Better."

Ezra leans forward, trapping my cock between our abs and bringing us face-to-face. There's an amused glint in his eyes I don't like. "Now what do you want?"

I lick my lips as I look at his.

"There's no way Anton Hayes wants to kiss me. We don't do that."

"And now you've made it weird again."

He hums as his lips brush my jaw, then licks under my chin. "You want my tongue in your mouth. Nothing weird about it."

"Ezra …"

"I am a fantastic kisser, you know. I totally get why you'd want to."

"Ezra …"

"You might get addicted, and it'll be kinda hard to skate in practice with our faces permanently meshed together though."

"Now there's a visual."

His lips brush the corner of mine. I'm breathless, waiting. Needing. Not able to ask for it. It's Ezra Palaszczuk, and he's right. We don't do this. I'm not even sure when that became a thing because I've never had issues kissing my hookups before. He's in my space, sharing my breath, splitting my body open, and it's this one small thing I can't seem to do?

He cups my face. "Kiss me, Anton."

Fuck it.

I twist my fingers in his caramel-colored hair and bring our mouths together. That neediness settles.

With his mouth on me, I can finally give up control.

A long moan builds between us, and I'm not even sure which of us made the sound, but Ezra finally starts to give me what I need. His thrusts pick up speed, hitting my prostate just right as he kisses me until I can barely breathe.

It's overpowering, indescribable to be owned like this. To finally let go and have him take over. My cock is trapped between us, teased with the friction between our bodies, the slickness as we start to build up a sweat, moving against each other, meeting each other halfway.

He doesn't slow down or let up as he literally fucks me into the mattress, and Ezra's stamina is blowing my mind. I've never hooked up with another athlete before, and I'm suddenly realizing what I was missing out on. Everything before with Ezra has been hot and fast and over when I want it to be over, but when I go to reach for my cock, Ezra pins my hands to the mattress.

"Not yet," he breathes against my lips.

I could sob. I'm so close, and he's hitting everything that drives me crazy, but I need that tiny bit more to tip me over the edge.

Ezra breaks our kiss and pulls back, looming over me as he starts to lose rhythm. He grunts with each thrust, eyes falling closed, and a moment later, his whole body goes tense as he comes.

I squirm, desperate, hands still pinned in his tightening hold.

I'm about to complain when Ezra pulls out suddenly and dives on my cock. His fingers slide inside my ass, and he pegs my prostate over and over as he swallows me deep into his throat. I grip his head, thighs trembling, fingers curling so tight I'm sure I'm about to rip out hair, but I'm so overwhelmed by the suction I forget to care.

And then I'm coming. It hits me so hard I swear stars burst in my vision, and I lose all track of who and where I am. I forget everything except this intense pleasure racing through me.

Ezra collapses against my chest. He's hot and sweaty, just like me, and I lean my face down to breathe in the smell of his skin and sex. It's intoxicating.

"Give me a second," he murmurs sleepily. "Then I'll be ready for round two."

It's ridiculous to think I'll ever be able to get it up after that. "I think I need more than a second."

He mumbles something that I miss, and then a long, deep inhale fills the air between us. He's passed out. Trying not to disturb him, I roll off the condom, toss it in the general direction of the trash can, then wipe us off with the sheets and pull the blankets over us.

His face is buried in my neck, so it feels natural to wrap my arms around him. To hold him to me. I blame the neediness that he's managed to silence for now.

Then I yawn widely and close my eyes.

I fall asleep next to him for the first time ever.

CHAPTER SEVENTEEN

EZRA

As we board the plane in Vegas to fly to Denver, I go to take my seat when Coach's voice fills the cabin.

"Palaszczuk, Hayes, you're at the back with me."

There are a few snarky comments, some jeers, and one big frown from Diedrich sent our way.

"What are we in trouble for now?" I ask when I reach his seat. "It's been almost a week on the road, and we haven't so much as got into a fight. Ooh, are you going to give us medals?"

Anton shoves me with a laugh.

"Sit," Coach says and nods to the row in front of him.

Oh shit. We're in a lot of trouble, then. Anton takes the window seat, me the aisle, leaving the middle seat as a buffer, and then we turn to Coach.

"When we get to Colorado, there's going to be some room changes."

"Room changes?" Anton asks.

"I've had the PR department, team management, and the owner chewing me out for my guys being more interested in pranks than playing hockey."

"Come on, it's all in good fun," I say.

"Is it though?" Coach glares at us, and I get the impression he doesn't want us to actually answer that. "Is it all in good fun that instead of being in the news for beating Arizona, the focus has been on our losses, and every sports reporter, fan, and even people who don't care about hockey are out there analyzing every look you send each other on the ice. Every pass, every scowl, every smile, and every prank you post on social media. You two are under the microscope, so the GM suggested we room you together to save on hotel property damage bills. I, personally, don't see how murdering each other will be better than pranking each other, but hey, it's worth a try."

I turn to Anton. "Who knew Coach had a sense of humor?"

"I'm a hoot," Coach says dryly. "That was all. Stop with the bullshit, and focus on what's important, okay? Focus on winning, and they won't care what you two do on or off the ice."

"Yes, sir," Anton says.

Coach makes a swirling motion with his finger. "You can turn around now."

Anton and I try not to laugh at each other and face the front.

We don't talk for the entire flight. Anton shoves his pods in his ears and watches something on his phone, while I dive headfirst into all the new articles online about Anton and me.

They're a little unnerving. Anton and I have always made waves with our known rivalry, but with the trade and rumors of us actually being friends, speculation is getting out of hand.

And when I read an article that implies there might be even more than friendship between us, my gut sinks.

West used to have these kinds of rumors swirling around about him all the time, and he didn't care, but he was ready to come out if he needed to. He didn't want to make a big song and dance about it, but he was fine if people knew.

Anton ... I don't think he's ready for any of that yet. I'm not sure how he'll take the news that rumors have started about him. He was fine coming out to that kid and his dad, but that's two people. It's not the whole damn world.

I stare over at him. He seems relaxed and not like his usual uptight self. I'm sure the fuckfest we had last night has something to do with that, but given the choice, would Anton put his reputation on the line for sex with Ezra Palaszczuk?

It's explosive sex, but there needs to be a line somewhere. At what point does this whole thing become not worth the risk? Obviously, my bar is probably set higher than a lot of people's. I get the impression Anton has a low threshold.

When we land in Denver, I haven't decided if I will show Anton or not.

Kosik sidles up to me as we head for the bus to go to the hotel. "Is it true? Have all my dreams come true?"

"Your nightmares maybe. You've lost me as a roommate. I know how devastating that is for you, but if you really miss me, I can sneak into your room and spoon you again if you like."

"Fuck off, Ez." He laughs. "Rooming with the rookie has to be ten times better than rooming with you."

"Good luck," Anton says behind us. "Moreau snores."

"It's true," Diedrich adds. "My kids are scared of him after he stayed with us a few weeks. They think when he sleeps, he turns into a monster."

Kosik purses his lips. "Hmm, nah, still has to be better than being dragged into the middle of some dumbass feud."

"Mm, we'll see. You can always come running back to me." I blow him a kiss.

"In your dreams. If you're hitting on me, you must be hard up for some action. Maybe you need to get laid."

"Normally, I'd disagree with you, but I think you might be right."

Anton's eyes lock with mine.

"Getting laid sounds like a brilliant idea."

Anton shifts and turns away, but not before I see his lips twitch.

We can't get to the hotel fast enough, and he must think so too, because the second we get our key cards to the room, he moves toward the elevators faster than lightning.

I'm about to follow him when I notice Diedrich watching. His gaze flits between the both of us, suspicion lacing his features, but then he shakes his head as if to say me and Anton hooking up is impossible.

"He's going to dead-bolt you out of the room," Diedrich says.

"Oh, shit." I rush after Anton, taking the excuse and running with it.

But it doesn't take long to process what happened just now with our captain. It might have only been a brief second before dismissing it, but he made the connection—the same one people in the media are starting to make.

I catch up to Anton as he opens our room, and he holds the door open for me.

"Don't pretend to be a gentleman now," I snark.

"Mm, what I want to do to you isn't gentlemanly at all."

We dump our bags, and then Anton backs us up so he can push me against the wall. His arms box me in, and my lips tingle to kiss him again.

"I have to say, this new rooming arrangement is kind of perfect," Anton says.

It is. It really is. Or, it would be if I didn't have this massive hesitance hanging over my head. My face must show it because Anton backs up a bit.

"What's wrong?" he asks.

"I want this. I really, really want to have all the orgasms with you, but …" I bite my lip. "I'm having an attack of conscience here."

"Really? *You*? It must be bad for that to happen."

I wave him off. "Insert argument here. But for real. After Coach told us we're being watched, I went online, and I think he's understating how much attention we're drawing."

Anton's face falls. "Oh, fuck, are there photos?"

"No, nothing like that. There's … speculation." I fish my phone out of my pocket and show him. "If you want out or whatever, I'm cool." I'm not really because I'm nowhere near done with him, but I'm not going to be the asshole who makes him take a step he's not ready to. The thought of pushing this and having Anton resent me for it doesn't sit right.

"Eh. It's more bullshit. Like our rivalry and bromance. They're trying to sell a story."

"Yeah, except our rivalry and this"—I point to my phone—"is damn near close to the truth. If we're going to keep doing this, you should probably be okay with the possibility of it getting out. Which would mean coming out or being outed."

Anton scrolls through the article again. "Well, now that we're being roomed together, it'll be a lot easier to hide, but you're right. I've always had the notion in the back of my head that if I do something risky, I have to be okay with the fallout, and this is no different. Hell, this might even help me. When I come out, it won't be a complete shock to everyone. And it's not like I'm holding back for any particular reason. So, yeah, this is fine."

"Are you sure?"

"Is that concern for me I hear in your voice?"

I want to say the expected—*Of course not*—but the smartass reply doesn't come. "I don't want to be the reason the world as you know it unravels."

"That ... might be the sweetest thing you've ever said to me."

"I mean it." And I do, which is so far beyond my realm of experience when it comes to men. I ... want to put Anton first. The only other person I've ever tried that with before was West, and I still messed that up.

With Anton, I want to do better.

"In that case, I appreciate it." He kisses me. "Now, stop being sincere. Your pretty head will explode."

I chuckle. "Okay, sorry. Back to all the sex. We should get to it. We have a game to win tomorrow night."

Anton strips off his shirt. "Who's bottoming tonight?"

"Flip you for it?" I grab my wallet and take out a quarter.

"I call heads."

"Being given tails has to be an omen." I toss the coin in the air and catch it, placing it on the top of my hand and covering it with the other.

It takes a moment to realize I don't even care what the result is.

—

Kosik and I are a solid wall on the ice tonight. Nothing is getting by us.

Anton's having the game of his life and has scored four fucking goals on his own.

It's the first game of the regular season where we've had synergy as a team. Sure, we've taken out two wins, but they were hard-fought wins. Tonight, we're back in preseason ass-kicking mode, and even though we still have nine minutes left on the clock in the third period, the score is 7-2 to us. We'd have to majorly fuck up to lose when we're this far ahead.

It's not impossible though, so we keep pushing. We keep scoring. Our plays are smooth, and we're clicking. It's one of those games where it comes easy, and we'll walk away tonight on a high.

The games where we have to fight tooth and nail and get by in a pinch might have an indescribable accomplished feeling attached to them, but when they're like this one? It feels historic.

We're half trying to run out the clock, half wanting to see how far we can really take this. Diedrich wins a face-off and passes the puck back to me.

I chill in our defending zone, faking a couple of moves like I'm going for it when I'm not, and skate circles around the puck a couple of times like I don't have a care in the world.

When I do finally pass, it's to Kosik, and then he passes it right back. Colorado has all my bases covered, though

Anton and Larsen are trying to skate their way out of their mess.

The second Anton is open, I pass to him. He spins and almost gets clipped by a D-man, so he passes off to Diedrich.

Play moves down the ice into the attack zone, and Diedrich circles around the back of the net and passes off to Anton, who shoots through the five-hole.

When the lamp lights up, the crowd screams so loud over the goal horn I can barely hear it.

The look of pure shock on Anton's face is going to be all over the media tonight. That goal is going to be on highlight reels for the rest of the season. Anton Hayes has made the very short list of players who have pulled off five goals in one game.

Where I should be jealous or bitter that it was Anton who did it, there's none of that. I'm actually … proud.

After the rest of our teammates attack him with hugs and claps on his ass, I barge through them all and wrap my arms around him.

Our helmets bounce off each other, and we almost topple over, but somehow, we manage to stay upright.

"Thank fuck you did that for our team," I say.

"The trade isn't looking so bad now, I take it?"

That's an understatement. I'm starting to think it was the best damn decision the B's has ever made. And not just because of the hockey.

CHAPTER EIGHTEEN

ANTON

I'm on the streak of my life. After Colorado, I score at least one goal in each of the next three home games, which goes a long way toward winning over the Boston fans and shutting up the haters. If you talk to Ezra, he claims it's all thanks to his dick, and while I'm not ready to believe something so ridiculous, I'm also happy to go along with his superstitions because I'm not going to say no to regular sex. With Ezra. I keep waiting for the itch to be around him to leave me, but instead, I swear it's getting worse.

Scoring five goals in one game is one of those career achievements every player dreams of, and I'm still riding the high.

At our next away game in Toronto, Ezra and I are roomed together again, which makes it easy to hook up, but back at home, we need to get more creative. We both agreed that me being seen at his apartment too often would be basically announcing to the world that we're sleeping together, and while I'm not apprehensive to officially come out, my need for privacy hasn't changed.

Then on top of that, I've found a place to volunteer at that collects food donations and packs and organizes distribution of the goods. On the down low. So no one, not even Ezra, knows about it. Having that take up most of my free time means fewer chances for hooking up, but somehow, we're making it work.

After a light day yesterday in the weight room, we're back on the ice today to prepare for our game tomorrow.

We go through an hour of line work with Diedrich and Larsen, then half an hour of firing bullets at Griffith in goals, but all I'm thinking about is what I have planned for when we're done today.

I'm sweaty and gross by the time we leave the ice.

I stretch out my neck as we strip off our hockey gear to head for the training room, and when Ezra falls into step beside me, his presence makes me immediately go stiff. Since we've started rooming together, I'm paranoid everyone knows what we're getting up to. I want to argue with myself that just because we're both gay, it doesn't mean people would assume we can't keep our dicks to ourselves, but … we can't. Not because we're gay, but because I'm very quickly becoming addicted to Ezra. Well, sex with Ezra. He's good. At sex.

Damn it. I shake the thoughts from my brain and try to focus on anything other than the heat rolling off his body. I've been avoiding spending too much time with him while the team is around because he makes it hard to concentrate.

All it would take is one heated look and everyone would know.

Do I care if they know I'm hooking up with Ezra?

It's … complicated.

Us sleeping together puts the team dynamic at risk. We're making it work now, but if this thing ends badly, it *will* affect our game. I don't want that thought getting into the other guys' heads.

"What are you doing later?" Ezra asks.

He doesn't bother to keep his voice down, and I can't help glancing around to see if anyone else heard us. And if they did, do they think it's a weird question? Or have they accepted that we're starting to get along? And if they *have* accepted that, do they think it's weird? Do they assume something's up?

Why did I think I could do this?

I clear my throat and match his volume. "I'm meeting up with someone." There. That'll throw them off. Maybe.

"Oh, really?"

"Yep." Then I pick up my pace and join Diedrich on the bikes. I can feel Ezra's eyes on me the whole time I work out, and I want to remind him to at least try to be subtle. When I move on to weights, his stare still burns into me, and then for my cooldown on the treadmill, he follows and takes the one next to me. Hearing his heavy breathing fills my mind with all sorts of indecent images. I torture myself with it for five minutes before calling it a day.

When I head for the showers, Ezra pulls me back.

"Who are you meeting up with?"

I check we're alone, then smile. "You."

"What if I have plans?"

"Considering we have a game tomorrow? You don't."

"Can't you at least let me pretend to play hard to get?"

"Fine." I arch an eyebrow at him. "Carry on."

"I'm actually *really* busy later. There're the things that need to be done and the other things that need attention. It's going to take the whole day."

I pretend like his fake resistance isn't endearing. "Feel better?"

"Much."

"What if I told you I finally have my apartment ready and we can meet up without worrying about being caught?"

"Did I say there were things that needed doing?" He taps his forehead. "I forgot. The things are actually you."

"That's better."

There's a sound behind me, and I immediately straighten and check we're still alone. I hadn't realized how close we were standing, which is another reason why I can't be trusted around him.

"I'll text you the address," I say before heading in to join the others in the showers.

When we're done, we all go our separate ways, and I drive to my new apartment. I'm only leasing it, because I'm still not sure if it's right for me, but things were getting desperate. I finally caved in picking a place and had people furnish it while we were away. I think Gerard is happy he can be done with my pickiness. For now.

The best part is no one knows I live here yet, and Ezra is on his way over.

I shave my face and fix my hair to get it looking halfway decent. It's still a bit damp from my shower, but if things tonight go the way they have most nights since Vegas, then I assume I'll end up in the shower again at some point.

My buzzer sounds, and I go to let Ezra in.

I find him scrolling through his phone.

"Have you seen the latest one?" he asks.

"Hello to you too." The rumors about us still haven't settled down, but where I avoid them, Ezra seeks them out. Apparently, he finds them amusing. I step aside so he can pass me, but instead he closes the door and tugs me into a kiss.

I go willingly, but the kissing thing still confuses me. My experience with long-term hookups is limited, but I would have assumed kissing was reserved for boyfriends and sex.

But since I asked him to kiss me that one time in bed, Ezra does it every chance he gets. Like asking for it was opening Pandora's box of affection.

I'm quickly realizing that Ezra is a tactile person. I don't even know if he knows it about himself. He's casually touchy with everyone, and I'm beginning to suspect his sleeping around isn't because he wants to give the impression of being a manwhore but because it gives him what he needs on a bigger level than celebratory hugs on the ice and arms slung around shoulders during after game drinks. Deep down, he's not craving sex. He craves *affection*.

He pulls back, and the bastard looks amused. "You almost felt like you enjoyed it that time."

"What can I say? You're wearing me down." I don't point out that if I wanted to end the kissing thing, I would, because I don't want to draw attention to the fact I ... don't hate it.

"And according to this Buzzfeed article, you like it."

"I don't want to know." I walk back down the hall to the living area, Ezra trailing after me.

"Do you know our ship name is Palayes? I don't hate it."

"It's terrible."

"Better than Hazczuk." He chuckles. "You should see the way you're looking at me in this GIF."

"Pretty sure I was looking at Kosik."

"You haven't even seen the ..." He pauses. "Fuck, you're right. First, how dare you smile like that at anyone but me. Second, have you already seen this? And third, that first thing again."

I laugh and pluck the phone from Ezra's grip before tossing it on the counter. "O'Ryan sent me the GIF last week. Thought it was a funny joke. But that was right after Kosik saved my ass from getting pummeled by Saager during the Tampa Bay game and you happened to skate between us."

Ezra narrows his eyes as though trying to work out whether he accepts that or not.

I step forward, tilting my mouth to his ear. "If it helps, I've never given Kosik that look from my knees."

"Surprisingly, that does." He pulls back, an evil glint in his eyes. "But now I'm trying to figure out how to be in the middle of a Hayes and Kosik sandwich."

I don't take his bait, even though the thought of him with Kosik makes me clench my teeth. We both know what he's doing. "Considering Kosik is straight and I don't share, you'd have to come up with something good."

"Well, my magic dick is what got you to the top of the scoring ladder, so I figure he'll probably want in on that once he finds out. All of the team will."

"Your dick. Of course. It has nothing to do with talent."

Ezra pats my cheek. "Exactly." His hand stills, thumb sliding over my face. I almost lean into it and catch myself in time. "You shaved."

"I did."

His nose wrinkles. "You smell like aftershave."

"Funny that." I step out of his reach and grab my phone to order us dinner.

"I don't like it."

"Good thing I didn't do it for you."

"Obviously. It was for all the other men you plan on having over." He steps up behind me, propping his chin on my shoulder and watching me scroll through the options. "Just so you know, I prefer when you smell all sweaty and like my cum. In case you were wondering."

"I wasn't."

"Well, I saved you from ever needing to. You're welcome." He reaches around me and taps on a Vietnamese place.

We end up ordering more than two people should reasonably consume, but there never seems to be any leftovers when we eat together.

"Now you need to give me the tour," he announces, taking a step back.

"There's not much of a tour. It's only two bedrooms."

"Aw, I get to have my own room? How sweet."

My lips twitch. "Who said you're staying over?"

"Me. And we both know I win at these things eventually." His voice drags out teasingly as he walks away, off exploring my place on his own. The problem is, Ezra's right. More and more lately, he's been getting his way. It's curious the way he wears me down because sometimes I don't even try to fight it. Like tonight. He'll be staying over, but it won't be in the spare room.

After a few minutes of waiting in the kitchen for Ezra to return, I realize he's not going to, so I go in search of him instead.

He's made himself comfortable on my bed. Shoes off, propped up on my pillows with his hands folded behind his head. "Good view." He gestures to the large window.

"It's not bad."

"Still miss your old place?"

I cross the room and sit near his feet. "Yes. It felt like home. This …"

"Will too. Eventually. No offense, but your other place was like a museum."

"Sure. Because why would that be offensive?" I nudge his bent knees, and he stretches his legs out over my lap instead. "It had character."

"So does this." He waves a hand toward the crown molding.

"If that's what you think gives a house character, your place is starting to make more sense."

"Hey," he protests. "My place is awesome."

"It looks like a man cave on steroids. You couldn't scream bachelor harder if you tried."

Ezra sucks in a deep breath and then, "*Bachelorrrr!*"

"Argh." I flinch at the sudden noise, then grab a pillow and whack him with it, cutting him off.

"You know your problem?" He pokes me with his foot. "You're a house snob."

"Having standards doesn't make me a snob."

"You can't claim standards when you're sleeping with me." His tone is light and playful, but it makes me wonder …

"What do you mean?"

"It's what you're thinking, isn't it?" His light blue eyes meet mine. "That I'm your way of slumming it. A fun way to pass time until you meet some guy you can be serious with. Kinda like this apartment."

"I didn't realize you were here to psychoanalyze me," I say.

Something churns in my gut at him thinking that, and I'm almost … offended? I might not be as openly affectionate as him, but that isn't because I don't value him or I think I'm better than him.

"Have you seriously not noticed how, even now, after we put all the bullshit behind us, you haven't acknowledged me around the team?"

That can't be right. "What are you talking about?"

"Like today, where you basically yelled you were meeting up with someone. I don't think it will be the end of the world if the guys know we're at least friends now."

"Are we friends?"

"Ouch, Anton. *Ouch*."

"My point is what do we do other than play hockey and fuck? Is that friendship?"

"To me, it sounds like we're besties. You also say that like we have time during the season to do other stuff. On the rare occasions we do get downtime, I tend to go golfing with some of the guys from the team. I'll get you an invite next time. If …"

"If I suck your dick?"

"I was going to say if you start acknowledging me in public, you fucking snob, but a blowjob might be better. Damn it, now you've made things hard for me."

"Okay, so in your own words, we're at the level of friendship where public acknowledgments are cool, but blowjobs are even better?"

"Exactly. Like I said. We're now besties."

I laugh, but our whole conversation has got me thinking. I know I try to avoid him in the locker room, but I'm scared that all it would take is one smile his way and everyone would know.

Now he's calling me out on it though, and being found out is scary, but losing this? I'm terrified I'm screwing it up, but I don't know how to balance a secret relationship and show Ezra he means ... *something*, all while not drawing attention. Because Ezra has enough people in his life devaluing him, and for maybe the first time since I met him, I don't want to be one of those people.

"What's up?" Ezra asks. "You have that look on your face like you're trying to think. I wouldn't waste my time if I were you."

I pinch his calf. "I didn't know I was ignoring you or making you think I thought less of you. So ..." This is actually difficult for me to say to anyone, let alone Ezra. "I'm sorry."

"Are you saying you don't think less of me?"

I want so badly to joke—say something like I don't think any less of him than I did before, which isn't saying much—but there's something about the vulnerability in his eyes that makes me think he needs the validation from me.

And for some reason, that makes my chest warm and fuzzy. I want him to want validation from me. It scares me because we might be *besties*, but Ezra doesn't do serious—not even with West—and if I let myself get carried away with this thing, I'll end up getting hurt. So I tell him the half-truth.

"I don't want to fuck with the team, and I think being friends—proper friends—might do that."

His face falls. "Sure. I get it." Ezra goes to climb off the bed, but I grab his wrist before he can walk out.

"I don't think you're less than," I say. "And I don't want to treat you like shit."

A hint of amusement starts to come back to Ezra's face. "Seems simple to me, then."

"Oh, really?"

"Yeah." He leans down to kiss me. "Don't."

CHAPTER NINETEEN

EZRA

I shouldn't have brought up the friends thing with Anton. I don't know why I even care. I never have before.

Maybe asking for friendship on top of what we're doing was premature, but all I know is his annoying traits—his ego, his condescension, all the things I used to hate—I don't hate anymore. Because I know it's Anton's way of protecting himself.

From scrutiny, from the media finding out about him, from every little thing. I understand it, I really do, but I thought …

I guess I thought after all this time that he might see me for who I really am too.

Anton's buzzer for the door sounds, and he taps my leg. "Food's here."

I head out to the kitchen when Anton says the guy's gone. I could have pushed for him to at least let the delivery guy see me, but we should start small. Team first. Then random strangers.

"Want me to set the table or anything?" I ask.

"Nah. Let's eat in front of the TV. Montreal's playing Columbus tonight before coming for us tomorrow."

"Back-to-backs. Sucks for them. Good for us."

"We'll have our turn next month."

"Fun times."

We pile up our plates with food and cross to Anton's living room, where he sits on what looks like a very new, very beige couch.

I choose to sit on the floor in front of him and put my plate on the coffee table because I don't trust myself not to ruin his expensive—albeit somewhat boring—taste in furniture.

Anton turns on the game while we eat, and I can tell he's doing exactly the same thing I am: assessing the competition we'll be facing tomorrow night.

"It's bad karma to wish a broken ankle on Foster Grant, isn't it?" Anton asks.

I almost choke on my food. "I can't believe that came out of your mouth. Mr. Nice. Mr. Good Guy. Mr. I'm So Charming to Everyone but Ezra Guy."

"I save my salty side for you."

"I feel ... special?"

"You should." Anton winks at me and leans forward. "Look at him though. When he came in as a free agent, everyone said he wasn't going to last. He ended up having the best rookie season I've seen in years, and he hasn't slowed down since. We're going to have to watch him."

"Or break his ankles."

"Hey." Anton points his chopsticks at me. "That is bad karma. I was joking. Mostly."

"He's part of the queer collective too, you know. He's a good kid."

Anton looks down at his food. "Yeah, I read that about him."

"I think he has the right balance between flaunting it and staying private. He's known for being queer, but his partner is really shy and introverted, so they're not seen out together much, and no one in the media seems to care."

Foster scores a goal, but Anton's attention is no longer on the TV.

"I don't think I'm scared of the attention," he says. "I just don't want people to define me and jump to conclusions."

"News flash, everyone defines everyone. Everyone makes snap judgments when they don't know you. Especially on the internet."

"Is it weird I'm okay with them doing it when it comes to hockey or something stupid I might've said in a press interview, but when it comes to who I sleep with, I want them all to fuck off?"

I think we've all been there, though maybe now at the same level. "That's understandable, and comments are inevitable, so I get being private about it. But I want to point out that Foster is managing a balance."

"And what if when I come out, it explodes everywhere, and I can't rein it back in?"

"And you call me egotistical," I tease. "Why are you more important than anyone else who's ever come out in hockey?"

He sighs. "I guess I'm not. But I'm having the best season of my life so far, and sure, it's still early, but if I do end this season with my highest-scoring record—"

"Duuuuude." I tap the solid wood coffee table a couple of times.

"*Hypothetically*—"

"Even hypotheticals are bad juju."

"Fine. Rephrase. What will happen if I achieve even a remotely decent season, and then I come out? What will everyone focus on?"

I adjust how I'm sitting so I'm facing him. "You have a point, but ... what if you come out now and then have the season of your life?"

"They'll say that coming out was the whole reason I played well because I did it as myself or some bullshit instead of what it's really from and that's years of hard work. There's no winning."

"I agree it sucks, and please don't think this is me pressuring you or whatever because I'm not, but can I point out one more teeny-tiny, small thing?"

"Is it your dick?"

"Hey, whoa, below the belt."

Anton snorts. "Literally. What's this teeny-tiny point?"

"Ollie, Tripp, Foster ... the media doesn't care about their sexuality anymore. For me, it's a separate thing. There's my hockey playing and my antics off the ice. Once the Band-Aid is ripped off, yeah, it'll sting for a while, but eventually, the attention will fade away."

"Unless I fuck a different guy every weekend and get photographed with them."

I scoff. "Please. You could never be a fuckboy like me. To get laid that often you need something called charisma."

Anton throws a piece of banh khot at me, but I catch it with my mouth.

"Mm, tasty."

"How did your dad react when you came out?" Anton asks out of nowhere.

For the second time in a few minutes, food gets stuck in my throat. "Hello, random subject change."

"Not really. We are talking about coming out."

"We're talking about you coming out. Not me."

Anton cocks his head. "What's with the sudden recoil? This is what you wanted, isn't it? Somewhat of a friendship in amongst all the sex?"

My neck is suddenly itchy, and I'm not hungry anymore.

I shuffle back and lean against the couch. "He's ... traditional. When I go over to Poland to see his family, none of them ever speak of it. For a few years after I came out, they'd still ask if I'd found a woman to settle down with. But even saying all that, they accept me for being gay now. They don't accept me for other reasons, but that's a whole other story."

"I have nothing but time and an understanding for parents who accept you but encourage you to keep your private life to yourself."

"Are your parents part of the reason you haven't come out publicly?"

"Yes and no. They love me. They accept me. They took my coming out as well as any gay kid could ask for. But then Dad asked if I was planning to tell the league. And it's like I can feel it, every time I visit them over the summer, it's like he's waiting for me to tell him I'm going to do it, so he cuts me off and reminds me how different it will be and how I'll be opening myself up for ridicule and embarrassment."

"Ouch. He said the word 'embarrassment'?"

"Yep."

"You said you visit them in the summer? They don't live in Massachusetts anymore?"

"Nope. Moved to South Carolina a few years back to take care of my grandmother."

Anton's sharing, which feels like a step in the right direction, but he's staring at me like he wants to ask more questions, and this conversation is getting a little too real for me.

I'm the Goldilocks of fuck buddy relationships. I want attention but not too much attention. I want a connection deeper than sex, but I don't want to get too personal.

I'm being an asshole. I called Anton out earlier for not treating me like a friend, but it's not like I'm giving him anything real either, am I?

Anton eventually goes back to his food, but I find myself saying, "When I came out, Dad was silent for a minute, and then he said, 'At least you won't get some gold-digging whore pregnant like I did.'"

Anton's mouth drops, and he blinks at me.

"And that in a nutshell is pretty much my relationship with my father. When I'm playing well, I don't hear from him. I haven't had a single phone call since preseason. When I screw up on the ice, my phone blows up so he can tell me how *he* could have played it better. He's narcissistic and always makes everything about him. He hates my mom, my mom hates him, and I always get caught in the middle of it. It's why I rarely speak to either of them."

And now I hold my breath. I don't talk to people about my parents. People barely remember Dad as a player because he wasn't one of the greats, so I don't get asked about him often.

"I'm starting to see why you are the way you are," Anton says.

"Ha ha, narcissism runs in the family. You're so funny."

"That's not …" His lips form a line. "I mean, yeah, that's totally what I meant."

It wasn't. We both know it wasn't. But I appreciate him backing off. He was going to say he's realizing why I only do cheap hookups.

Because when you're raised by two people who are more interested in bitching each other out than showing their kid love and support, you can't help growing up to be closed off to anything more.

People. Relationships. Love.

I don't want any of it.

Except when he leans over and presses a kiss to the top of my head, I'm starting to suspect that I really, really do.

CHAPTER TWENTY

ANTON

The whole game, Montreal has had us on the back foot. Their offense is on point, but luckily, so is our defense. Ezra's playing an incredible game, and whenever I'm in the team box and he's out there, I can't keep my eyes off him.

There's nothing but the roar of the fans, the cool ice, and Montreal standing between me and adding another point to this season's tally.

Coach is on edge, arms crossed, jaw set. He hasn't stopped pacing.

For the first time all night, Montreal sends their third line out, and I watch Foster Grant hit the ice.

Coach calls for a line change, calling for me to go up against the kid who's breaking records all over the place.

Diedrich, Larsen, and I are over the barrier the second we can, and we're straight into it.

Grant is fucking fast. Griffith stops his first two attempts on goal, but that doesn't slow him down. I want to school him to pace himself, but when you only get a few minutes of ice time each game, you're hungry for it, and Foster Grant always skates like he has something to prove.

He's like an eel, constantly slipping free of Diedrich and breaking away from defense, and when he's got the puck, none of us can take it from him.

Fuck.

I'm not losing this game.

Time is ticking down, and I know Grant will be pulled from the ice soon. I'm determined not to let him leave until I've shown him what someone with years of experience can do.

The second I see Torson pass to him, I tear down the ice. The crowd drowns out, my legs burn, and my focus narrows down to the puck.

Then everything falls into place.

Ezra shoots past me, legally checking Grant into the boards before he can get a pass off. I change course, scoop the puck up on my way past, and head straight for the blue line.

I catch sight of Torson to my left and send a bullet right by him to Diedrich, who passes to Larsen. Excitement flooding my veins when I'm hit with a wild thought: *we're about to score.*

There's not a shred of doubt with that statement. Superstitions be damned, Ezra and I made this happen.

I push harder, falling in line with Larsen as he shoots—and misses. The puck bounces off the goalie's pads and rebounds right into my blade, and I fire it back to Larsen, who now has a clear shot.

The lamp lights up.

"*Fuck yes!*"

I knock my helmet against Larsen's as Coach calls us off again.

When the game ends 2-1, I haul Ezra against me. It's safe, because the rest of the team is doing the same, but I keep it short—shorter than when I hug the other guys.

And the moment that thought hits me and I step off the ice to head down the chute, our conversation from last night runs through my head.

This is what he was talking about, and now that it's been pointed out to me, I can see where he's coming from. I didn't mean to treat him that way at all, but the problem is, I'm worried about getting *too* friendly with Ezra. The moment last night where we talked about our families really toed that line of what we are and highlighted exactly why I've been trying to keep my distance.

The impossible has happened. I like Ezra *as a person*.

And I'm beginning to think if we become actual friends, I'm going to end up liking him a whole lot more than that. I'm scared I already do.

I watch as he takes off his gloves and shoves them under his arm, then pulls his helmet off. I do the same. I remind myself that being friendly in public with Ezra isn't going to make me fall for him unless I let it.

So I won't let it.

I reach over and ruffle his sweaty hair. "It wasn't broken ankles, but we sure showed Grant."

"I know, it was like"—Ezra makes a gagging noise—"*teamwork*."

"You meeting up with him after this?"

"Yep. Queer collective rules."

Sometimes I wonder if Ezra takes this queer collective more seriously than the others, but then I think back on the bond he has with Tripp, and it makes me curious. I have friends in the league, and I love them, but there's something about shared experiences that can't be beat.

One day, when I retire, will I regret not getting to know these guys better?

I'm already regretting not getting to know Ezra sooner.

"Maybe I could come?" The words leave me before I give myself time to think them through.

Ezra stops in his tracks. We're midway between the locker room with the waiting press and the fans hanging over the railings, so I'm confident neither will overhear.

He looks as surprised as I feel, but thankfully, he doesn't question me. "I dunno, I sort of feel like you'd be cramping my style. Foster Grant is *hot*."

"And taken," I point out.

"Maybe his boyfriend is the sharing kind."

"I know what you're doing."

Ezra blinks at me innocently, and it makes me equal parts amused and stabby. "I don't know what you mean."

I grab the collar of his jersey and tug him to me, thankful that our conversation has made us fall behind the others. "You're trying to get me jealous."

"You look so sexy when you're trying not to deck someone."

"Why do I always need to remind you who you belong to?"

His eyes fly up to meet mine and *fuck*. Umm. I'm still trying to think of how to make those words go away without sounding like a complete dick and making him feel bad again, when he starts to smile.

"I think you like it," he points out. And of course, Ezra is able to see right through me. "Do you like seeing me flirt with other guys? Knowing that they can't have what you can?"

Somehow, I hold back from groaning. "Not the place to be having this conversation." I loosen my hold on his jersey and can't help subtly brushing my fingers along his neck as I release him. He fights back a shiver that makes me grin. "But I give you full permission to flirt with whoever you want. We both know whose dick you're going to finish the night on."

I really want to kiss him to prove my point, but this isn't the place to do it. So instead, we both head inside the locker room to cool down and shower. Even with a room full of men, I can feel Ezra's presence like it's the only one that matters. My body is so in tune with where he is at all times that it makes it hard not to chub up as I'm washing myself.

Once we're finished and getting dressed, I glance over at Ezra pulling on a suit with what looks like a leaf print. He catches me watching him, and I hurry to turn my attention back to my cubby.

"You serious about coming to meet Foster with me?"

"Yeah." I swipe my tongue over my bottom lip. "Think he'll care?"

"Nah, he's pretty laid-back."

Ezra is right. When we walk into the hotel bar where the rest of the Montreal team is mourning their loss, the first words out of Grant's mouth are "Fuck you very much, Palaszczuk."

His team behind him laughs, but then he breaks away from them and leads us to a cocktail table with stools.

"How's the shoulder, sweetheart?" Ezra asks.

"You two really couldn't go easy on a rookie like me?"

"Rookie?" I take the stool beside him. "Yeah, you can't play that card in your third year, and you *really* can't play it when you've been offered another three years on your contract and the media can't shut up about you."

"To be fair, it's Canada," Ezra points out. "They don't have much else to talk about up there."

"True. Tell me, do they pay you guys in real money or just, like, Timbits?"

"Your jokes would be so much funnier if I was actually Canadian," Grant says.

"You've been there over two years," I point out. "You're basically one of them now."

"Shut up and buy me a drink. I have sorrows to drown."

Despite his words, he doesn't look all that upset. Disappointed, sure.

"Funny, but, Ez, didn't we win?" I ask.

"I think we did."

"So shouldn't the loser be buying *us* drinks?"

"That *is* how it works, I hear."

Grant flips us off but heads for the bar.

"I think we teamworked again," I point out.

Ezra shudders. "We *have* to stop doing that."

"He's cool." I look at where Grant is waiting.

"Uh-oh."

"What?"

Ezra leans in close. "You gave me permission to flirt. Not the other way around."

"Aw … would you get jealous?"

"Jealous? You're cute. Thinking of you and Foster together?" He moans. "Turned on is more like it."

My fingers bite into his thigh. "Careful. I'm getting the urge to teach you a lesson."

An evil look crosses Ezra's face, and I'm certain I won't like what comes next. And not because I'm against it. But because he already knows how to read me too well.

Grant gets back with the drinks and slides ours across to us. He eyes us strangely for a moment, and I realize I'm still leaning into Ezra's space and my hand is still on his thigh. I quickly straighten.

"That's the only round you're getting out of me," he says.

"Maybe I could get something else out of you later." Ezra winks.

"You wish."

"Your loss. My cock's basically a good-luck charm. Or like Aladdin's lamp. You rub it and all your dreams come true."

"Has that line ever worked before?" I ask.

"It depends." He turns to me. "Want to try it out?"

"Oh, no, I wouldn't want to cockblock Grant."

Grant lifts his hand. "Solidly taken and committed, thank you."

We both ignore him.

"You should have heard the guy I was with the other night," Ezra continues. "Thought my name was Jesus."

My cheeks heat as I remember exactly what night he's talking about. We'd fucked so hard and fast I'm pretty sure I lost brain cells in the process. "Maybe what he really wanted was divine intervention to stop him from making a big mistake like sleeping with you."

"I'll ask when I meet up with him later. You know, if I can get anything other than babbled pleas in response."

"Might want to check in with him. I think he just got busy."

There's a laugh from the other side of the table, and Ezra and I both turn to Grant at the same time. "Sorry." He holds up his hands. "Didn't mean to interrupt … whatever that was."

"Banter between teammates," I suggest.

"Right. Yeah, I've seen that kind of"—he uses air quotes—"banter between teammates before."

"What are you trying to say?"

"No, nothing." And like he can't help himself, he continues. "Though I didn't know you were queer. Are you closeted, or …?"

I could deny it. I don't want to though. "There are plenty of people who know. But they respect my privacy enough not to spread it around."

He lifts his hands. "Noted."

"But now that you *do* know," Ezra says, propping his elbows on the bar table. "Interested in a threesome? *Ohh*, a foursome. You can bring your little guy and—"

I grab Ezra's thigh again in warning. "Stop talking."

"What are you gonna do, Hayes?"

"Not something I need to hear," Grant hurries to cut in. "And Zach and I do the monogamy thing. If I saw another guy touch my boyfriend, I'd probably break their fingers."

"I'm exactly the same," I say, and it takes me a moment to realize why Grant is looking at me weird again. I quickly remove my hand from Ezra's leg. "When I have a boyfriend. Which I don't. But I *would be* the same."

I'm failing terribly at being subtle. I don't know how to do this. How to walk the line between being friendly with Ezra and keeping things under wraps. I might as well have clubbed him over the head and carried him back to my den where Grant is concerned.

Ah, fuck it all.

We don't stay too long with Grant—just long enough for Ezra to check in with him and catch up—and as soon as we leave the bar to go back to where our team is celebrating, I can't wait any longer to touch him.

I drag Ezra down into a side alley and push him up against the wall between a dumpster and a fence. Then I kiss him. My tongue surges forward into his mouth, and all the doubts calm. *This*, I know. Sex between us is easy. It makes sense.

So I pull back from the kiss to undo his belt, then spit into my hand.

"I think I failed at the flirting thing," Ezra says.

"I don't know. You went so over the top with it that Grant knows exactly what's going on between us now." I slide my hand down the front of his pants and wrap my fingers around his half-hard cock.

Ezra moans. "Yeah, but I was meant to be flirting with *him*, not you."

"It's not your fault. I'm extremely irresistible."

"Yeah, my favorite quality is your humility."

I don't respond, kissing him again, stroking him until he's fully hard.

"Also, so you know, you didn't fail," I say.

He looks at me like he's struggling to stay focused. "What do you mean?"

"Your aim was to flirt with him to turn me on." I press my hard cock into his thigh. "Mission accomplished."

Ezra goes to reach for me, but I swat his hand away.

"What are you—"

"I'm saving that for later."

"Ohh, tell me more."

I pick up the pace of my strokes, tightening my grip and twisting over the head. "We're going to meet up with the team, have some drinks, and you'll be your usual charismatic self."

"Like I can be any different."

I lean closer, lips brushing his. "And the whole time you'll know this is what's waiting for you. The second we walk into my apartment, I'm going to bend you over and make you take my cock like you were made for it."

Ezra's eyes roll back, and his dick jerks in my hand. He's so close. So turned on. He's leaking so much I want to drop to my knees and swallow him down, but instead, I twist a hand through the hair at the back of his neck and bring my lips to his ear. "I'm going to fuck your gorgeous brains out, Ez."

He cries out, and his cock pulses right before warmth floods my hand. He comes and comes, and my hard-on is begging me to let it get some action, but I push that thought away.

When he finally slumps back against the brick wall, breathing returning to normal, I tuck his dick back inside his briefs and use the inside of them to clean up the mess.

He cringes. "That's going to be uncomfortable."

"That's going to be your reminder."

He furrows his brow, clearly not totally with it. "What do you mean?"

"It's going to be all you can focus on." I press him into the wall with my body. "Every little cringe, I'm going to know you're thinking of me."

"You really are a possessive motherfucker, aren't you?" There's a teasing note coming back to his voice.

I tilt his chin up so he meets my eyes. "Are you okay with that? Despite our history, I don't *actually* want to make you uncomfortable or feel like you can't say no."

His gaze softens. "Look at you, being almost sweet."

I go to argue, but he cuts me off.

"And when have you ever known me to do anything I don't want to? If I didn't like it, I'd tell you. But so far, I'm loving every minute of it, Hay—*Anton*."

"Even though it's me?"

"*Especially* because it's you." There's a brief flicker of panic that crosses his face, so I kiss him.

I don't ask him to elaborate because I don't think either of us could handle it. Whether he meant the animosity made things hotter, or the teammates aspect, or it just being me? I don't know, and I don't want to.

So I keep kissing him.

Until we're both out of breath and we can pretend like his words are forgotten.

CHAPTER TWENTY-ONE

EZRA

I stretch out in bed, so wrung out I have no idea what day, time, or week it is. I also don't know where the hell I am.

Then I open my eyes and remember.

Oh. Right. Anton's apartment.

We ran into each other at weight training this morning, and after watching him do squats for twenty minutes, there was no way I wasn't following him home to get in a workout of our own.

Only, I must've passed out immediately afterward.

"Good morning, Sleeping Beauty," Anton says from somewhere in the room.

I open one eye a crack and roll onto my back, finding Anton in the doorway dressed in jeans and a Henley. "You're wearing too many clothes. Come back to bed."

"You slept through lunch."

"That must be why my stomach's rumbling."

"Are you planning to go to Diedrich's thing?"

"His kind of baby announcement party? He already has a billion children—why do we have to celebrate every time his wife gets pregnant? Isn't that like throwing a party for getting laid?"

"Imagine if the gays did that."

"Oh, they would never. Too many calories in cake. And you can't have a party without cake."

Anton plays with the hem of his shirt. "I was wondering if you wanted to go ... maybe together."

"Like a date?" My gut flips. "To a team event?"

"Like *friends*. I'm paying attention, see? You want the team to know we're friends, so I figured—"

"You figured going to a *baby shower* together screams friends?"

He huffs. "Forget it. It was just an idea. I'm *trying* here."

"I would love to go with you. As your friend. But the team is definitely going to give us shit about it."

Anton shrugs. "Let them."

"What time do we have to leave?"

"In twenty."

"Will they have food there? I'm starving."

"Go shower. I'll make you something to eat on the way."

"Aww, thanks."

"I'm not doing it for you. I'm sure they'll have food there, but I don't want to have to drive out to Chestnut Hill with you whining the whole time about being hungry."

"You know me too well." I roll out of bed and jump in Anton's shower, and when I get out, I'm greeted with a peanut butter and jelly sandwich. "Wow. Don't outdo yourself."

"Eat at the party. This is purely to stop you from complaining."

I shove the whole thing in my mouth in under a minute. "Let's go."

"That was both horrifying and impressive."

"I'm good with fitting a lot in my mouth, but you should know that by now." I wink at him.

He doesn't even fight me on that or call me ridiculous. I think this is what we call progress.

Anton's relaxed on the drive out to Chestnut Hill, and I can't help trying to make him crack.

"So, bestie …"

He raises an eyebrow at me. "Bestie?"

"Well, we're friends now. This is our friend date. And I have been looking for a replacement for West, so it all fits."

"I'm not West's replacement." He pouts. It's adorable.

"Ooh, do I sense a little jealousy there?"

"Not at all. I just refuse to be your fuckboy like West was."

"You still worried about that? If it makes you feel any better, what West and I had was completely different."

"How so?"

"Well, for one, we actually liked each other. Never fought. Always fell back on each other because it was easy. It wasn't—" I slam my mouth shut because I don't know what was about to come out of it.

"Wasn't what?"

I struggle to find any word that describes Anton. "*Intense*."

"You think what we have is intense?"

"You don't? You have to admit our sexual chemistry is off the charts. You can go head-to-head slinging snark back and forth with me without even blinking." I pause. "You challenge me to be a better player." *And a better person.* But I don't say that part even though I kind of like it. "It's the opposite to what I had with West. He was happy to come along for the ride. He was easygoing."

"Are you calling me uptight?"

"Are you arguing that you're not?"

A muscle ticks in his jaw. I need to give him a bit more.

"You see through my crap and pick up on things I don't even like talking about. I hate it and … I don't."

His gaze moves slowly from the road to me. Something in his expression relaxes. "Of course I challenge you. I'm better than you at almost everything."

I laugh, relieved and unsettled at how easily he reads me. "You wish."

"Excuse me, but who's having the season of their life?"

"Whose dick is responsible for that?"

"Here you go with your magic dick again."

"I was thinking I should approach a sex toy company. Get my bad boy molded for replication. I'll call it the Good Luck Fuck. Guaranteed to improve your game."

Anton sighs instead of enabling me.

"Yep. We're definitely besties. You don't even call me on my shit anymore."

"It's because I know when I'm wasting my breath."

"I've been called a waste of breath many times."

"*What*?" His jaw ticks.

"I'm a terrible person sometimes. I get under people's skin. Even I know that."

He pulls into Diedrich's long drive, but it looks like we're close to being the last ones to arrive. We park behind Larsen's Bentley, and Anton turns to me.

"You are not a terrible person."

"Because I'm an aweso—"

"Nope." He pinches my chin and leans in, dark eyes locked with mine. "No joking. You *are* an awesome person, Ez. And while we do this thing, you're also *my* person. If anyone says that shit to you, they get to face *both* of us."

I ... have no idea how to respond to that because my brain has gone blank on the jokes. Hearing him say there's an *us*, as fragile as it might be, is sort of ... nice. Actually, a lot nice. West and I always had each other's backs, but in a way where we'd defend the other separately. Not together. I've always loved being part of a team. Is that what a relationship thingy is like?

No wonder so many of my friends have fallen victim.

Anton lets me go, and we get out of the car to approach the front door together.

Diedrich and his wife answer, and her pregnant-glowing face lights up.

"Anton! It's nice to finally officially meet you," Gretchen says and hugs him.

"You too."

Then she turns to me. "Ezra. Always nice to see you."

"Lies. Congrats on baby number ..."

"Five," she says, pulling a face. "I swear it happens after every road trip longer than eight days."

That's ... information I didn't need to know about my team captain.

"When are you due?" I ask.

"Somewhere around the Stanley Cup finals. Is it mean of me to hope you guys don't make the playoffs so he'll actually be present for this one's birth?"

I automatically knock on the doorframe to avoid that bad juju.

"Hey, I was there for one and four, thank you very much," Diedrich says.

"Are those their names? One, Two, Three, Four?" I ask.

"It's how I remember them," Diedrich says, but then his gaze flicks between me and Anton. "You two ... came together? Or did you arrive at the same time?"

I throw my arm around Anton's shoulder. "Together. We're besties. It's a new development."

"Kill me now," Anton mutters.

Diedrich steps aside. "That sounds about right. Come on in. The guys are already out the back."

We walk past a group of women, some I recognize as other players' girlfriends and wives and others I haven't met before—presumably Gretchen's friends. We give them a wave and head out back to the team, who are standing around the backyard, all with drinks already.

"Looks like we have some catching up to do," I say.

Anton touches the small of my back. "I'll get us drinks."

I make my way over to Larsen and Kosik, but they too do a double take.

"Did you walk in with Hayes?" Larsen asks.

"What's so wrong about that?"

"It's you. And Hayes."

Anton appears and shoves a beer in my hand. "We're besties ... apparently."

"Hey, I'm just doing what team management asked. I'm playing nice."

Kosik leans in closer to Anton. "Don't turn your back on him tonight. This prank has to be epic."

"Please. I am past all the pranks." I sip my beer. "I am a mature adult."

Everyone laughs.

"Fucking whatever."

"Nothing says mature adult like muttering the words 'Fucking whatever,'" Larsen says.

Apart from the initial comments about Anton and me coming together and having to defend that we have actually become somewhat friends—which we expected to face—Anton finally starts to relax around the team in my presence.

I take that as a good sign, but who knows how long it will last.

CHAPTER TWENTY-TWO

ANTON

It takes a solid week or two for the team to calm down on the teasing. I get why they're so surprised, but it's also a relief when they start to move on from it because then I don't need to be on edge all the time. It makes it easier to treat Ezra like any of the other guys on the team.

The problem is, though, he's not any of the other guys.

When we joke together, there's more subtext. While we're laughing over something, it holds heavier meaning. The lingering gazes, the beat-too-long touches, the way my jaw starts to hurt from holding back from smiling at everything he says.

There's no way to deny we're friends now.

On the flight home from our away game yesterday, a couple of us organized a game of golf once our morning workout was done. It will be the second time Ezra and I are hanging out with the team as friends, and I'm … excited?

This is different.

Celebrating after games is more about our push and pull. He flirts with men, it turns me on, I pull rank, and Ezra basically melts for me.

Today, we get to be friends without all the other nonsense. We're allowed to like each other without things getting weird or twisted.

The problem is, they're already getting weird and twisted in my head.

I've started noticing this pang that hits me right in the chest whenever Ezra is being, well, Ezra. All the bad qualities I used to hate about him no longer seem as irritating.

Diedrich has a membership with his local country club, so I drive out there and meet the guys. Ezra's already there, caramel-colored hair brightened by the sun, and I immediately grin as I pull into a parking space.

"About time, Hayes," Diedrich says as I grab my clubs from the trunk and lock up.

"Gotta save the best for last."

Ezra snorts. "I can't imagine why anyone would call you egotistical."

"Tell me you're not already thinking of how to make me eat my words."

We catch eyes. Smile wide.

"All right, besties," Diedrich says, heavy on the sarcasm. "Let's get moving. Kosik is already inside."

It doesn't take much brainpower to guess why. He's leaning on the counter, chatting with the woman behind the desk. Ezra and I trade a glance before he walks over to them.

"You know," Ezra says, and I immediately pick up on his shit-stirring tone. "This guy's a real catch."

The woman lifts her eyebrows. "Oh, really?"

"Yup. Decent at hockey, still has most of his own teeth, barely snores. His personal hygiene could use work, but look at this face …" He squeezes Kosik's cheeks for emphasis, and while Kosik bats Ezra away, I approach on his other side.

"Not to mention he's great at spooning, right, Ez?" I turn to the woman, who looks more amused than interested. "Want to see the photos? They're adorable together."

"I'll pass." She looks back at Kosik. "Was it just the balls?"

Ezra nudges him. "You're in."

"Leave her alone," our captain says, joining us.

Ezra snickers. "We're double-teaming Kosik."

"Fuck you guys," Kosik grumbles.

"Welcome back, Mr. Diedrich," the woman says, like she's trying to ignore the three stooges in front of her.

"Ooh, Mr. Diedrich. I like that. You can call me Mr. Palaszczuk." Ezra stresses the Polish pronunciation.

At the woman's blank face, I say, "You can call him Hayes two-point-oh. He basically wants to be me anyway."

Her lips quirk, and she holds eye contact a little too long before she grabs Kosik's golf balls and the keys to the golf carts Ezra insists we need.

He's less than friendly as he collects it and steers me outside while Diedrich pays.

His pouty face is pouty.

I poke his cheek. "Are you sulking?"

"She thought you were hot."

"And?"

"And? You're mine."

That word hits me with a surge of satisfaction. Whenever I say it, it's on a sexual level. I own his body and all the ways to make him feel good, but there's something in his tone that covers more than that, and I love it.

"Ez …" I soften my voice. "I'm gay."

"I know that. But if you were anyone else, I would have walked right up and claimed you." He tosses me a key. "She got lucky."

I frown. Not because I object, but because that's his *I'm pretending to joke but am actually serious* voice. Is that what he wants? I've given him the acknowledgment and friendship he wanted, but claiming is a whole other step. A big one. That's relationship levels. I'm not sure what to think about that.

The little pang hits me again, leaving an echo that sounds suspiciously like "liar" behind.

I shake it off and point to the closest cart. "This one is mine."

"Deal."

We climb into our carts as soon as Kosik joins me—after pointing out how much he hates us both—and Diedrich joins Ezra. From the drive to the first hole, our egos take over.

We race to see who can get there the quickest. We're both determined to make the best score on the first hole, and then we compete for the first hole-in-one. Every time we make a hole under par, we're quick to goad the other, and it reaches a point where I barely register Diedrich and Kosik are still with us. They're in their world; Ez and I are in ours.

"Race you to the ninth," Ezra says the second Diedrich makes his shot, and the four of us break into a run.

Kosik and I all but jump into our cart, and then I turn it over and put my foot down. These things gain speed for something so small.

We're tearing across the perfectly manicured turf, pushing the fifteen-miles-an-hour limit to its max and probably breaking about a hundred of the country club rules, but fuck if any of us care.

It's been a long, long time since I switched off and had fun like this.

Kosik's laughing and white-knuckling the handgrip as we round the small crop of trees toward the ninth and head downhill. The small bumps in the terrain jolt us in our seats, and I can feel the cart starting to become unstable. Reluctantly, I ease up on the accelerator, and Ezra and Diedrich start to pull ahead, until—

"Ez!"

He sees the pond a second after me and hits the brakes. The back end kicks up, and it's like slow motion as Ezra and Diedrich jump from the cart as it flips. It tumbles downhill and hits the pond with a massive splash.

The sound of the water is still ringing in my ears as I bring the golf cart to a stop beside them. The four of us are silent for a second as we stare at the mess.

"Fuck …" Diedrich hisses.

"You both okay?" I ask.

Ezra nods, but Diedrich shakes his head.

"You're hurt?"

"I will be. My wife is going to kill me if I get us kicked out of the club."

I smirk. "Not the pain I was talking about."

"If it helps," Ezra says, "I'll make sure your funeral is awesome. Lots of tears and sappy stories."

"I think the only thing that's going to help is us going back in time and not being dickheads," Diedrich answers.

I hum in agreement.

"The tabloids are gonna love this," Kosik says.

My back tenses painfully, and Ezra's gaze shoots to mine.

I lick my lips. "Nothing none of us haven't dealt with before." I sound way more confident than I feel, but thanks to Ezra, I've been in the tabloids more this season than any other. I take a deep breath and remind myself I can get through this.

"Okay, plan," Ezra says. "I'll offer to buy them two golf carts to replace this one."

"We all will," I cut in, because this wasn't all on Ezra. "We'll split the costs."

The others quickly agree.

"Sweet, so we'll replace the carts under the provision they keep this quiet."

"And I get to keep my membership," Diedrich adds.

"Yeah, sure." Ezra waves him off. "One last thing though."

I wait for him to continue.

"We all agree not to tell Coach." He grimaces. "This is the last thing I need for him to hold against me."

To my surprise, I actually laugh.

Sure, the knot of anxiety is there over the idea that this will get out, but no one got hurt, and we were having fun until right now.

The whole—slow—drive back to the clubhouse, we're mostly quiet. I can tell that even though it isn't all on him, Ezra still feels bad. He keeps glancing at me out of the corner of his eye, like he's waiting to see what my reaction will be.

So I give him time, and when he finally meets my gaze again, I wink.

His relief is immediate.

As is that stupid, dumb little pang.

CHAPTER TWENTY-THREE

EZRA

It's easy for Anton and me to fall into a rhythm, and I never thought I'd love away games as much as I have this season. It's easier for us to hook up when we're rooming together instead of doing the stupid cloak-and-dagger bullshit sneaking around Boston when we're home.

The coaches and team management are happy that we're behaving like good little boys and getting along, though there are still stories about us in the media across the entire spectrum from us hating each other to we're getting married and having a surrogate carry our babies.

Either way, the team doesn't really care what might or might not be going on with us because we're winning every damn game.

We're on a streak, and we're all holding our breaths for the inevitable day where something goes wrong and breaks it.

Today, we have a quick morning skate to stay loose, and then some of us get the rest of the day off. Some—as in, the lucky ones. Us unlucky ones have to go home and get ready for the B's annual charity gala. Black-tie event. Stuffy, rich people wanting to meet hockey players. Begging for donations for the thousands of different charities the B Foundation contributes to.

Fun times.

Like I told Anton when he dragged me to the animal shelter, I don't mind the charity work. It totally has a purpose. But our schedule is so grueling, all I really want to be focused on during the season is hockey. The in-between times should be reserved for fucking and resting. Oh, and eating.

I'm a simple man. Food, sex, sleep, and hockey. That's all I need.

I don't need to get all dolled up in a penguin suit and schmooze rich people while I can't even get drunk because we have a game tomorrow.

After our skate, in the locker room, Anton approaches me. "You get tapped for that dinner tonight too?" he asks.

"Yep."

"Want to, uh, go?"

"It's mandatory, so yeah."

"I mean … with me."

Okay, this is new. I glance around at the rest of the guys stripping down to see if any of them are in on this. Like asking me out in front of everyone is some elaborate prank. No one is paying attention. When I look up at him, usually meticulously neat black hair a mess and expression guarded, I can't make out what he means.

I lower my voice. "Like a date or …"

"I figure we live close by, we both have to go, but never mind—"

"I'll go. With you."

"Meet at mine at seven?"

My smile is almost painful.

Anton hits the showers, but I stay at my cubby, trying to dissect what just happened.

He didn't answer my question if this is an actual date or not. Maybe it's as friends. And, scarily, maybe I don't want it to be.

Anton's relaxing around me more and more, which is great, but now he might be overshooting it. I wanted public acknowledgment as a friend and teammate, nothing more. Does he think I need public dates? Or is this *him* wanting public dates?

Or is this his way of being friends?

Am I freaking out at the prospect of more? Surprisingly, no. And I don't know why that is either.

I'm not sure of anything, especially the answer to why Anton is different than anyone I've ever been with before.

Normally, I'd freak out at his demand for exclusivity. Initially, I didn't want to agree to it because that's not how I operate. Knowing there was an end date on it made it easier for me, but now … I don't see an end date in sight, and I'm weirdly okay with it.

I try to shake all those thoughts free, but they come back intermittently throughout the day.

I think about Anton when I get home and hit the gym to stretch out my muscles from this morning's skate, when I'm grooming my beard and manscaping my junk to get ready for tonight, and particularly when I'm donning my tux and getting ready to show up at this gala together.

I doubt any more could be said in the media about us, so arriving together isn't going to cause a stir. It will look like we're teammates.

Yet, there's a ball of nerves in my gut as I text Anton that I'm leaving and to meet me out front. I can't tell if it's from dread or excitement.

Anton confuses me in the best possible way. Or the worst. It could be either. Or both. I'm a confused mess, and it's all Anton's fault.

One thing I do know is when Anton steps out of his building, I'm not prepared for seeing him in a tux.

A tailored suit, sure. I see that every other day.

But a tux? With a bow tie and his Armani jacket?

I'm hard just looking at him.

His hair is back to usual—perfectly styled and parted on the side.

He climbs into my passenger seat. "Couldn't even come up to knock on my door like a gentleman? Why am I not surprised?"

Instead of a smartass remark about there being nothing gentlemanly about either of us, nothing passes my lips. My analytical side kicks in again, and I overthink every word in his sentence until nothing makes sense.

Was I supposed to pick him up from his door like it's a date?

"Wow, you really hate being charitable," Anton says. "It's the animal shelter all over again."

"Huh?" I pull out onto the road.

"You look tense. What's up?"

"Nothing's up. Other than my dick. You look hot."

Anton releases a small smile.

"And I don't look too bad either," I prompt.

"You scrub up nice."

"You mean for a fuckboy?"

Anton sighs. "I can't believe I'm going to say this, and I will deny I ever did, but ... you're not a fuckboy."

"Oh no, are you dying? Retiring? Is the world ending? Did I miss the alien zombie invasion? Or are you trying to make us crash?"

"Yep. I take it back already."

"You can't. No backsies. That's how it works with actual compliments, not the half-assed ones you throw at me sometimes."

"You really don't want to push me right now, Ez. I'm on the brink of making things really uncomfortable for you."

"Uncomfortable how? You gonna reach over and tease me through my pants? Ooh, road head?" I reach for my fly, but his words stop me cold.

"You're not a fuckboy, but you act like one because deep down you don't want to feel the rejection your parents inflicted on you your whole life. You treat people as disposable so they can't do it to you first."

I grip the steering wheel tight and grit my teeth.

"I told you," Anton says.

"That's some grade A psychoanalyzing you did there, but you're wrong."

"Am I?"

"People are disposable to me because I'm literally too much of a fuckboy to care about anyone but myself."

Anton stares at me for a moment, and I can feel the heat of his gaze on the side of my neck, but he turns away and looks out his window.

He says something, and it's so low I miss half of it, but it sounds like "Keep telling yourself that."

—

Walking into this function together is no big deal. Getting photographed while a million questions are thrown our way about our friendship is the same old shit on another night. But Anton's words keep replaying in my head, and it's taking all my energy to be my usual carefree self.

I manage because I have to. Not for the rich attendees who I couldn't care less about or because the team's management expects me to. I need to do it to prove to Anton that he can't see through me.

Even though he can. He's the only one who's paid close enough attention to me to see past the smokescreen. Not even my parents care enough to put in the effort. I make it deliberately hard for people to love me, and I sabotage when they're getting too close. It's easier than them being disappointed by who I really am. But Anton sees. And he's not disappointed.

Yet.

It's only a matter of time until I screw up though. And I'm not sure how I'm going to get past when it happens because I don't want to disappoint him. That's a completely new experience for me.

"Drink?" I ask Anton, and he nods. "I'll be right back."

I'm suddenly regretting driving because despite being told not to drink by Coach, I want to drown out all the overthinking.

This is not me.

A presence and familiar cologne appears next to me, along with a deep voice. "What, I retire and you replace me with Anton Hayes?"

I turn to find my best friend, Westly Dalton, standing there, and next to him is his sexy professor boyfriend.

"You escaped prison!" I exclaim, and everyone's heads in the immediate vicinity turn to look.

"Uh, five kids is not prison."

"If you say so." I don't hesitate to throw my arms around him. "I can't believe you're here." Then I shove him. "Why didn't you tell me?"

"And ruin the surprise? There's no fun in that."

His partner, Jasper, rolls his eyes. "He didn't tell you because up until a few hours ago, he wasn't sure he was going to come. He still struggles to leave the kids for longer than an hour."

I turn to West. "Can I ask you something?"

"I'm scared," Jasper says. "He's going to ask for a threesome, isn't he?"

I hold my heart. "I'm touched you know me so well already. This is fate. We should get married."

I swear West's partner loves me. He really does. Even when he inhales a long breath, tells West he'll be at the bar, and leaves us alone.

"What's up?" West asks.

"How did you know ... like ... how did you know you wanted more. Umm, with me?"

West's gaze narrows. "Why do you want to—" His gaze ping-pongs all over the room, trying to find Anton, no doubt. "Are you and Hayes still—"

I tug on his arm. "Not here."

There are two doors leading outside to a balcony where smokers can have a cigarette, but there's no one out here right now.

"Yes, Anton and I are still fucking around."

West puts his hands in his pockets. "And you're scared he wants more from you?"

Of course he'd think that.

"I'm scared *I* do."

West flinches as if I hit him.

"Sorry. Maybe I shouldn't talk to you about this, but you were and always will be my best friend, even if things got weird for a while, and I don't know why I'm getting confused over him when I never did with you. It would've made so much more sense for this to happen with you, and maybe our timing was off or something—"

West starts laughing his ass off.

My neck burns, my skin tingles, and even as he bends to try to catch his breath, I'm struggling to see what's so funny.

"Sorry. I'm not laughing," he says ... through laughter. "I just don't know how else to react to that."

"Neither do I, but with hysterical laughter isn't even on my list."

West stands upright. "Okay. Sorry. I'm done. I swear."

"You sure?"

His face screws up, and he laughs some more.

"Oh, fuck you. Forget I said anything." I turn to go back inside when West catches my arm.

"Sorry. Again. I ... I don't think my mind can comprehend this. When we were together, I thought maybe, possibly one day you'd think about settling down but you hadn't got all the sleeping around out of your system. I was kinda over that scene by the end, and I was waiting for you to catch up. But you never did. Then—"

"Then you found yourself having to move home with an insta-family, and you realized you could never be serious about someone like me."

"Aww, Ez. That's not it at all. Our paths went in two different directions. You were in no way ready to settle down. But if you're standing here telling me that you want to try to have a relationship with Anton, then I'm going to give you all the support in the world."

"So again, how did you know?"

West is clearly struggling to find the words. "I ... realized that when the night ended, I'd rather hook up with you than anyone else. But ... don't take offense to this, it was different with Jasper. With you, I didn't care if you hooked up with anyone else. With him, I would cut a bitch who looked at him too long."

I snigger, because we both know that West is all talk. He's a big kitten who would skate away from fights on the ice.

"How do you feel when he's with someone else?" West asks.

I start to feel really, really awkward about that. "You mean like talking …" Of course I know what he means, but I suddenly don't want to admit that we're exclusive.

"Fucking. Duh." He eyes me funny.

"I wouldn't know because he doesn't sleep with anyone else."

West looks surprised. "Okay, well—"

"And neither do I."

"*What*? You're exclusive?"

"Would we call it exclusive …" I try for dismissive, but West isn't having any of it.

"Yes. That's literally what that means." He lets out a low whistle. "Are you guys already in a relationship?"

"No." But when I think about it, we do hang out a lot. And talk. About things other than sex.

"But you want to be?"

"Maybe. I don't know." I pause. "Why him?"

"You're …" West cocks his head. "You're asking me why you like Anton?"

"I guess? Because I sure as hell don't know. We still bicker, and up until a few weeks ago, I wasn't sure if we were even friends."

"What's changed over the last few weeks?"

"That's what's driving me crazy. I can't figure it out."

West's lips flatten.

"What is it?" I ask. "That's your *I have the solution but don't want to say it* face."

"I didn't realize I had a face that said that."

"You do, and I want to know what you were thinking."

"I was thinking that maybe you're falling for Anton, and because you've never done that with anyone before, you're freaking out."

"I'm not freaking out. That's not it."

Oh fuck, is it?

CHAPTER TWENTY-FOUR

ANTON

I press my tongue harder into my cheek to try and push down the rising emotions. Ezra left to get us drinks, and the second Westly Dalton approached him, I was completely forgotten about.

I'm still staring at the doorway they disappeared through as my overactive imagination conjures wild images that are impossible but I'm convinced are true.

Ezra on his knees for West.

Ezra bent over the banister.

Ezra moaning with West's hand down his pants.

And then when another guy I don't recognize joins them on the balcony, suddenly he's in on the action going on in my mind too, even though he's probably only going out there for a cigarette. My insecurities don't make sense, and logically I know that, but that doesn't stop my jaw clenching so hard I swear I crack a molar.

I remind myself Ezra's aware of our arrangement and I trust him. Despite everything, that thought catches me off guard every time, but if Ezra wanted to fuck around, I know he'd tell me first.

Still, even the thought of him out there flirting with West, reliving old memories, makes my gut turn. I like him harmlessly flirting in front of me, behind my back? No. Nope. Don't like it.

I don't like any of this.

Okay, this is bad.

Ezra shouldn't have this kind of power over me.

I haven't slept with anyone else since our first time together, and I don't even want to. I'm sure he got laid plenty over the summer, and even that makes me uncomfortable. We weren't together, we didn't even like each other, yet the thought sends a simmering rage under my skin that I can't shake.

Maybe if we weren't some kind of filthy secret, this wouldn't be such an issue.

Whose fault is that though, moron?

I look around the room, determined not to go after him.

The alcohol is flowing freely, everyone seems to be laughing or joking, and fat checks are swapping hands. There are more than a few people on the dance floor now. I spot Diedrich and his wife and, surprisingly, a handful of same-sex couples.

My gaze catches on them. Discomfort creeps over me as I watch them in their own happy bubbles, proud to be who they are.

Goddamn it.

I want that.

I don't want to want that. I'm happy. I know who I am. What does it matter that the rest of the world doesn't? Why should it be a thing?

The reality is, though, that people still care. And they'll continue to care until it's normalized, and the only way for that to happen is for people to live their truth.

But the thing that's making me keep my mouth closed is that if I come out, I won't want to hide this thing with Ezra anymore.

Whatever it is.

Being out to me means dinner dates and holding hands and starting a life with someone.

Ezra might never feel that way. It has never been part of our deal. And if I come out and don't hide being with him, that will be where the attention comes from and when this whole thing blows up in our faces, I doubt I'll ever live it down.

I don't want to be remembered as that NHL player who dated Ezra Palaszczuk and walked away brokenhearted.

I look back over at where Ezra disappeared, my anxiousness ramping up again.

They've been gone a long time.

To distract myself, I go and buy my own damn drink, but they're still not back.

I'm not going to go after him.

I refuse.

I have no idea if Ezra has told West about us, and that bothers me so much I'm not sure I want the answer. I'm beginning to suspect this is how Ezra felt when I couldn't even be friendly toward him. It sucks.

I finish my drink and weigh my options. I could go out there and be friendly to Dalton, having to look into his eyes and know he's fucked the man I can't stop thinking about. It's no secret to me that Ezra's slept around, but so far I've managed to avoid coming face-to-face with anyone he's slept with.

My other option is to leave. But I already know that's not going to happen. I'll end up tormenting myself all night.

The third option is to walk out there and make it very clear where I stand with him.

Damn, that's tempting.

So, so tempting.

It would only be West. I wouldn't have to make a big deal out of it. I could walk out there, and so long as there was no one else around, all I'd need to do is slide my hand over his ass and my message would be clear.

Ezra is mine.

I groan at the thought.

At doing what no one else has ever done.

The thing is, I don't want to rein him in. I don't want to change him. He's light. He's attention. People are drawn to him and his larger-than-life personality. I want to wind him up and watch him fly, then be the safe place where he can land. The one he always comes back to. I'm okay with the flirting and the teasing, the only thing I'd expect from him is commitment.

Fuck.

Commitment.

With Ezra.

What is wrong with me?

Ezra is all of those things and more, but I'm … not. I'm hockey. I'm ego, and not in a fun way like him. How long until my possessiveness stops being hot and feels like a noose around his neck?

My foot taps as I contemplate ordering another drink.

I'm not going to go out there.

I'm not.

I won't.

I refuse.

And yet I head in that direction anyway.

The second I step outside and see Ezra, something jitters inside me so hard it makes me hesitate.

I'm about to convince myself to go back inside when he looks up and catches me. Something passes between us that I can't name, and when Ezra gives me a small, private smile, it brings the fire inside me alive.

Mine.

I close the distance between us, completely ignoring West and the man next to him and not stopping until I'm in Ezra's space. My hand finds his lower back.

"Hayes," he says.

"Remembered I exist, did you?"

"Aw, is someone feeling neglected?"

"Thirsty," I correct. "What happened to my drink?"

He steps closer, shoulder pressed to mine, and turns back toward West. "You remember Dalton."

I turn slowly to find West watching me. "Yes."

"Anton Hayes." West holds out his hand. "I've heard your name a lot lately."

I hesitate before shaking it. "Well, I have the most points scored in the league this season, so I'm not surprised."

The guy beside him groans. "Oh no, there are two of them."

"Anton," I say, holding out my hand to him.

"Jasper." We shake quickly, and I swear he drops my hand faster than West did. Then there's a beat of awkward silence before Ezra starts to laugh.

"What's so funny?" I ask.

"I don't actually know."

"So, West," I say, trying to be civil and not focused on him being hot and sweaty with Ezra. "How's domestic life suiting you?"

"Best decision I ever made." He points to Jasper. "This is my partner."

Well, that makes me feel a fraction better. I lick my bottom lip and glance at Ezra to find him already looking at me. "What?"

"You're not as growly as I was expecting you to be."

"I'm trying hard to play nice."

"That's no fun. Do you need me to ask these two for a threesome to bring it out of you?" Ezra's flirty smile is back in place, and I have the feeling that maybe he did tell West about us.

It makes me irrationally happy. I slide my hand up to grip the back of Ezra's neck, fingers tangling in the hair at his nape. "Don't worry, when we get home later, I'll show you exactly how annoyed I am with you." I can barely believe the words I'm saying in front of people.

His heated gaze meets mine. "Is that a promise?"

"We don't need to hear this," West cuts in.

"No problem." I hold Ezra's stare. "We were going to dance anyway."

"We were?" Ezra asks.

"Unless you have any reason why we shouldn't?"

"Did you take a hit to the head?"

"Is that your way of saying no?" That would be embarrassing.

"Oh, I'm all for it. But unlike you, I'm more than happy to make a scene."

I lean in close to his ear, and my fingers tighten on his neck. "Then dance with me, Ez?"

As soon as he agrees, I turn on my heel and head back inside, not pausing to check if Ezra is following me. I have no idea what I'm doing, or what's possessed me, but with all the rumors circulating lately, it's not like this could cause any more damage.

At least, that's what I'm trying to convince myself of right up until I reach the dance floor and turn to find Ezra's thankfully right behind me. He's eyeing me strangely, and I can't blame him.

My stomach is in knots, and I'm second-guessing myself, but then I think of losing all this, and my determination overrides everything else.

I hold out my hand, and after a fraction of hesitation, he takes it.

"I have questions," he says as I pull him in close.

"I can imagine."

"This is going to blow some shit up. Are you ready for the theories about us going from five to one hundred?"

"People are speculating anyway. This doesn't confirm anything."

"Sure, keep telling yourself that." He drums his fingers on my shoulder. "The question is, though, which rumors does this support? Because the dancing would fuel the dating rumors, but the look on your face makes me think you want to punch something, and people probably, correctly, assume that something is me."

Huh. Time to ditch the murderous expression, then. I force myself to relax. "I didn't like being forgotten about."

His gaze darts away from me. "Yeah, so not what happened."

"It wasn't?"

"No. I got excited to see West, obviously, but then we ended up talking about you."

Interesting. "What about me?"

"That you're a giant idiot who bones like a beast."

"Eh, I'll take it." My grip on his waist tightens, and I feel better than I have all night.

"You're smiling."

"Why wouldn't I be?"

Ezra studies me for a moment. "I, uh, I like when you smile."

"What else do you like?"

"There's no way I'm going to stand here and give you compliments."

"Fine." I know this kind of conversation is hard for him, but I'm not backing down. "My turn. I like how other people don't get to you."

"Oh, really?"

"Your turn."

He hesitates, clearly needing to think about it.

"Wow," I say. "I didn't think it would be that hard to find something you like about me." Because, ouch.

"Shut up, I'm trying to choose. Okay … I like … your hair."

"My hair?"

Ezra nods. "Yeah, it's soft."

I hang my head back. "Well, fucking fuck. Slow down with those praises, Ez. Here I am thinking you're fun and"—I glance around to make sure we're not overheard— "sexy. You always think the best of people, have a positive outlook on life, hate getting vulnerable, so when you do it's—" I cut off. "Anyway."

A long silence stretches and then, "I like … you," he finally says.

"Me?"

"Hear me out." He stares in the direction of my chest, avoiding my eyes. "I never thought I would. I always thought you were an asshole and had a stick up your ass, but now I know it's because you put pressure on yourself to be the best. And I like being around you. You know more about the real me than maybe anyone."

"There's still a lot I don't know. Like, a lot. What's your favorite color? All-time favorite hockey player?"

"Red. It's good luck in Poland. And all-time player? Me, duh."

I'm grinning again. "Superstition and ego. I should have guessed."

"Let me guess, your favorites are blue and Gretzky."

"How did you—"

"They're safe." He gives me a knowing look.

"Okay, smartass."

"This though"—his grip on me tightens—"is not. Did you want me to hunt down Diedrich after this and force him to dance with me too? Take the heat off a bit?"

The fact he would do that, would even suggest it, sets off those jitters in my gut again. "Careful, Palaszczuk. I'm starting to like you too."

"Oh no," he gasps. "I take it all back. Everyone check out Anton with the fuckboy."

"Stop." I pinch his waist and lean closer to him. "I was wrong. You're actually a"—I have to force the words past my throat because I mean them—"good person."

He swallows. "I don't think anyone has ever said that to me before."

"Because no one knows you like I do." Instead of kissing him like I want to, I give him a small smile. "You're *my* fuckboy now."

"I should hate that, but ... I don't." He lowers his voice. "I really, really don't."

I pull him closer than two friends would comfortably dance, half-terrified, half-high from the moment. From dancing openly with a man. Especially when that man is Ezra.

"I hope you know what you're doing," he says.

I'm actually clueless, but I can deal with the fallout tomorrow. "It's Thanksgiving next week. What are you doing for it?"

"Nothing. It's the day after a game, my dad doesn't celebrate it, and my mom ... uh, yeah, let's say we're not the *see each other for the holidays* type. Usually Kosik and I go to Diedrich's, but I think they're visiting family in Quincy this year."

"Well, I'll be free too," I say. "I won't have time to go see my parents in South Carolina, and they only come to see me in summer when it's not freezing up here, so ..."

"So ..."

"You're going to make me say it, aren't you?"

His eyes shine in amusement. "I don't know what you mean."

"Fine. Want to come over? I'll cook us lunch, and we can watch the parade together. There's a game the next day, so we need to have our mandatory pregame ritual, but otherwise, friends hang out, right?"

"They do." I catch a moment of doubt passing across his face, but it's gone before I can question him. "You're on."

CHAPTER TWENTY-FIVE

EZRA

The annoying, obnoxious sound of the oven timer going off destroys my bliss.

We're on the couch, and Anton is on top of me with my cock still in his ass. He's slumped on my chest, breathing heavily as we both come down from killer orgasms. It would be perfect if it weren't for the damn kitchen noises.

"Make it stop," I whine.

Anton goes to move, but I grip his hips.

"No, don't leave."

He laughs. "Which do you want? For the noise to stop or to stay buried in my ass. You can't have both."

"Fine." I release him.

He eases off my dick and stands. Fuck, I want to lick his cum-covered abs. I sit up and lean forward to do just that, but he steps away.

"You want the noise to stop or not?"

"What noise?"

It's all but forgotten when Anton's perfect body is naked in front of me.

He picks up his shirt and wipes himself down. "You go deal with the condom. I'll deal with lunch."

"Best Thanksgiving ever. Sex and food? You're spoiling me."

"Don't forget the parade." He points toward the TV and finally—finally—hits the button on the oven to turn off the noise.

I stand and deal with the condom, ditching it in the trash. "Eh, I could take or leave that. It's how we ended up fucking before lunch in the first place. Pure boredom."

"Wow. Here I was thinking I'm so irresistible you couldn't help it, but good to know it was to cure your boredom. Noted."

I step up behind him where he's pulling plates off a shelf. His ass is round and delectable, all the muscles in his back taut and contracting. "Your irresistibility is a given."

I kiss the back of his neck, and he leans forward and grips the counter, pushing his ass back against my cock. It goes from spent to a semi instantly.

"Mm," I hum against his skin. "Someone isn't done with me."

"I can't help it. I'm *bored*."

I chuckle. "I'm not going to live that one down, am I?"

"Nope. You'll be paying for it for a while." Anton grinds his ass against me, and my eyes roll back into my head.

"You feel so good."

"I'm still prepped. Do it."

"You sure you're ready to go again already?"

"We have a game tomorrow. If we don't have all the sex now, we'll lose."

"You're the one who said I can't stay over tonight." Fully hard now, I run my cock down his ass crack. "Look who's suddenly superstitious."

"Not superstitious," he breathes. "I just know how to play you."

Yeah, he really does. But it's not my superstitions making me want to sink inside him again. It's him. All him.

I still haven't worked out how to deal with those thoughts yet, but I figure I don't need to either. When the tabloids ran with news of our dance together, instead of getting tense or annoyed, Anton has shrugged and said at least their stories were close this time.

Anton and I are together in most senses of the word. We're sleeping together, we're exclusive, we're … fuck, I don't know what we are, but as he reaches behind him to grip my cock and press it against his hole, I don't care.

"Condom," I murmur and try to step away.

The hand not guiding me to his entrance wraps around to grip my ass and push me inside him just a little.

"Anton …" I warn. This is *his* rule.

"It's okay," he says. "I trust you."

I don't question it, even though I should, and when I sink inside him completely, the tight heat of his body with nothing between us sends ripples of pleasure crackling along my skin.

I literally came not that long ago, so I thought round two would be long and drawn out, but the way he takes me, the grip his ass has on my cock, I worry my only issue will be getting Anton off again fast enough.

I slowly move in and out of him, enjoying every thrust, every second of having him like this.

"Harder," Anton says.

"I can't," I grit out.

"Yes, you can." He takes things into his own hands and thrusts backward.

"Fuck," I pant.

"That's the point." Anton drops his head.

The pressure surrounding my cock makes my brain fuzzy and my control slip. I give him what he wants, but that only gets me closer to the edge. After only a minute or so, I have to slow down again.

"Are you trying to torture me?" he asks.

"I'm trying not to come until you do."

"How can I come when you won't fuck me harder?"

"Maybe if I can get you close enough …" I reach around him and take his heavy cock in one hand while the other pulls on his balls.

Fucking him while giving the best handjob of my life? It's awkward, but hey, I'm good at multitasking. Having to focus so hard on what I'm doing brings me back from the edge too.

Anton's breaths come in short gasps. I fuck him as hard and wild as I can, using my hand that's jerking him off to steady my thrusts.

We both hold out, our orgasms from before making us last longer than I thought I could. But when Anton stiffens and warm cum hits my hand, I take my opportunity to let go for real.

I release him and grip his hips hard, pounding into him. He calls out because I'm hitting his prostate over and over, and I can only imagine the sweet torture his sore and wrecked ass is giving him right now.

"Ez," he whines. "Come. Come inside me."

I unleash, possibly coming even harder than I did before on the couch. Before, it was Anton riding me, so he was the one in control. Here, it was all me, and I might not need it all the time, but when I do get it? It heightens everything, and I love it.

But when I pull out of him and my cum dribbles from his hole and all over his ass and thighs, the weight of the condom issue hits me again.

I should have questioned it more.

What if it was a spur-of-the-moment thing, and now he regrets it? What if I'm reading into it?

Anton looks at me over his shoulder. "Are you okay?"

"Dead. I'm dead." My voice is croaky and shaky.

Anton laughs. "Me too. I'm also really hungry. I should get back to the food."

"You mind if I jump in the shower real quick?"

"Go for it. The food will be out when you're done."

I shower quickly because I don't want to give Anton too much time to overthink it like I am, and when I get out and wander into the living room, where we ditched our clothes earlier, Anton's got his jeans back on but is still shirtless.

He moves about his kitchen, putting everything together. He bought turkey pieces instead of a whole one seeing as it's just us, but he made stuffing to go on top, despite my argument that it's called stuffing because you're supposed to stuff the turkey with it. He also has cranberry sauce, vegetables …

"I had no idea you could cook. Whenever I've been here, we've gotten takeout."

"That's because we're both lazy asses."

I snap my fingers. "Oh right. That."

Anton smiles. "I don't mind cooking, but I hate the cleanup afterward. I don't have time or effort for that shit."

"Well, seeing as you cooked, I promise I'll clean after we're done."

"In everything we do?" Anton waggles his eyebrows.

"You want to go again? My dick is honestly asking for a time-out."

"No. I'm too hungry to go again. But later. You know … for the team."

My heart twinges. "Right. The team."

I stand awkwardly while I wait for him to plate up the food. I would offer to help, but I'm too busy trying to assess where his head is at and if he's okay.

Going bareback isn't something to freak out about, especially considering I'm on PrEP. I have no idea of his status, but if he hasn't lied about being exclusive, and we've had full medicals since we first made the agreement, I figure I should be okay. But from the beginning, Anton was adamant, and I worry he's regretting it.

Though, he shows no signs of regret. He's his usual self.

Even when he brings me my plate where I'm standing, he hands it to me with a soft kiss on my lips.

"Go sit in front of the TV," he says and swats at my ass.

I take my spot on the floor next to the coffee table, still refusing to stain his couches with my messy eating. Apparently, I have different standards when it comes to sex.

I stare at the couch, thinking about how watching the parade led to getting naked on it. It was Anton who disappeared, saying he'd be right back, and then the next minute he was on top of me. He brought out the supplies. Including the condom.

"You okay?" Anton asks as he takes his seat on the other couch.

"Yeah. Just … thinking."

"About?" He shoves some mashed potato in his mouth.

"Why you were suddenly so willing to go without a condom."

Anton chokes on his food, coughing and spluttering. "Blunt, but umm, okay." He thinks for a second. "It felt right in the moment."

"You're not freaking out and regretting it now? I should've gotten one. I know your rules, and—"

"I wasn't freaking out about it, but it seems you are."

"No, I …" Is it stupid to read so much into one teeny-tiny thing I've never thought was a big deal? There's a voice screaming in my head, one that's been nagging for weeks since Westly put it there. The one asking *what does it all mean?*

"You what?"

"Never mind. I didn't want you to think I took advantage."

Anton levels me with his dark stare. "Ez. If I didn't want to do something, you know I wouldn't. You don't have that much of an effect on me."

I can't help smirking. "Uh-huh. That's how I got you to fuck me when you despised me."

"I always wanted to fuck you. Though, in my fantasies, you were wearing a ball gag."

"That checks out."

He's still watching me, and I squirm a little at how intense his gaze is. "Come here."

I hesitate, then push onto my knees, and he pulls me between his thighs.

"Thank you."

"For?"

"Caring about whether I was worried or not. But I'm not. At all. I think I've caught an illness where you're concerned, and it's affecting my decision-making abilities."

I have a lump in my throat as I ask, "I'm guessing you don't mean chlamydia?"

Anton drops his forehead to mine. "I *trust* you, Ez."

That about does me in. Trust is a big thing, especially from someone like Anton who doesn't do it easily. I'm not sure if I'm worthy of it, but I want to be.

I kiss him softly. "Here's hoping you don't regret that."

"I'm confident." He kisses me once more before letting me go.

I turn and drop back onto my spot on the floor. "Does that mean … Can we ditch them altogether now?"

"Damn straight. I want to know what it feels like to be inside you with nothing between us."

"Okay. Good to know."

He points at my food. "Now we've gotten that out of the way, eat. Your food is getting cold."

"Yes, Mom."

As if perfectly timed, Anton's phone lights up on the coffee table.

"Speaking of moms, yours is trying to call."

He quickly reaches for it to answer. "Hey, Mom. Happy Thanksgiving to you too. And you, Dad." He pauses for whatever they say and follows it up with, "All good here. I have a teammate over, and we're having a quiet one." He continues to talk to her while I stare at the blank screen on my phone.

I don't expect my dad to call, and my mom hasn't invited me to her place for Thanksgiving in years. She has a new husband, new kids … Still, it would be nice if one of them picked up their phone to call me.

"Sorry," Anton says when he finishes up.

"It's fine. You have parents who obviously care."

His lips flatten into a thin line. "You said your dad doesn't do Thanksgiving."

"Yeah. I'm not expecting anything from him. Or my mom. It's fine. I've never been their priority."

"It's okay to still want them to make an effort though."

"Nah, only a dumbass would still want it."

"Well, you are you, so like you said, it checks out." He leans back and sips his drink smugly.

"Stop showering me with all this affection and sweet words. You will spoil me for other men," I deadpan.

"You're welcome."

"How do you think we'll play tomorrow after eating all this food?" I point to my plate.

"Sluggish. But hey, the other team will be full of turkey too, so it'll all even out. And if we get in another orgasm tonight, there's no way we can lose. Our streak is still hot."

"Better do it soon since apparently I can't stay over."

He clears his throat and leans forward to place his glass on the table. "About that."

Ooh, I don't like that tone. "What?"

"Maybe I do want you to stay over."

"O … kay?"

"But I want you to do something with me first."

He sounds uncharacteristically serious, and when he shifts, linking his fingers together and releasing them, I bite back my response of *Sacrifice to the hockey gods?* and wait.

"On the afternoons we're home and I'm not with you, I spend a lot of time volunteering. No one knows. Not my agent, not our PR team, sometimes not even the charities I'm there for because I don't give my real name. I do it for me because I think it's important to give back."

I narrow my eyes. "No one's noticed you?"

"One of the soup kitchens I go to frequently knows who I am, but they respect my privacy. It's not something I want the media getting wind of and making into a big deal."

Wow. I know Anton is always going on about his privacy, but I know a lot of guys who volunteer or give money, and even when they do it privately or anonymously, it always gets out. Everyone loves recognition.

Then it hits me what's happening here. "You're telling me."

"Yes."

"When no one else knows?"

"Correct."

Something warm creeps through my chest, making me smile.

"I want you to come with me today," he says.

The smile drops right off my face. "If this is another animal shelter …"

Anton laughs loud and uninhibited. "I promise it's not. I've actually filled my trunk with donations, and I was going to take it to a soup kitchen I help at and drop it all off. We'll stay and help cook everything and get it set up, then the other volunteers will take over to do the actual serving."

It's not how I wanted to spend my afternoon, but I'm interested.

"You don't have to," he rushes to say. "No obligation, I just thought …"

"Yeah?"

He clears his throat. "I thought it might be nice for us to do together."

"You're on."

And it's hard to imagine that spending an afternoon with Anton where we play delivery driver and then cart boxes back and forth before joining a production line of people preparing food could be fun, but when we get back to his place and climb into bed, I'm hit with the strangest thought: there was nowhere else I'd rather be today.

Anton wraps his arms around me and yawns widely. "You did good today."

"Thanks."

"Now go to sleep. We have a game to win tomorrow."

"There you go trying to jinx us again."

"Please. It's *Buffalo*. We have nothing to worry about."

It's true we've been kicking ass. We haven't lost a game since Anton and I started sleeping together regularly. We're high on the leaderboard and should easily skate into the playoffs at this rate.

But like all good players, I'm not delusional.

Hot streaks always end. It's only a matter of when and how we bounce back.

CHAPTER TWENTY-SIX

ANTON

After our morning skate at the arena, we head back to Ezra's with a couple of the guys and hang out. It's low-key while we all try to get in the right mindset, and when my gaze constantly strays to Ezra and whoever he's talking to, I don't try to hide it.

I warn myself about getting in too deep, but I think I'm already there. Does it freak me out?

A little. But not because it's Ezra.

My concerns are centered around coming out. Whether one of us will be traded. If a relationship even works in this high-pressure environment. Sure, we're making sex work for us now, but I've seen way too many of my teammates get wrapped up in a relationship only to have it end in heartbreak or bitter divorces.

There are some people who make it work, but they're the exception, not the rule.

After everything we've been through, I can't go back to how it was before.

When we're getting ready to head back to TD Garden, I catch Ezra as he's leaving his bathroom and shove him back inside. I close the door behind us, push him up against the wall, and bring our mouths together in a searing kiss. "Whose idea was it to invite people over?"

"Diedrich's," he says against my lips. "I'm really starting to hate that guy."

I chuckle and squeeze his ass. "Let's go win that game, then it's my turn to take you bare."

"Normally I'd punch you for jinxing us, but you did get some added magic yesterday."

I cringe. "The only thing that could make that sentence worse is if you called your cum magic juice."

"Oh, I like that."

"I had to open my big mouth."

"If it makes you feel any better, I would have got there myself eventually. You just gave me a head start." He brushes his lips against mine. "Plus, we're playing Buffalo. Those guys have had a rough season. Even by their standards."

"Maybe I'll beat my points record. Reckon I can go for six goals this game?"

This time, Ezra does thump me. "Dude. You're really pushing it."

We catch up with the rest of the team before it looks suspicious and head for the arena. Even though I'm confident, game days wouldn't be the same without nerves. We show up in our suits, get changed, and start to warm up. The hours tick closer to the game starting, and half the team gets loud while the others go quiet. It's no surprise Ezra and I are on opposite ends of the spectrum, and I sit and watch as he kicks a ball back and forth with some of the team.

"You ready, Hayes?" Kosik asks.

"Let's do this."

The atmosphere of a live game is like nothing else. I can still remember the first time I walked out with Philly and looked around, completely awed that this is my life. The impact has lessened slightly after a few years, but every now and then, I hit the ice and take it all in.

We're on the streak of the season, and Buffalo is at the bottom of the table. There's nothing in this game, but I know not to get too far ahead of myself. Every team is capable of having a good game and a bad one.

And apparently, tonight is one of those times.

As soon as the puck drops, it's clear something is off. Buffalo doesn't make a wrong move. They're constantly in our half, taking shots on goal, and the only thing between them and a high score is Kosik defending like a champ and Griffith shutting down all attempts.

I can barely find the puck, and when I do, no one is where I need them to be. It's the same when Diedrich makes a steal and flicks it in my direction. I'm too slow to get on top of it, and it lands in the blade of a Buffalo forward.

Our second and third lines are playing better than we are tonight.

By the time the first period ends and we get back to the locker room, Coach is beside himself. He reams us, and I don't blame him. We're playing worse than we did when I was first traded.

I meet Ezra's eyes briefly and have to quickly look away. I'm not the only one playing like shit tonight, but I feel like I'm the only one letting the team down.

An athlete's ego goes both ways.

The second period is no better than the first, except this time, Buffalo slips two goals past us. Griffith is frustrated, Kosik is starting to get desperate with some of the hits he's making, and the worse we get, the more I can tell we're losing Ezra.

He's in his head, and he's missing some really easy plays.

Coach tries the new tactic of trying to motivate us before the final period, but I can't help thinking it's too little too late.

I try to turn my mindset around. Try to remind myself that two goals is nothing. We can do this. We can get back out there and pull a win out of our asses. It isn't theirs to celebrate yet.

My brain doesn't manage to convince my body though. I give away an easy pass, and barely five minutes in, I'm chasing down rookie Ayri Quinn from Buffalo and make a play for the puck too late.

He passes as I reach him, but my blade clips his skates, and he goes down. The ref calls a penalty.

"Fuck." I pull up beside Ayri and crouch down. "You okay?"

"Jesus, Hayes." He shoves me as I try to help him to his feet.

Another Buffalo player slams into me from the side, and I'm about to go back in for him when Ezra drags me away.

"Asshole," I bite out, trying to shove Ezra off.

"You're already off for two. Don't make it worse."

You know things are bad when Ezra is the voice of reason. I shove him away and head for the penalty box, the crowd's jeers deafening.

I pride myself on playing clean, and as I enter the penalty box for the first time this season, I can feel my ears burning. The weight of an arena full of stares prickles the back of my neck, and I have to force my face to stay passive because I know there are cameras trained on me.

Especially when thirty seconds later, Kosik joins me.

I want to pull out my hair in frustration that the game is quickly slipping away from us. Kosik is right on the edge of the bench, and we're both glued to the play happening on the ice.

A five-on-three power play is the worst thing to happen right now.

Buffalo charges past the blue line. There are too many of them and not enough of us.

Kosik and I jump to our feet, watching in horror as Ayri gets his payback. He dekes out Ezra and shoots. Griffith is a millisecond too late, and the puck hits the net.

The lamp lights up, and I'm straight back on the ice, but no matter how hard I fight, the seconds tick down. Nothing is smooth. Diedrich and I can't find each other. Larsen is fuck knows where.

I try a shot back to Ezra, who passes to Diedrich, but it's intercepted again. I almost throw my goddamn stick.

The buzzer sounds, and as the home crowd around us goes into half-hearted cheers and encouraging applause, I stand there, heaving, barely able to believe the last hour.

We lost.

In a fucking shutout.

I can't say a word as I shake the other team's hands and head back to the locker room. Thankfully, it's only Coach at the press conference tonight, because there's no way any of us want to go face the media after that mess. We played like a pack of clowns.

The locker room is subdued. I strip down to my undershirt and cool down on a bike, but none of us are talking.

"Next game will be better," Diedrich says when we head back to the locker room to shower. I nod but don't look at him. Kosik agrees, and so do some of the others, but I drown them out.

In the NHL, you win games, and you lose games. It just is.

But tonight, I'm not only disappointed, I'm embarrassed. I played like shit. I got a penalty. And I didn't make even one halfway decent shot on goal.

Then a new worry hits me ... what will this do to me and Ez? It's our first loss since the start of ... whatever we are, and the pretense of it being good luck obviously won't hold weight after tonight's disaster.

The fact I'm questioning what this monumental loss means for me and Ezra instead of focusing on what this means for the team makes me realize one glaringly obvious detail I might have missed somewhere along the way.

I told myself I wouldn't fall for him.

I lied.

CHAPTER TWENTY-SEVEN

EZRA

We fucking lost.

It was inevitable. The record for longest streak in the history of the league is seventeen. Did I really think my stupid superstition would somehow break that?

No.

Was I using that stupid good-luck-charm stuff as an excuse to keep sleeping with Anton without any consequences? You bet.

But there are consequences. Like being forced to either play it off or lay it all out there that I want to keep doing what we're doing because I like being with him.

I'm half out of my hockey gear, my jersey and chest pads off but my hockey pants still on, and I stare at my phone for the inevitable call I'm dreading. I'm in no mood to talk to my father—or anyone—and it's not just about the game.

This is the inevitable moment I never saw coming. Or, I didn't want to see. Because I knew it would make me sit back and evaluate everything. And what I see, I don't like.

I mean, I really do like it.

I like the way Anton makes me feel.

I love getting along with him, but we've never lost that spark between us—the one that made us want each other in the first place. It's lust and snark rolled into an intense sexual connection ... and then so much more. I've never cared about someone else's happiness more than my own. I've never wanted to spend every moment with someone. I've never wanted to be vulnerable and feel safe with one person while protecting him with everything I have.

But telling him that and having him say this is still nothing? A lump gets stuck in my throat at the thought. I don't think I could handle that kind of rejection after the loss we've endured.

Maybe I'm more like my father than I realized because when it comes to feelings, it's hard for me to express myself.

"Expecting a call?" Anton asks.

I flinch at his voice and find him sitting on the bench in front of his cubby, watching me.

"You know I am. Any minute now, this will start ringing, and I'll be reminded how all those years of private coaching were put to waste, and I'll never make a name big enough to be in the hall of fame. I'll never win the Cup if I don't step up. All the fun things I love to hear when I'm down."

"So maybe don't answer it?"

"I may as well get it over with. If I ignore it, I get it twice as hard the next time." And there will be a next time. Because superstition sex isn't the key to winning the season. No matter how much I wanted to try to convince myself that it was the key to holding this team together.

"Are you okay?" Anton asks.

I huff. "Did you really just ask that?"

"Well, shit. Sorry for checking in."

Fuck. I've somehow reverted back to asshole Ezra, and Anton hasn't even done anything but see if I'm all right.

Way to go, fuckboy.

I go to apologize when my phone lights up. I take a deep breath and answer. "Hey, Dad."

"What happened out there?"

"Why don't you tell me, seeing as you always know how to play my game better than me." Maybe I shouldn't have answered.

"It was my game first. I know what I'm talking about."

"Even if I've been playing for longer than you ever did?"

"Not at this level."

Yet. Come next year, I will have met his five years in the NHL.

"You were sluggish on the ice tonight. What has your diet been like?"

I want to yell that I'm not a kid anymore and that one bad night on the ice doesn't mean I'm neglecting my diet or the exercise regime the team sets for me.

"Apart from the thousand calories on Thanksgiving dinner last night, I stick to team-approved diets. You know that. Even during the off-season, I tend to watch what I eat." What I drink and who I sleep with, however, that could go either way. I don't say that though.

"Thanksgiving and Christmas and any other holiday doesn't give you the excuse to slack off."

"You're not telling me anything the coaches haven't already reamed me for, so what do you want from me?" Heat rises up my neck and floods my face.

I've never felt so out of control of my emotions in my life.

"You might be a screwup and an attention whore off the ice like your mother, and I let your antics slide, but when it comes to hockey, you can't be half-assed about it. You need to put in more of an effort and take the game seriously."

The comparison to my mother, calling me out for the public antics that Anton also hates about me, and insinuating I don't take my career very fucking seriously is too much. Even for him.

"If you think I don't take hockey seriously, you haven't been paying attention. Maybe if you actually saw the good in me and not the traits you claim I got from Mom, you wouldn't treat me like the mud under your shoe."

"I don't—"

"You do. You always have, and I'm sick of it." What am I doing? Yelling at my elders? I send up an imaginary apology to my grandmother in Poland, whose heart just twinged and she doesn't know why. But now that I've started, I can't stop. "You only call when you want to feel superior. Like putting me down makes you feel better about yourself and your *failed* career. I know what I'm doing. I've already made it to more playoffs than you ever did."

Dad goes silent for possibly the first time ever, but then he mutters the one thing that just digs the knife in deeper. "I shouldn't have wasted all my time and money on you. You're a disappointment."

"Pierdol się." *Fuck you.* There's some Polish I do know. I hit the End button and throw my phone in my cubby.

"What happened?" Anton asks.

I shake my head. I can't do this now. Not after that. I just ... can't. "Nothing. It's not important. I'm going to go shower."

I strip off the rest of my gear, grab a towel, and walk away. I'm usually good at it—walking away. But this time, it feels wrong.

My heart wants me to stay, to put myself out there, but my mind is telling me to run instead.

CHAPTER TWENTY-EIGHT

ANTON

Ezra looks totally dejected when he comes back from his shower. I waited here the whole time for him because I want to get him to talk. I want him to know I'm here for him after witnessing the epicness of that phone call, but I'm also suddenly hit with the need to be reassured that everything is still okay with us.

The whole reason we agreed to keep sleeping together, the reason he humored me with my request to be exclusive, is because of some kind of ridiculous superstition. If he gets it into his head that the good luck has worn off—or worse, that sleeping with me is *bad* luck— what then?

He doesn't say anything, and I can't think of anything *to* say.

I'm not used to this. I confront things head-on, but there's something about Ezra that's holding me back. I almost don't want to ask why he looks so defeated because I get the distinct impression the answer won't be the game, and the fear of what he could say is clogging my throat.

I glance toward the showers, where the guys are talking loud enough to be heard over the water, and drop my voice.

"Wanna wait while I shower and get out of here?" I don't want to ask, but I have to know. "Are you coming to my place?"

"Is there really a need to?" His careless tone is back. "Our streak is broken."

I blink at him like he's hit me. "Are you serious?"

"Come on, Hayes." His blue eyes pin me in place. "We both know what this was. Just like Larsen's dirty socks. You were a superstition. That's all. You don't want to be with a fuckup like me."

Wow. "Maybe I shouldn't have enabled you and your stupid good-luck theory because you can't seriously be sitting there thinking we lost because of something we did or didn't do off the ice. Losses happen—"

"How did it all go so epically bad?"

"It's the game. We had an off night. Maybe we were getting too cocky and comfortable in our standings. And I know you're going to be reading into it, trying to pinpoint which thing you did that brought us bad luck, but blaming *us* isn't going to fix what was broken on the ice tonight. That's something we have to work on as a team. A whole team. You and I aren't the only ones out there." I can hear the panic in my voice, but I can't make it stop.

"No, but we're the only ones fooling around off the ice." His expression is closed off, and the fear of rejection hits me right in the face. I don't want to ask what he wants.

I get the distinct impression the answer will be *not me*.

We can't have this conversation right now. I know Ezra, and I know what phone calls with his dad do to him. If he's doubting the game and has had a hit to his confidence, he's going to latch onto anything he thinks he can control—like his superstitions—and will put up walls to protect himself.

If we keep talking, he's going to lash out, and I'm scared he'll say something we can't come back from.

So I force my worry and panic down and swallow so my voice comes out low and even. "If you really think that after all this time I was only a superstition, then I've been giving you too much credit. If you want to stop sleeping together, say it. Don't use some good-luck-fuck bullshit as an excuse."

"I told you early on that I'm only temporary." He says each word carefully like he's trying to make a point. "That I'm no one's forever home."

My heart breaks for him. And us. I want to shake some goddamn sense into him. He's disappointed and hurting, but I'm the person he's supposed to share that with. That's what a partner is for.

But … we're not partners. Not really. I want to grab him and drag him back to his place and show him that alone isn't an option because we're in this together. Or, I want us to be in it together.

But I don't have the guts to say that in a locker room that's filling with our teammates who are finishing up their showers. Instead, I say, "Okay then."

"Coming out, Palaszczuk?" Kosik asks.

"Nope, I'm heading home. *Alone.*" Ezra stands abruptly and storms away without another word. I watch his retreating back, feeling sick.

"What about you, Hayes?" Kosik asks, and it's only now I remember they're even in the room.

Instead of answering them, I numbly grab my bag from my cubby and leave.

Screw the suit. I'll take the fine.

Maybe Ezra and I never got along in the past, but this is our first real fight. Our first real moment where I'm actually worried we could lose everything. I'm determined to talk to him in the morning, hopefully once he's calmed down, but that doesn't help the gut-clenching anxiety that won't go away.

I shove through the arena doors to the parking lot and thank goddamn Gretzky that I left my car here before our practice skate.

There's a hollow feeling deep in my chest that won't go away.

I shower at home, and by the time I'm done, I've calmed down a fraction.

Only a fraction.

I can't stop pacing. I can't stop stewing over that fight.

Leaving things so open-ended doesn't sit right with me. Is he so superstitious he'd throw everything between us away?

Does he even feel the same connection I do? Ezra is used to casual sex, but I'm not. Is this me building things up to more than it is?

Yeah, there's no way I'm sleeping tonight. Not until I have some answers.

I try his phone, but he doesn't answer. Ignoring the pit in my gut, I grab my keys and head out. I know the smarter option is to leave this conversation until morning, but I can't do it. If there's a chance Ezra feels even a fraction of what I'm feeling right now, I need to do whatever I can to fix it.

The faster I can get to Ezra, the faster we can get this conversation over with. Starting it in the locker room of all places was a dumb move, but I'm not someone who can sit around overthinking things. There's still a lot of traffic out for how late it is, and by the time I pull up at a red light down from Ezra's apartment, I'm clenching the steering wheel hard. I still have no idea what I'm going to say, but I have to try.

I glance toward his apartment block and see two figures approaching. When they step into the light from the foyer, I pick out Ezra immediately and with him … Ayri Quinn from Buffalo.

They're chatting, and even from this distance, I pick out Ezra's easy charisma out in full force. Something about how close they're walking, how Ezra holds the door for him to pass and gives him the same cocky grin that never fails to get me into bed—

Beeeep.

I swear and almost jump out of my skin, noticing way too late the light has turned green. I step on the gas, glancing back in my rearview mirror in an attempt to spot them, but I can't.

My heart is pounding as I try to convince myself I didn't see what I thought I saw.

We've had one fight.

One.

Going home alone, my ass.

I try to tell myself it doesn't mean anything.

So what if Ezra took Ayri home? After telling me he was going home alone. And ignoring my call.

I'm completely torn over what my next move should be.

What I want to do is go to Ezra's apartment and demand answers.

But what if this is exactly what it looks like?

My gut rolls.

I can't see that.

I *can't*.

So instead of driving to Ezra's, I head back home, trying to convince myself that tonight never happened.

CHAPTER TWENTY-NINE

EZRA

My head feels like it has its very own drumbeat going on inside. It goes hand in hand with the ache in my back and neck from passing out on my couch last night. The last thing I remember was taking Ayri Quinn back to my apartment to drown our sorrows but for very different reasons. Or maybe they were the same.

Me, over the loss of the game, my phone call with Dad, and Anton not picking up that I wanted him to fight for us, to give me a hint of something real. Him, because the poor kid is experiencing his first setback as an NHL player. The twenty-two-year-old's boyfriend broke up with him because a couple of months of long-distance was too tough to handle.

Ayri being gay was news to me, and I don't think he would have turned to me for advice if he had the choice, but I was the only out player there last night. I bet he wishes he'd been playing New York or Vegas instead. I kind of do too. I was far from being in a comforting mood.

But then Ayri Quinn cornered me on my way out of the arena and very awkwardly asked if he could pick my brain about something. I could tell by his demeanor I couldn't say no. Just like those kids who have come out to me, I got a sense of what he wanted to say before he said it.

Once he told me his story, I brought him here to drink away his problems because ... healthy.

Probably not the best example I should be setting.

Especially because now, as we're waking up, me on one couch, him on the other, both hungover as fuck, it's clear that maybe I should have lent a comforting ear instead of telling him, "Relationships suck. Here, drink up."

"What's that banging?" he complains.

"You can hear the drum kit that's in my head?"

"Ezra!" *Bang, bang, bang, bang.*

"Is that in my head too?" I ask Ayri.

"No, I think it's coming from your front door."

"If you and Ayri Quinn are naked, you better get some fucking clothes on before I break down this door. Getting an ass kicking while naked is too gay, even for me."

Anton.

I try to get off my couch but kind of roll off it instead and hit the ground with a thump. "Ow."

"Fuck, who is that?" Ayri asks. He sits up, looking as disheveled as I am, his eyes squinty and skin ashen.

"My stupid boyfriend. Who's stupid. The one I was telling you about in my drunken ramble." Okay, Anton isn't stupid. Last night was stupid.

Lashing out was stupid.

Challenging him to see what he would do was stupid.

Most of all, hanging our whole relationship on the outcome of one game is stupid.

And yeah, maybe we haven't had that conversation yet—that we're actually together—and yes, we need to have it. But last night, I needed to lick my wounds and sulk.

Now, apparently, I have to explain myself. How did he even know Ayri was here?

I open the door, my vision blurry through still-squinted eyes to find Anton standing there looking murderous. The bags under his eyes probably rival my own. "What time is it?" I rumble.

"Six."

I groan. "I've only had like three hours' sleep. Can you yell at me after I've had coffee?"

I turn and let him in and head for my kitchen, but as we round the corner, Anton's eyes land on Ayri.

Ayri frowns. "Anton Hayes?"

"Fuck this," Anton says. "I just needed to make sure I was right, and I am. So fuck you"—he points at me—"and fuck you." He points at Ayri. Then he turns to leave, but I catch his wrist and pull him against me.

"Where do you think you're going?"

"Away from you. You're still free to hook up with whoever you want, Ez, but I thought you'd at least have the decency to tell me before you did it. The worst part is I actually *trusted* you. I never, *never* would have thought—"

I chuckle and wrap my arms around him.

"You think this is funny?"

"A bit."

"Why?"

"Does it really look like either of us spent half the night having sex?" I gesture to where Ayri still sits in his rumpled suit. Hell, he hasn't even taken his tie off.

Anton glances around at all the empty beer bottles scattered around the place, the almost empty bottle of tequila on the coffee table, and he lets out a little "Oh."

"If I let you go, can I explain without you running off?"

He looks around again. "Okay."

I release him and click on my coffee maker. "Now." I spin and lean against the counter. "All we did was talk. And mostly, I talked about *you*. I left your name out of it, of course, because I'm not going to out you to anyone, but—"

"It's true." Ayri stands from my dark leather couch. "It got pretty ugly in here both with alcohol and emotional shit. You really didn't want to see it."

Anton glances between the two of us. "I'm confused."

"I …" Ayri starts.

I nod in encouragement. Last night, it was like pulling teeth trying to get it out of him because he's not used to coming out yet.

"My boyfriend broke up with me, and I knew Ezra was out. I … I wanted advice."

Anton cocks his head. "And you thought Ezra would be the best choice? For relationship advice."

"I would have come to you, but I didn't even know you were … with Ezra."

"Oh dear God, he didn't encourage you to drunk dial your ex, did he?"

I laugh. "I think I did at one point."

"I was drunk, but not that drunk," Ayri says. "I should get back to the hotel before the team leaves without me." He steps up to Anton. "Nothing happened—"

"I know. I trust Ez."

"Yes, because I totally got that impression when you were banging down my door," I say.

"Urgh, I was scared I'd lost you, you idiot, but if you tell me nothing happened, I trust your word. You've never lied to me even when you hated me." He turns to Ayri. "I'm sorry for threatening to kick your ass."

Ayri tsks. "Tripping me and threatening to kick my ass in a twelve-hour span? You guys don't take it easy on us rookies, do you?"

Anton snorts. "Nope."

"I'll leave you guys to it."

As he heads for the door, I say, "Think about my offer from last night too—about the queer collective. We're trying to get the bingo of guys in the league. One on every team."

Ayri smiles. "I'll definitely think about it."

"No pressure." I point my thumb in Anton's direction. "This guy makes being closeted work. Even if you need someone to talk to like you did last night, you don't have to be out to approach any of us."

"Thank you."

As soon as he's gone, Anton opens his mouth, but I hold up my hand.

"I know you have a thing about rejection, but you *really* don't take it well, do you?"

"Well—"

"Coffee first. Then you can yell at me."

"I don't want to yell," he says.

I make us two cups and slide his over. "Last night—"

"We were both crushed by the loss of what should have been an easy win," Anton says.

"Well, that, and ..." I stare down at my cup. "I thought you could've used it as an excuse. To stop"—I wave my finger between us—"this. I think I was looking for you to take the out, and I didn't want to deal with that, so I ... didn't. I was going to come back here and sleep it off, but then Ayri caught up to me, and he looked like a sad little puppy dog."

Anton rounds the kitchen counter and presses himself against me. "Just so you know, I was never going to take the out, and deep down, I know you were trying to push me away last night, and maybe I should've stood my ground and fought for you, but I was terrified it was more than that—that you were actually done with me. I wasn't ready to hear that, so I left. Then I changed my mind and drove to your apartment, only to see you on the street with Ayri."

"Is that why you're over here so early? To make sure we weren't fucking?"

"No. I came over this early because I haven't slept." Anton runs his hand over his hair. "But when I saw him here …"

"He slept on the couch. I slept on the other. And by slept, I mean we passed out. It was literally hours of talking about our boyfriends, saying how relationships are hard, and basically bitching you and Chandler's name out all night."

"Oh, well, that makes me feel so much better—wait, boyfriend?"

I take a deep breath. "Well, yeah. That's what I kind of realized. If you take the superstition out of our relationship, supposedly we don't have one. But last night while Ayri was crying over his ex, I realized I didn't want that to be us. We may not have said we're together officially, but … we're together, aren't we? At least, I want to be. And that's scary in its own right because I've never done the relationship thing before. But I've also never tried. I'd never done the monogamous thing before you, and it's surprisingly easy because … you're the only one I want to be with."

"Really?" Anton's voice is a rasp.

"Then we won't have to keep up this ruse that it's good for team—"

"Something I have never believed, by the way."

"I know, but maybe … maybe this means we can start being real with each other?"

"Real how?"

I swallow hard because I don't want to say this next part. "I'm falling for you."

Anton sucks in a short gasp. I can't tell if it's genuine or sarcastic.

"I broke you," he says.

Sarcastic it is.

I throw my hands up. "This is why I've never told someone that before. Because it encourages mockery."

"Aww, baby." Anton pulls me closer, wrapping me in his arms. "I think I'm falling for you too."

"You think? You … *think*? I'm gonna have to work on that."

"No, I know it. I just can't trust this is actually happening yet."

"It's happening. We're being real with each other, remember?"

"Okay, so we're together. What does that mean? Do you expect me to come out or—"

I shake my head. "Never if you don't want to. Do I think it would be easier than sneaking around? Sure, but you're worth pretending I'm a secret spy doing secret spy stuff."

He pats my shoulder. "You're a real James Bond."

"James isn't even a real name. It should be Jame. Because they're only *one* Jame."

Anton sighs. "It's scary how your brain works sometimes."

"I didn't make it up. I saw it on a meme, but thank you."

"Wasn't paying you a compliment."

"Yes you were because we're together now. You have to love everything I do from this moment on."

"Never going to happen."

Mm, we'll see. "Stay for coffee and hungover sex?"

"I don't really want to be puked all over during sex, so I'm going to pass on that. But I'll stay for coffee."

"In an official relationship for thirty seconds and the sex stops. I knew it would happen, but I don't think it's supposed to happen this fast."

"I'll fuck you tomorrow. After you get unstanky and gross. You smell like you bathed in tequila and beer."

I narrow my eyes, trying to remember. "I think ... I think at one point I might have spilled my drink on me."

"Probably more than once," Anton points out. "And, hey, what happened with your dad? It sounded like an intense conversation."

"I really don't want to talk about it."

"Well, I'm your boyfriend now, and apparently that means I can force you to talk to me. Cool perks, huh?"

I grumble. "He didn't like that I stood up to him, obviously. Talking back to a parent in Polish culture is a big no-no."

"Holy shit. How did you survive teenhood?"

"Easy. I lived with Mom. Dad only ever saw me if he'd come to hockey practice to yell at me. His version of parenting and doing what's right by his kid was throwing money at the problem and then complaining what a waste it was. Nothing's really changed, but back then I was a good little boy, and I stood there and took it because he'd threatened to take hockey away from me." My eyes begin to water, but I push it down. "I don't need to take it anymore. I made my career. I did. Not him."

"Is that why you said 'Fuck you' to him when you hung up on him?"

"Yep. Wait, you speak Polish?"

"I googled."

"Wow. We really are together, huh? You googled because you were concerned about me."

"I was." Anton cups my cheek. "I am. I could see you were hurting, and I wanted to tell you everything was going to be okay, but you were lashing out at me, and I didn't know where I stood, and—"

"It was misplaced anger from the game and my dad and the fear that I was going to lose you. I didn't have the courage last night to put my feelings on the line, but I'd rather tell you a thousand times and have you reject me than lose you because I didn't have the guts to say six simple words: I want to be with you." I lower my forehead to his. "I'm sorry."

Anton breathes in and closes his eyes. "That's the hottest thing you've ever said to me."

My cock twitches. "Hot enough to change your mind on the hungover sex?"

"Nope. But maybe some shower handjobs aren't out of the question."

I race my boyfriend to the bathroom.

Wow. My boyfriend.

CHAPTER THIRTY

ANTON

We lose the next two games, which really tests Ezra's superstition, but then we hit another streak. The whole team's game is smooth, but something clicks with Ezra, and the two of us play together like we never have before. It's easily my best season, but there's still one thing nagging in the back of my mind.

I want to come out.

Because while my career is at an all-time high and I'm in a relationship that fulfills me in a way that's caught me completely off guard, not being able to combine the two is wearing thin.

I let my fingers trail along Ezra's spine, and he shifts in his sleep. We're both totally naked after a night celebrating, and we leave to fly home in just over an hour.

"Time to wake up, Ez."

He grunts at me, which is his equivalent of "five more minutes." Apparently, I can speak Ezra now.

"Nuh-uh. I'm not packing your bags this time."

"I'd do it for you," he grumbles.

"And yet, you never have." I bring my hand down on his bare ass cheek, and it lets out a satisfying *crack*. Ezra's back tenses, muscles tightening, and if I had the time, I'd map out every one of them with my mouth.

Ezra finally pushes up onto his elbows and blinks sleepily at me, the vivid blue of his eyes peeking out from behind dark lashes. I run a hand over his rough cheek, remembering how his beard felt on my ass last night, and damn if that doesn't make me want to go again.

"Okay, get up before I maul you," I say.

Ezra slowly climbs out of bed. "You coming straight to my place once we're back?"

"I might head home for a bit. I have some washing and things to do."

He nods as he heads for the bathroom, and I wonder if I should tell him what's on my mind. Ezra supports me either way. Whether I'm out or closeted is all the same to him, but I'm finally starting to get what he means about wanting to live by his own rules, not someone else's. And my rules state I need to take my boyfriend on an actual date.

The problem is, Ezra and I are making it work *now*. While we're on the same team, in the same city. I have another year contracted to Boston, and I think Ezra has two, but that doesn't mean that we won't be traded or be offered a better contract somewhere else.

If management thinks us being together is bad for the B's, they wouldn't hesitate to ship one of us off.

I have to believe we're playing well enough that they'll want to keep us.

And if not, well, there's a good chance we'll have to face that eventually.

So while we're here, I want to make the most of our time together.

We fly back to Boston and each go our separate ways. Only, instead of heading back to my car, I catch Coach in his office.

I knock lightly on the doorframe, and Coach looks up.

"Hayes, what can I do for you?"

"Nothing, actually." I shift, trying not to let my nerves show. "But I figured I should give you the heads-up I'm planning to come out."

"That's good. Do you need me to set anything up? We can get the PR department onto it."

"I can go to them next. I want to go low-key about it and don't want to make it a big thing. But … it's probably going to be a big deal."

He leans back in his chair. "Is there a reason for doing it now? You know you have all of our support."

"There is a reason. You might not like it."

"Hayes, I've been in this industry for a long time, and when a player tells me I won't like something, I know it's going to be bad."

"Could be a PR nightmare."

"If it's something illegal, we're not going to stand behind that."

I laugh. "Not illegal. Well … I mean, it's always hard to tell when it comes to Ezra."

"What does Palasz—wait. Tell me you're not sleeping together."

"I'm not sure how it works in your household, Coach, but that's something I like to do with my partner."

"Your—fuck. You two are dating?"

"Yep. And this is me letting you know, not coming to you for permission. It's going to get out, so I thought you might want to get ahead of things and …" This is the hard part. "I really hope it doesn't impact our places on this team."

Coach shakes his head. "You're both playing the best hockey of your careers. Keep that up, and keep the team a drama-free zone, we'll have no problems. I'll talk to management and make sure they know."

"Thanks."

"You know, when I said for you guys to play nice and get along, this isn't really what I meant."

"It's not in us to do anything by halves."

"Apparently not." He picks up his phone. "So when are you planning to do this?"

"I haven't worked that out yet."

"If a press conference is out, how are you going to do it? Social media?"

That still seems like too much. "No, I don't want to feel like I need to announce it. I'm going to do what any other teammate does when they're seeing someone ... I'm going to take Ezra on a date."

"Okay. Good luck."

"Thanks, Coach."

"And I have to warn you, because I know the history you two have, I don't care if things get messy or you break up or whatever, but that shit stays out of my locker room and off the ice. Got it?"

"Neither of us want to risk our careers, so that's a given."

"Good." He points at me. "And no funny business on these premises."

"It's like you know Ezra or something."

"I've been coaching him far too long to think he wouldn't sneak you in here to fuck with me."

Poor choice of words. My lips quirk, because sex in here actually sounds like fun. "I'll let him know."

That's one conversation done, and once I'm done telling my agent and the PR department the same thing so they can prepare the team's statement, I only have one more awkward conversation to go before I can pick Ezra up for a date tonight.

On the way home, I call and make a reservation at a restaurant Diedrich recommended to me when I first moved here. It's always busy, which is exactly what I want.

The more people who see us, the better.

Back home, I put on a load of laundry so I didn't actually lie to Ez, then grab my phone and flop back onto my couch. I have a great view of the city from here, but I'm still not sold on the place. It's pretty sad when I feel more at home at Ezra's bachelor pad than here. Though that could be the Ezra factor.

Which is why I need to do this. I'm serious about him, and I don't want some stupid stigmas holding me back. It's that reminder that makes me hit Dad's number.

It only rings a handful of times before he answers with a cheerful, "Anton."

"Hey, Dad."

"I caught the game last night. You were amazing. Never thought I'd see my boy top of the points board for the season."

"I never thought I'd be there either," I agree.

"Clearly that trade was good for you. We were worried at first of course, but I shoulda known you would make it work."

"It's been the best move I've made." I suck in a breath. "For more than one reason."

"Oh yeah? Sounds like you've got good news. Want me to grab your ma?"

"Umm ... yeah." Might as well get this over with both of them. A moment later, the phone clicks over to speaker, and Mom immediately starts gushing over the game too.

"Thanks." I'm glad they're proud. "But I actually wanted to talk to you about something other than hockey."

"Okay ..." Mom sounds confused.

"I'm seeing someone."

She lets out a long breath. "That's wonderful. Does he make you happy?"

"Very."

"And what's he like?"

I pause, trying to come up with a way to tell her Ezra is perfect, when saying things like *cocky, loud, and high-energy* are always seen as negatives. "He's really fun, and he knows who he is, so that's helped me work out who I am as well. He has a big heart, and I love how I get to see sides of him no one else does."

Dad hums skeptically.

That's it. His whole response.

"He sounds lovely," Mom says.

"Dad?"

He doesn't answer right away. "Look, I'm real happy for you. You know that. But you need to be careful. People will see you with this man, and they're going to figure it out."

It's so hard not to be frustrated with him. The thing is, my dad *does* want me to be happy. When I came out to him, he hugged me and told me he loved me, which was a big thing from a blue-collar worker who grew up in the generation he did. A lot of his friends still use slurs and say things that make me uncomfortable, and while he corrects them, the mindset is so completely different. I'm so privileged to be surrounded by a queer-positive community, but having a safe space doesn't just happen.

It's the result of years and years of hard work. Of all the people before me owning who they are. It comes from visibility and open conversations; it comes from challenging people's beliefs and from people who have influence, people like me, showing we're proud of who we are.

"That's actually the plan," I say.

"What?"

"My agent, my team, and my coach know. And I'm not the only queer player on the team, so the fans we have clearly don't have a problem with it, and if they do, they can fuck off out of hockey, because there are a bunch of out and closeted guys, and the more acceptance there is from the league, the more it will attract queer players. I … I want to be part of that."

"I don't want you being targeted."

"I won't be. I'm sure there'll be people with things to say, but I don't care about them. My team and my boyfriend have my back. I hope my family does as well."

"Well, yeah, of course," Dad says. "You always have our support, but I want you to think about this. Don't make the decision lightly."

"I haven't. I've been thinking about it for a really long time, and I wanted to let you know first."

There's silence for a moment. "Okay. You're a grown man, and you know what you're doing," he says gruffly. "Anyone who gives you shit, you send them to see me."

I laugh at the thought of my fifty-five-year-old dad, who's barely five ten and one hundred and seventy pounds, still trying to scare off bullies for me. "You're the best. Both of you are."

"Yeah, we know."

Mom jumps in. "So what's his name? When do we get to meet him?"

"Well, if we're together in the off-season"—I slap the wooden coffee table before realizing what I'm doing—"we'll fly down then. But, ah, you already kind of know him."

"We do?"

I clear my throat. "Ezra Palaszczuk."

There's silence.

"The one you hate?" Mom asks.

"Hate-d. Past tense."

"Oh," Dad says.

"So the tabloid gossip is true?"

"Ma, you read that trash?"

"It was about my son!"

"Wow." I don't want to know what sort of stories she's come across. "Yes, it's true. Now I'm gonna let you go so I can get ready for my date. I'm sure the tabloids will have even more to tell you after tonight."

"Good luck," Dad says.

"I don't need luck. I have Ezra."

Later that afternoon, I text Ezra to dress nice and let him know I'll be by in an hour to pick him up. He agrees immediately, but I refuse to tell him why.

It doesn't deter him from going all out though, because when he answers his door, wearing a navy velvet suit, the man takes my goddamn breath away.

"Why are you always so hot?" I ask, stepping forward to kiss him. "You're making me regret wanting to leave the apartment."

"We don't have to," he murmurs against my lips. His voice is all deep and sexy, and if tonight wasn't so important to me, I'd take him up on that offer.

I step back so I have the space I need to think clearly. "We do. I'm taking my boyfriend out."

"Really?" His gaze sweeps over me, and when his stare lands on my tie, he smiles. "I don't think I've ever seen you wear anything other than black."

My hand smooths over the silk self-consciously. "Red's good luck, right?" Because okay, *maybe* I do need a little of it.

"Anton Hayes, is that superstition coming from you?"

"I'm more stacking the cards in our favor."

"Admit it, I'm rubbing off on you."

I snort. "You would be if I let you. But ... no. Tonight we keep our clothes on. We're going to be attracting enough attention as it is."

"You? Willingly attracting attention?" Ezra presses his hand to my forehead. "Are you okay, or have you been taken over by aliens? Blink twice if it's the aliens."

"I'm taking my boyfriend to dinner." I drop my voice. "And I don't plan on hiding it."

Ezra's face lights up. "You're sure?"

"Completely."

I'm not as nervous as I thought I would be. Ezra keeps his hand on the back of my neck as I drive, and when we pull up to the valet and I hand over my keys, he catches my eyes and I know what he's saying.

Last chance to back out.

Instead, I take his hand. "Let's go cause a scene."

CHAPTER THIRTY-ONE

EZRA

Anton makes a *pfft* noise. It's not the first one he's made since parking his ass next to me on my couch twenty minutes ago. He's scrolling through his phone, something he has been constantly doing since our date last week.

We went out, we held hands over the top of the dinner table, we waved to fans and signed some stuff on the street, and then we came home, where Anton proceeded to wait for his life to implode.

It hasn't.

The rumors still run rampant, but they haven't changed much. They're all speculation and no substance.

"Are we going to have to have sex in public for them to get it?" Anton asks.

"Or … and hear me out … You could *tell them* we're together instead of hoping someone else confirms it for you."

"I didn't want to make a big deal of coming out."

"I know, but this isn't working. I still don't care either way, and I understand you not wanting to address it directly, but—"

"What if I get a tattoo across my forehead that says *I'm with Ezra*? They'll have to assume which Ezra because your last name won't fit."

"You could get it across your ass. *Property of Palaszczuk.* Then you can walk around without pants. I won't be complaining."

"Let's save that for plan B."

"What's the new plan A? Because even I'm a no on public sex and being arrested."

Anton hums. "I don't know yet."

I wrap my arm around him. "However you do it, I don't care. If you're second-guessing, that's okay too. Maybe the moment will present itself. Ooh, sex tape."

"Not on your life."

"We could at least kiss in public."

"Nah, I don't like that either."

"Why not?"

"Because when I kiss you, I want to do other things to you—things we *can't* do in public."

"Maybe I'm having second thoughts, and we should revisit the coming out sex idea."

"Let's make that plan C."

"Hey, if it's on CCTV, we can knock off sex tape and plan C in one go."

"No sex tape."

I sigh. "Fine. However you decide to do it, I'll support you. This is your moment, and I'll go along with whatever you want."

Anton squeezes my thigh. "This is *our* moment."

I lean in and whisper, "I don't know if you know this, but I'm already out." I mock gasp. "Shocking."

He shoves me. "I mean that it's not just me coming out. This will blow back on both of us."

"I think the only blowback I'll get is accusations of being taken over by some body-snatching-type thing.

Ezra Palaszczuk in a …" I gag. "Relationship? Gay men around the country will be crying."

"In sympathy for me?"

"I think you should leave being funny to me. I'm better at it."

Anton kisses my cheek. "You think you're better. There's a difference."

I tackle him on the couch and climb on top of him to straddle his waist. "I can show you how I'm better."

"Better at being funny? By having sex with me? Hmm, yeah, I can—"

I cover his mouth with my hand. "Ha ha ha, I'm bad at sex. You're soooo funny. See, this is why you should leave it to me. In the meantime …" I snake my free hand between us and rub his cock over his pants. "Think we have time to get off before we have to get to the arena for the game tonight?"

Anton reaches above him to grab his phone and check the time. "Maybe if we jerk off with the urgency of teenagers."

"Challenge accepted."

He shoves down our sweats while I spit on my palm and then wrap it around both of us.

I'm not going to lie, since our streak was broken, there might be a teeny-tiny voice in the back of my head saying this could be bad luck, but we've proven since then that we can fuck and have good games or bad games. I know, logically, the actual sex has nothing to do with whether we win or lose, but going into games being scared of losing is when it'll most likely happen.

Head games are the worst, which is why I do all my superstitious crap. If I have any seed of doubt, I'm too distracted and not focused on what I should be—hockey.

And when we do lose, I need to acknowledge that it's not because a black cat walked by or not because one of the team walked under a ladder or opened an umbrella inside. It's because it's the game.

Anton grips the back of my hair and pulls my head down to touch my lips to his. He drinks me in while I stroke us fast and hard.

I spill first, the taunt about beating him getting swallowed by him moaning into my mouth and then coming right there with me.

Cum splashes between us, our kisses get sloppy and slow, but when I eventually slump on top of him, he doesn't even give me the chance to recover.

He slaps my ass. "Come on. We have to go, or Coach will ream us for being late."

"I'd never let Coach ream me. The only person who's allowed to ream me is you."

"Aww. Thank you. I think."

"You're totally welcome. This ass is yours now."

Anton grabs a handful of it. "Mm, maybe you should get the ass tattoo, then."

"Ooh, matching tattoos!"

"Okay, I was joking, and now I'm terrified you thought I was serious."

I finally climb off him, and we clean up and get ready to head across the street to the arena.

We've been arriving to games together more and more, but still no one picks up on it.

We're playing against Edmonton tonight, who are having a really good season so far, so even though it's a home game and that goes in our favor, it doesn't mean shit when both teams have been playing well.

I expect it to be a huge scramble and fight for the win, but the minute we get out there, it's like my blade is magnetized. I'm intercepting passes, stripping the puck, and staying out of the sin bin while I do it.

Not only that, but Anton's on one of his scoring streaks, and Edmonton's goalie is having an off night.

By the time we head into the third period, Anton's got two goals under his belt, I have one, and Larsen and Diedrich have one apiece.

The score is 5-2, and even though that's a decent lead, we're not going to let it get to us in the last period.

A three-goal difference is nothing.

When we're sent back out there though, our lead becomes four when Larsen passes back to me and I take a slapshot that flies past everyone and right by the goalie. Then it feels like I blink and Anton is scoring again.

I practically tackle him to the ice.

It's my man's third hat trick of the season already.

Anton might not be able to say that us being together is good for our game, but we have to admit, it's not bad for it. We're both having our best season.

I'm starting to think we should've been on the same team all along. Think of all the Stanley Cups we could've won.

If I wasn't so superstitious, I'd say we have a good chance at one this season. But I won't say that. I'm not as reckless as Anton.

We leave the ice victorious and on a high that never gets old, even after the countless wins I've walked away with in my career.

When we get to the locker room, our PR manager flags down both Anton and me for the press conference, so we strip out of our gear and into our B's shirts and head for the press room.

We're led to the podium and take our seats next to each other.

I run my hand through my hair that's still damp with sweat and take a sip of the bottled water they've put out for us.

The first question gets fired off. "At the start of the season, it was said Anton Hayes's trade could be the smartest thing the B's have ever done or the dumbest. What do you both think about that now?"

"Well, we're winning, so of course we think it was smart," I say, the attitude I'm known for slipping through.

Anton's response is much more dignified. "The trade was a risk for all involved, but I can say without a doubt, it was the best move for my career. I'm having the best season I've ever had."

Another reporter adds, "You got your third hat trick for the season tonight, including that impressive five-goal game you had against Colorado, and we're not even halfway through the season yet. Do you see yourself breaking records this year?"

I slash at my throat. "Dude. Don't jinx the poor man."

Half the room laughs, including Anton.

Then, totally casual like he's done it a million times, Anton reaches for my hand. "Ignore my boyfriend. He's the superstitious type."

My eyes widen, but he keeps going.

"But I do know I wouldn't be having such a great season if he wasn't there on the ice with me."

I don't think this has ever happened before ... but I'm completely speechless.

CHAPTER THIRTY-TWO

ANTON

I reach over and close Ezra's mouth. "Don't worry, he's usually shocked into silence around me."

There're hesitant chuckles as my news seems to seep through the room. I hadn't been planning on saying that, but a second before I said the word, it felt right.

And now it's finally out there, just like I wanted it to be.

When I watched Caleb Sorenson and Ollie Strömberg address the media when they came out, I felt sorry for them. It felt like they'd been forced into letting people into a part of their lives that no one had business knowing, but now, sitting here myself, I don't feel trapped.

I'm free.

"When did this start?" a reporter asks.

"It's been a while now, but if you don't mind, we're keeping details of our relationship private."

"Do you worry about how the relationship will affect your games?"

"I'm the highest point scorer this season, what do you think?"

"Does this mean you're gay?" someone else asks.

"I am. I'm gay, Ez and I are together, and no matter what happens there, it isn't going to impact our team.

We're both professionals who have a job to do, and nothing will change that."

I keep expecting Ezra to jump in with a smartassed comment, but when I finally glance over at him, he's sitting back watching me, soft smile on his face. It makes my heart flip for a second, and I badly want to reach for him, but even though I can now, even though people know about us, I do want things to stay private. Right now, we're teammates. The second we're off the clock, he's my boyfriend, my partner in crime, the man who's helping me discover a lot of things about myself.

"Given Ezra's past history, fans will have a right to be worried that if there's a breakup, the team will suffer."

Before I can jump in and tell the guy to mind his business, Ezra leans forward. "It's no secret I like to have fun, but rest assured Anton has that more than covered."

I whack him lightly on the back of his head as he starts to laugh, and apparently that's enough for Coach.

He stands. "If there's no more questions about hockey, these two have a game to celebrate."

Voices and questions start to fire at us, but Coach gestures for us to get up and leave. We follow him off the platform and out of the room, and the second we're in private, he turns on us, hands on hips.

"You had to say that last thing, didn't you, Palaszczuk?"

"I might be in a relationship, but I'm still the same guy. You really should have expected something like that."

Coach sighs. "People are gonna be worried about you two breaking up when what they should be worried about is how big your damn egos will get when you're spurring each other on."

"Egos?" I pretend to be offended. "Would we call it an ego when it's totally justified?"

"Don't worry, babe," Ezra says. "He's jealous of how awesome and talented we are."

Coach lets out a string of swear words and what sounds like a cry for help under his breath. "Go celebrate. And stay away from the media for a couple of days. They'll be looking for you two."

Ezra shrugs. "Apparently the way I want to celebrate was plan B ... or C? And according to Anton, it can't be done in public, so I think we're going to head home."

"Right-o. Good game tonight."

"Thanks," I say at the same time as Ezra says, "Duh."

Coach throws his hands up and walks away.

I turn to Ezra. "You know, no matter what he says, I think you'll always have me beat for being the most egotistical player in the NHL."

"And the sexiest?"

"Nah, I have that tied up."

He narrows his eyes, but then his gaze runs down my body. "Damn it, I think you're right."

I step closer and pull him into my arms, every muscle relaxing as he squeezes me back.

"I'm proud of you."

I want to give him shit on reflex, but it's nice to hear. "Thanks. It actually felt good."

"You know what else feels good?" His hand trails down to grab my ass.

I laugh and pull back, then cup his face so I can kiss him. "We almost had a serious moment there, Ez."

"I know, close call."

"Appreciate it," I say dryly. "But to risk being serious again for a second, you don't know what it means that you were with me in there."

"Of course. We're a package deal. Your shit is my shit and vice versa. You're lucky I'm so incredibly low-maintenance that you won't have to support me through anything."

I grin. "Including meeting my parents?"

"Ah …"

"And I wanna meet yours one day."

Ezra cringes. "Have you been listening to any of my stories about them?"

I drop a kiss on his nose. "I have. Package deal, remember? You don't need to deal with that alone."

"Careful. You're dangerously close to being too perfect, and I don't think I can compete with that."

"Don't worry. There was never any competition anyway." Because he'll always have me beat.

He pulls back to take my hand as we make our way back to the locker room.

I'm not expecting our whole team to still be there waiting.

Close to twenty guys look up when we enter.

Ezra bows. "I know, you do have me to thank for the epic win. Tonight was all on my shoulders, you're welcome."

Kosik throws a towel at him. "You two are dating?"

"Oh, that." Ezra waves him off. "That doesn't seem anywhere near as exciting as the two goals I scored tonight."

"Are you forgetting who got a hat trick?" I ask.

"Yeah, but you're supposed to get those. Honestly, it's sort of embarrassing how few of those you have."

"Talk to me at the end of the season when we're taking out the Stanley Cup, and we'll see if you still think that."

I'm met by groans from nearly everyone in the room, and Ezra slaps a hand over my mouth. "It's like you want us to fail."

"Early vacation?" Luckily, my reply is muffled by his hand. He lets me go when he thinks I can be trusted. "I'll let you punish me later."

Larsen throws his hands up. "There are two of them. This is going to be unbearable."

Diedrich points at me. "Remember the rules. No kissing and telling. And this time, it's not even because you're talking about a dude. It's because you'd be talking about Ezra, and—" He shudders.

"No one needs to hear that," Kosik finishes.

"But I'm cool to give details?" Ezra asks innocently. "Since it'd be about Anton, that makes it totally fine."

"Same rules for you," Diedrich says. "Always same rules, especially for you. None of us need the types of visuals you're capable of coming up with."

I cross my arms. "I'm beginning to think they're under the impression that I'm innocent."

"With the things you did to me last night, you have nothing to worry about."

Kosik covers his ears, while Larsen points at Ezra with a solid "No."

We both laugh, and I hold up a hand. "Promise that's it. From both of us."

"I don't promise," Ezra says.

"That ball gag is still an option. You don't need your mouth to play hockey."

"No, but I do need it for other things."

Good argument. "You know what, I can't be held responsible for what Ezra says."

A few of the guys grab their bags to head out. They pat us on the back as they pass and say they'll see us later.

A handful hang back, and Diedrich smiles.

"I knew there was something going on."

"I figured you did," Ezra says.

"What?" It's the first I'm hearing of that.

"The pranks. Suddenly getting along …"

Kosik jumps in again. "Ezra spooning me to send you the photo. It all makes sense."

"You knew too?" I ask.

"Nah, but now I do, I'm seriously concerned for your guys' mating ritual."

Ezra slings an arm around my waist. "Trust me when I say that's not something you need to worry about."

Diedrich's teasing expression turns serious. "I'm not saying this to be a dick, but I am worried."

"Yeah, I get it," I say. "We have … history. That makes it hard. But if it helps, I'm prepared to stick it out for as long as he'll have me."

"In that case, you better not die first, because I won't be done with you, and then things will get dark," Ezra says.

"Maybe I should have said for as long as he'll have me or I die. Whichever comes first."

"It's an important distinction to make."

Diedrich shakes his head with amusement. "I'm guessing you feel the same, Palaszczuk?"

He looks at me. "Eh."

"Eh?" I echo.

"I mean, you have a nice butt."

"A nice butt?"

"And I suppose it's sorta cute when you get those frown lines when you're thinking."

"Did you just ... say I have wrinkles?"

"Don't be stupid."

"Okay ..."

"The wrinkles are around your mouth."

I rub my temple. "Amendment number two is as long as he'll have me, I die, or he gets so annoying I spontaneously combust."

Ezra nods sagely. "That's fair."

"You guys have the old married couple thing down pat," Kosik says.

Marriage?

Ezra and I look at each other. Our eyes lock, and somehow I know we're both on the same page when it comes to our future.

We burst out laughing.

"Ah, maybe in theory, but I don't think marriage is for me."

"Or me," Ezra says.

Larsen pulls a face. "It's still so weird to see you two agree. Even on something like not wanting to marry each other."

I don't point out that Ezra and I are getting good at agreeing. Like whose apartment to stay at and who gets to top, which of us needs to buy the lube when we're running out ...

We grab our bags and follow the others out.

"You guys coming for drinks?" Diedrich asks.

"Actually, I think we're going to head home tonight."

After that press conference, I don't need to explain why.

All I want is some time alone with Ezra.

We go our separate ways, but Ezra and I cross the street holding hands. The media is still lurking, and I'm sure they get some shots of it, but I don't care.

When we reach the safety of inside and get on the elevator, I lean against the back wall and tug him close. "You know I mean it, don't you? That this is it for me."

"Yeah. And I meant what I said as well. You really do have a nice butt."

"Ezra …"

"Fine." His voice drops so it's raw and husky. "I love you."

"You know I love you too, right?"

"Actually, I do. And I've never said that before, because it's not something I feel lightly, and I never let myself be vulnerable around people. But I let you see all that, and it doesn't make me embarrassed. You don't make me feel like I need to hide that side of me or be someone else. You and me, Anton, we don't need to justify this for anyone else, because we know what it is."

"Oh yeah? And what's that?"

There's no hesitation as he answers me with one perfect word. "Forever."

EPILOGUE

EZRA

STANLEY CUP FINAL

If anything, Anton's game only got stronger after our relationship became public knowledge. Ollie Strömberg and Caleb Sorensen might be known as the first out players, but Anton and I will forever be known as the first couple in the NHL. And if we take out the game tonight, we will also be the first couple to win the Stanley Cup.

As we hang out in the visitor locker room before we need to get ready, I can't help thinking the odds are stacked against us. We're fighting it out with Vegas, in Vegas, in the longest seven-game series of my life. Three of the games, Vegas won easily. The other three were hard-fought, two of which were won in overtime. Vegas has sailed through the playoffs, while we've had to fight tooth and nail just to be here.

After our great regular season, the playoffs have almost killed us. Every single game, we pulled the win out of our asses. Somehow. Making it this far has been nothing short of a miracle.

I know better than to go into this with a defeated attitude, but it's hard to tune out.

The voice inside my head trying to psych me up reminds me that Vegas might've had it *too easy*. We could use that to our advantage if we're smart.

Some of the guys are stretching in the weight room, and others are sitting near their cubbies, trying to get in the zone. That's where I am too, but my phone buzzes in my pocket.

Normally, I wouldn't piss off the team by taking it, but when I see who the video call is from, I know they won't mind.

I hit the Answer button and yell out to everyone. "Hey, guys, say hello to Westly."

There're rounds of shouting from all angles of the locker room along with a few "We miss you."

I face the phone back toward me. "Aww, they love you."

"No," Diedrich yells. "It's that Ezra is more tolerable when West is around."

"What about me?" Anton asks.

"If anything, Ezra has been a bad influence on you," Diedrich says.

I take that as a compliment. "That's true. Anton's not so uptight anymore. Not since he's been getting the—"

Anton's hand slaps over my mouth. Then he leans in so West can see him. "Hey, West. One day, you really need to teach me how to shut this guy up."

"You know one way," I mumble.

He releases me. "Huh?"

"Nothing."

"I thought so." His big palm pats my leg. "I'm gonna go stretch."

"Good luck tonight," West calls out to him.

"Is that why you're calling? To wish my boyfriend good luck? What about me?"

West winces. "Is it still way too weird hearing you say *boyfriend*. I don't like it. It's *unnatural*."

"That sounds mildly homophobic of you, Westly Ann Dalton."

"Ann is not my middle name. Also—" He gives me the finger. "It's not because you're two guys. It's because you're *you*. Last summer, you couldn't even say relationship without calling it a *thingy*."

"Well, I did say you and Jasper were so cute it made me want a relationship thingy. So I went out and got one."

West shakes his head and mutters, "So unnatural."

"Love you too, brother."

A low growl comes through the phone.

"Ah. Jasper's there, I'm guessing?" I yell, "I mean in a platonic way, dude! You might find Westly's boyish good looks attractive, but I need my men to be rugged, manly men who don't faint at the sight of blood."

"Okay, on that note, I'm going to go," West says. "I just called to wish you good luck and to apologize for not being able to be there."

"It sucks you'll miss out on this year's queer collective meetup. You're going to miss Anton's initiation."

"I know. I wish I could be there, but—"

"You have a billion kids. I get it."

West's gaze flicks off-screen, and when his bright green eyes meet mine again, they hold something like regret, but I know for a fact Westly doesn't regret retiring to be with his family.

"This was our dream," West says solemnly. "I might not have made it, but you will. Drown out everything around you, and do what you do best."

The need to lighten the mood hits like it always does. "I don't think I can have sex on the ice. That won't win us the game. I should focus on what I do second best."

"I can't even with you …"

"Sure you can because I'm me, and you're you."

West smiles. "Go win this thing."

"No pressure."

"Hey, you've gotten further than any other year you've played. Even if Tripp doesn't let a single puck past him tonight and you walk away empty-handed, you've played in a Stanley Cup final. You've worked hard for this."

I have. This is what I've been working for since my dad put me in my first pair of skates before I could even walk properly. He called me last week, but I didn't answer it because nothing's changed. Even after swearing at him, the only times he has made contact were to tell me what I've done wrong on the ice. I've let his calls go to voicemail ever since.

His latest was to tell me he'll be here tonight. It almost makes me want to throw the game because I know, without fail, if we win tonight, he'll want his photo op.

I'll do it for him to keep family drama out of the press, but that's all the time I have for him.

He might have been in the NHL for five years, but he wasn't able to make a big name for himself. Still, whenever I succeed, he'll ride those coattails as much as he can. He's the reason I'm so good at what I do. He's the reason I am where I am today if you ask him.

If anything, the pressure he used to put on me as a child could've crippled any desire I had to play in the NHL. It's lucky I love the game more than I hate him.

Both of my parents love to brag about their NHL-playing son, but neither of them wants to be an active part of my life. I have no delusion that winning tonight will change any of that.

And where I used to despise it, in the last couple of months I have realized that I'm worth more than that. People always make a big deal about not turning your back on family. You respect your elders, and cutting people out of your life is wrong, but putting up with toxic relationships because you share DNA with someone is way too stressful, and I don't know why people do it. I can't believe I did it for so long.

I'm worthy of healthy relationships. It *is* possible to love me.

Just ask Anton and his family.

Anton's parents are nothing like mine. They drove up to North Carolina when we played there. They seemed so loving and caring even if they had reservations about Anton and me being out. And when they said, "We don't want either of you to be hurt," I almost damn near cried because no one has ever cared about me before.

Maybe Westly has, but not … not like that. In one meeting, I felt closer to Anton's parents than I ever have my own.

Anton comes back from stretching as Coach walks in to give us his pep talk before telling us to suit up.

My leg bounces while Coach tells us to go out there and play the game of our lives.

Anton places his hand on my thigh and squeezes, trying to reassure me and calm my nerves. "We've got this," he says quietly so he doesn't interrupt Coach.

I really hope so.

It's just another game.

One more win. That's all we need.

It's not the end of the world if we walk away empty-handed.

Only, no matter how many times I tell myself that, my stupid inner voice reminds me that this isn't just one more game.

It's the fucking Stanley Cup.

—

Heading into the third period, the score is two apiece. Vegas scored early in the first, and we followed it up with a goal of our own. Then when we scored in the second, they turned around and evened it up. It's like neither team is willing to let the other get away with holding a lead.

Now we need to seal the deal.

I was really hoping Anton would get his sixth hat trick for this season and put him on a very short list of guys who have done that, but at this rate, he'll have to be happy with the amazing five he did get. There are still only thirty or so players on that list.

Time ticks down, and neither team manages to put one past the goalies. Both Tripp and Griffith are having a tight game.

I swear every time we've gotten remotely close, Tripp gets bigger and takes up the whole net.

In between plays, I skate past him. "Come on, man, you guys won three years ago. Give us something. Please."

Tripp laughs. "You know I'm immune to your begging, dude. Try harder."

And try harder, we do. We manage to spend a chunk of time in our zone, taking shots on goal and getting shut down every time.

I may love Tripp Mitchell to death off the ice, but holy shit, I want to break one of his legs. Or his arms. Either one. I want him to not be so damn good. Just long enough for one of the B's guys to score.

Then, with only a couple of minutes left on the clock, Dex intercepts a pass between Diedrich and Larsen.

Dex comes flying at Kosik and me, but Kosik and I have played defense together for a long time now. We make sure to keep his path blocked while getting ready to break off if Dex passes to one of his wingers.

He doesn't.

He tries to split us, but Kosik and I hold strong.

Dex gets so close, I can see his smirk, and that's when I know things are about to go downhill.

He looks like he's about to take his shot. Griffith throws himself on the ice, while Kosik and I create a wall the puck can't get through. But instead of shooting, Dex passes to Walker.

There's a practically empty net, and Walker is in prime position to score.

Fuck, fuck, fuck, fuck, fuck.

This is it.

This is the end.

There's no way Kosik can get in position to block the bullet Walker is about to unleash.

Then, as if in slow motion, Walker pulls back for a killer slapshot, but on the follow-through, Anton gets in the puck's way. It bounces off his pads, and then it's an all-out scramble to take possession.

Diedrich gets to it first but is shoved from behind. Then there's a mess of bodies, and I lose sight of the puck, but as soon as it gets loose, I'm on top of it. So is Vegas though.

I crash into Selby but come out victorious when the puck hits my blade.

Anton has already detangled himself from the others, and I quickly pass to him.

And then he's on the breakaway of his career. Anton shoots before the Vegas guys gain on him.

Tripp raises his glove as he does the splits, trying to protect as much of the net as he can, but it's no match for Anton's shot.

When the lamp lights up, I almost fucking cry. If I really wanted to make a scene, I'd kiss the hell out of my boyfriend right here on the ice.

But I won't. Because Anton might be out now, but he's still private. Instead, I practically crush him in a hug.

The team celebrates until Anton reminds us it's not over yet.

"Don't let these guys tie up the score again. I for one am sick of overtime."

What's even worse is Coach calls Kosik and me off, so all I can do is sit back and watch.

I swear the clock has never moved slower, and for the full one and a half minutes, I hold my breath.

Anton looks cool under pressure out there. He's confident. But I can't help that my superstitious side is in overdrive. I can't celebrate yet.

We haven't won yet.

Why the fuck is one second so slow let alone ninety of them.

When the final buzzer sounds, a weight lifts off my chest. While everyone else jumps over the railing to celebrate, I'm slow to respond.

I shake it off and storm the ice, looking for the one teammate I want most. And when our eyes lock, Anton flies toward me like a bull on skates. We almost topple over when we slam into each other, but somehow, we manage to stay upright. Then Anton does something he's never done before.

He kisses me in front of twenty thousand people and a shit ton of cameras.

What do you do when your lifelong dream comes true?

You create new dreams.

EPILOGUE

ANTON

STANLEY CUP CELEBRATIONS

The night is a blur. The game, the crowd, winning. I still can't believe it.

Seeing that Cup, being on the team presented with it, and watching Diedrich carry it into the locker room and lift it into the air …

The celebration with the team is over-the-top and manic. We all drink from the Cup before Diedrich puts his newborn baby in it. I would've spent all night drinking from it had that not happened. After that, all I could think about was how many babies had been placed in that thing and how many had pooped in it.

It's almost midnight before we finally leave the locker room, heading out. The team is meeting at a bar on the Strip, but before Ezra and I join them, we've got a stop to make first.

Ezra and I hold hands in the elevator the whole way to the rooftop of the hotel Tripp said to meet them at.

When the doors open, obnoxiously loud cheers come from one of the rooftop cabanas, and the first person I see is Tripp standing in the entrance, pumping the air with both fists.

"You're a lot happier than I was expecting you to be," I say as he attacks Ezra with a hug.

"Don't get me wrong, I'm pissed you guys won." He's smiling though, so he's obviously not *too* pissed. "But a queer collective win is a very close second to winning ourselves. A gay *couple* just won the Stanley Cup. That's epic!"

Ezra shrugs. "Clearly the only reason I'm dating Anton. Leveling up from awesome to epic is my destiny."

We join the others in the cabana, and even though I still don't know these guys all that well, it feels like coming home. Foster, Ollie, Oskar, and Tripp are here, but Soren and West are both missing. Ayri still isn't sure if he wants to join, but I do.

And as if Tripp can read the thoughts going through my head, he asks, "You finally in, Hayes?"

"Yep," Ezra answers for me. "Tonight is his initiation."

Ollie claps his hands, grin stretching across his face. "Perfect. It's been a while since I've had some Macallan."

"Macallan?" I ask, looking around at them all.

"It's a queer collective tradition. When you join us, you solemnly swear to never take a sip of Macallan outside of an initiation."

That's definitely not what I expected. Or, not all I expected. "That's it?"

"Oh, and you have to buy the bottle."

"Of course I do." But hey, what's a few thousand dollars when I've just won the Stanley Cup? "You know, this is a thousand percent tamer than what I was imagining."

Oskar snorts. "We're not a frat. We're a group of highly sophisticated gentlemen," he says with a shitty British accent.

"Who like to beat the crap out of other guys at work," Foster adds.

"Can you blame me for picturing the worst when Ezra is in charge of these things?"

He pats my arm seriously. "If you're that distressed over getting off easy, I can paddle your ass later."

"That's what he said," Ollie mutters.

"I'm starting to understand why Ezra loves you guys so much." I leave to buy the expensive-as-fuck alcohol, and I get the feeling there's a good chance Ezra and I will be puking by the time the night is over. Tripp joins me at the bar to help carry the glasses.

"No Dex tonight?" I ask.

"He wanted to come, but I said it was for the collective."

"Why?"

"This is my space. Maybe that sounds a bit childish, but the next hour or so is for us. That's sacred. I'll catch up with him later."

I can read the subtext in his words though. He needs space. I have no idea how long he's been in love with Dex for, but I bet it can't be easy.

His mood lightens considerably when we get back to the cabana, and it's like our own oasis on top of the world. The lights from the Strip are all around us, soft music playing and mixing with the laughter and conversation around us.

We pour the Macallan for everyone, but as I go to take a sip, Ezra's hand catches my arm.

"You're forgetting the most important part of the initiation."

"I knew there had to be more to it."

He pats my hand. "It's just a toast, calm down."

"A toast?"

"Yep. All you have to do is lift your glass and say 'Hey'o, I'm gay'o.'"

"Or however-you-identify'o," Foster adds. "Because I'm bi."

"'Hey'o, I'm bi'o' sounds like you're saying *you're science*," Ezra says. "And it doesn't rhyme."

I lift my glass. "Cheer'o to being queer'o? Is that inclusive?"

Ezra's eyes soften toward me. "You're perfect."

"I know."

We all cheers and drink down the extremely expensive whiskey that tastes like regular whiskey. At least to me.

"You know," Ezra says after a few moments. "One day, when we have a queer member in every team in the league, we'll need to book out the whole rooftop. Now that's a goal."

Ollie shifts. "Well, you might need to start looking for someone new to cover New York."

"What?" I lean forward, pretty sure I know where this is going but not wanting to hear it anyway. NHL players, we're all for the sport. It's our lives. So when someone brings up the "r" word, I feel it in my soul, because I know that's going to be me one day. To have to walk away and leave this part of my life behind.

Well ... I glance at Ezra. *Part* of it behind. With any luck, Ezra will be right there alongside me.

"I've got one year left on my contract," Ollie says, "and I don't think I'm going to renew it."

"What will you do?"

"Lennon was talking about creating my own hockey segment on his sports show. I don't know if being on TV is for me, but I'd love to give it a try."

"That's awesome."

Ezra lets out a long sigh. "Whose ass am I going to check out when we play New York now?"

He gives me an evil look, and I squeeze his thigh in warning.

"I think the right answer here is your boyfriend's," Tripp answers, and the others laugh.

"Real talk though." Ezra leans forward. "NHL or not, you're queer collective for life. Same as Soren. Same as any of us. We don't need to replace you because while you might not be a hockey player anymore, you'll still be one of us."

He and Ollie share a smile. The kind that can only be understood by them. Ollie and Soren were first, but Ezra wasn't far behind them. He came out after being signed to his first team. They only ever had each other, and I understand why he needed this. Why we all do.

"Better make it one hell of a last season, then," Foster says.

Ollie lifts his glass. "Cheers to that."

We all tap our drinks together, but then Tripp lets out a loud groan.

I turn in the direction he's looking and see Dex heading right for us. At the look on his face, Tripp goes from annoyed to concerned in a second flat.

"What's wrong?" There's an edge to his voice that sounds like he's ready to attack whoever made Dex look so dejected.

Dex steps up into the cabana, takes Tripp's glass, and downs the entire contents.

"Fuck, Dex," Ezra says. "You don't shoot this shit. You're supposed to sip it."

"What's the point?" He slumps into Tripp's side and face-plants into his shoulder.

I exchange a look with Ezra.

"Ah, Dex? What's up, buddy?" Ezra asks.

"Jessica."

Tripp immediately scowls. "What's she done now?"

"She used the '*I*' word again."

I'm confused. "Idiot?"

"*Irresponsible.*" Dex looks up to pout at Tripp. "Is it true? Am I an irresponsible fuckboy who will never be ready to get married? I can commit." The panicked look on his face and the way he tugs at his collar says otherwise. "I can—could. If I wanted to. Obviously."

"Uh-huh." Tripp pats his head, avoiding eye contact with the rest of us.

"Hug me, Trippy." Dex pulls Tripp's arm around him and buries his face again. Tripp's eyes fall closed, and the poor guy looks in pain.

"Hey, Dex," Ezra says, standing suddenly. "You look like you could use some shots. Come get them with me."

The two of them disappear, and Tripp slumps forward, letting out a long breath.

"You okay?" I ask.

"Yep," he says, sounding more like he's trying to convince himself than us.

"You need to get over that," Ollie warns.

"I'm working on it."

"The best way to get over someone is to get under someone else," Oskar says at the exact moment one of the servers arrives to collect empty glasses and bottles from the table.

The server almost trips over himself and then turns bright red.

"Hey," Oskar says to him. "This is our man Tripp. He's a professional hockey player and is *very* bendy."

"Hi, I'm going to go die now." Tripp tries to get up, but Oskar pushes him back down on his seat.

"What do you say?" Oskar says.

The server looks back toward the bar and then to Tripp. "I get off in an hour."

As he walks away, Oskar calls after him, "I promise Tripp can get you off faster than that."

Tripp sinks farther into his seat while the rest of us laugh.

Ezra comes back, and I pull him down into my lap. I've never been more grateful to have found him than I am at this exact moment.

"What are you doing?" he asks playfully.

I press a hard kiss to his lips. "Holding my prize."

"Normally I'd call you out on being cheesy, but do go on."

I tug him down so my lips are pressed to his ear. "Remember what I said our first time together?"

"What part?"

"That when you see me lift that Stanley Cup, all you're going to think about is me fucking you."

Ezra shivers.

"Did it work?" I ask.

"No."

Well, fuck.

He pulls back and laughs at the look on my face. "Because I'm constantly thinking about it. Always. Whenever I look at you, whether you have the Stanley Cup or not."

I stroke his cheek. "Okay, I like your way better."

When he kisses me, it's softer, slower. "Want to head out soon?"

"Yeah, we should probably meet the team."

"We should ... after a celebratory quickie?"

"You're on."

"Ah, guys?" Foster says. "We can hear you."

The others shake their heads at us.

"Well then," I say, standing and taking Ezra's hand. "I guess we don't need to make an excuse to leave, then, do we?" I grab the bottle on the table. "And we'll be taking this with us. See you guys in a few weeks."

Ezra's organized a trip with them that I'm more than ready for.

We leave the way we came, hand in hand, and when the elevator doors slide closed, I step in close. "Where are we going?"

"I've got a room."

"Smart man."

"I've been telling you this the whole time." He squeezes my hand. "We're going to be celebrating for a bit, but once that's finished ... we have the whole summer. Just us. No practice, no games, no hockey."

"That sounds perfect."

"And I was thinking, since you're not in love with your place, maybe, while you look for something else, you could stay with me?"

"Move in with you?"

"If you want," he hurries to say. "No pressure. We've been basically together the whole season, and let's face it, with all this free time, I'm going to want to spend at least ninety percent of it naked, and being naked at home alone feels sort of sad—"

I cut him off with a kiss. "Let's do it."

"Yeah?"

"You're pretty great, you know that?"

His smile is huge. "You know, I distinctly remember you saying you'd never say those words."

"I can admit when I'm wrong."

"You'll be doing that a lot, then." Ezra kisses me. "But you're pretty great too, babe."

The thing is, nothing with us is guaranteed. Our careers, our teams, even the cities we live in. I want to spend as much time as I can with Ezra while I have it, so then if we are ever separated, we'll be stronger and ready to face that together too.

The NHL might be a big part of our lives now, but that won't always be the case.

Ezra will be though.

I can feel it.

No matter what happens, no matter what we go through, we're going to do it together.

Boyfriends who win Stanley Cups together stay together.

That's my superstition.

And I'm sticking to it.

Read on for a preview of *Irresponsible Puckboy* …

DEX

I'm an eternally happy person.

It's my thing.

Everyone has a thing. My best friend, Tripp, he's the sweet one off the ice but has a razor edge when he's being the best goaltender in the NHL.

I'm the one with bricks for brains who's always smiling.

Well, I'm not smiling today.

Losing the Stanley Cup to Boston last night stung like a bitch, especially when it was followed up by yet another fight with my girlfriend, but then instead of drowning my sorrows with my best friend, he ditched me for half the night. I spent most of it drinking with the team before they headed home and I holed up in an all-night diner and ate my weight in pie.

My gut is hating me for it, but not as much as my head is hating me for all that whiskey I consumed.

All I want is to go to bed and sleep it off, but she will be there. She's always there. I don't even remember when she moved in. Tripp came over one day and asked if Jessica lived with me. When I said no, he pointed out she'd redecorated and all her stuff was there. I'd never lived with someone before, but it didn't take long for me to realize the worst part of sharing your space with someone. When you fight, you can't get away. Hence the all-nighter of whiskey and pie.

Hmm. Sounds like a country song.

She called me *irresponsible*. Again. I want to be offended, but then the waitress asks if I want another slice of pie, and my stomach lets me know it regrets all of my life choices up to this point.

The thing is, I *can* be responsible. Sometimes. When it's important. I just don't see why people choose maturity when the alternative is having fun. She resents my away games, my celebrating and commiserating with the team, and my friendship with Tripp.

Jessica wants to be my whole world, and yeah, I want a relationship, a person I can spend my life with, but that can't be all I have. I need hockey, my mom, my baby sister I adore, and then there's Tripp. Tripp's my bro, and he owns a good chunk of me.

Other women have tried to come between us, and it's never worked. Without him around, everything is ... claustrophobic. Suffocating.

She doesn't understand.

Jessica mentioned a ring. *Again*. When I told her I wasn't ready for that, she got pissed, and then when I said I was going to go out with the team, that was unreasonable. She said she was leaving and to call her when I grow up, but she's threatened to leave countless times, and I don't know what to do anymore.

Would she be more forgiving of me staying out all night if we got married? I doubt it. If anything, my teammates' marriages have shown getting hitched weighs you down even more. I don't want to stand at the other end of an aisle and promise forever when everyone knows forever doesn't mean shit these days. Not for normal people, let alone NHL players.

Marriage isn't something I want, and as much as I want to blame hockey for that, I was anti-marriage even before making it into the NHL.

After my parents' divorce, Dad took off, and Phoebe and I didn't have much to do with him anymore. Mom was distraught, and we had to pick up the pieces. But then she became a serial bride, and every breakup was worse than the last. Lawyers, alimony, fighting …

Phoebe and I love our mother, but she's a disaster when it comes to love. Growing up and seeing what divorce does, both my sister and I vowed we'd never put ourselves through that.

I don't understand why it's so important to Jessica. Bragging rights? My money?

We already live together, so how would a piece of paper change anything?

Maybe I should do it and get it over with. It's important to her, but it's not to me. But then the thought of being married sends a shiver through me. How could I commit when I'm not even sure I could say "I do" without running from the church or setting myself on fire to get out of it?

I need advice, and there's only one person I trust to have my best interests at heart. I'm sure he won't mind me interrupting his hookup now. I've given them all damn night.

I leave the diner and take a car to Tripp's penthouse apartment just off the Strip.

He'll still be in bed since it's officially off-season, and it's where I'd be if not for the shitshow of a night, so I let myself in with my key.

Tripp's apartment overlooks the Wynn golf course, where we'll be spending a lot of time together this summer, and the whole living area is flooded with morning sunlight. His bedroom door is closed, so before I go barging through it, I knock loudly and shout, "Cover up, I'm coming in."

I give them a minute, then push inside.

Apparently, I wasn't loud enough, because Tripp is still fast asleep, and his hookup is staring at the door through weary eyes.

"Move over," I tell him before crawling along the middle of the bed and flopping down between them.

Tripp barely stirs, so I lean right into his face, then shout his name.

His hazel eyes fly wide as he shoots upright. "What the fuck, Dex?"

I crack up laughing even as Tripp stares at me in shock. Then his gaze slides across to the other guy.

"Fucking hell." He turns to face-plant into his pillow. All I can see is the top of his messy red hair.

"Ah, should I go?" the guy asks.

"Actually, maybe you could help." It doesn't look like Tripp is planning to resurface anytime soon, so I settle back into the pillows and tuck my hands behind my head. "I think my girlfriend broke up with me."

The guy's gaze flicks over my head toward Tripp, looking like he isn't sure what to do.

"It's fine," I tell him. "Dex Mitchale, Tripp's bestie. This is nothing I haven't seen before."

"Okay …" He adjusts the sheets around his waist and gets comfortable again. "Austin."

"You were our server last night, right?"

"Yup. So, this girlfriend. Why do you only *think* she broke up with you? Isn't that kind of thing obvious?"

"She said to call her when I grow up or whatever. So does that mean it's over for now? Or we're still together and she wants me to fix my shit before she comes back?"

He cringes. "That sounds like a breakup."

"Damn." I rub my hand over my face, thinking. "She said I was irresponsible, so if I fixed that, do you think she'd come back?"

"Why are you irresponsible?"

"How am I supposed to know?"

Tripp snorts behind me.

I turn my head to grin at him, but his face is still firmly buried. "Feel free to contribute to this conversation."

Nothing. Fine. Back to Austin, then.

Austin is staring at the window. "Look, talking emotions isn't something I thought I'd be doing the day after a hookup, so I'm a bit rusty on advice, but if you have to change for someone, it's probably not worth it."

"I think she wants to get married."

"Is that something *you* want?" he asks.

"Umm … yes? Well, no, not really, but I could want it. If it made her stop acting like a …" I cut my words off. My momma taught me to only speak nicely of women, and if I can't say nothing nice, I shouldn't talk at all.

Tripp starts to chuckle behind me and finally reappears. "There is no way you're marrying her when you can't even give a straight answer."

"You're alive!" I cheer.

He gives me a dry look, and I glance back at Austin.

"He loves me. I swear he does."

"I'd love you more if you didn't wake me at the butt crack of dawn to talk about … *her*."

"You two need to start getting along if you're going to be my best man, Trippy," I say.

"I guess I won't be your best man, then."

I gasp. "You'd let me go through that alone?"

"If you're desperate enough to force yourself to get married when you've never wanted that, then yeah. You can go through it alone."

"You're breaking my heart here."

Tripp lets out a disbelieving noise. "Go home and let us sleep, Dex."

I yawn. "That's a good idea. I'm beat. Let's all sleep and talk about this when we wake up."

Austin doesn't look ready to sleep. "Actually, as fun as this is, I'm going to head out."

"You don't have to," Tripp hurries to say.

"*Sure*," I say, trying not to be offended. "He can stay, but you're ready to kick me out. I'm feeling very unloved this morning."

Tripp's jaw tightens. "Well, I'd like my dick sucked, so if you're planning to do that, by all means, stay."

My eyebrows shoot up.

"Yeah. That's what I thought."

"You two are cute," Austin says, which dissolves my shock as I glow under the praise.

We *are* cute.

Everyone says so.

Tripp and Dex.

Dex and Tripp.

The Mitchell Brothers.

Not that we're brothers. We're closer than that.

"Thanks for last night," Austin says, his voice taking on a husky quality.

"I think I should be thanking you."

I look from one to the other. I'm no stranger to Tripp's hookups, but the way they're looking at each other, like they've got a shared secret—that I guess involves the other's dick—makes me squirm.

Then Austin leans over me and gives Tripp a soft, way-too-slow-to-be-comfortable-for-me kiss, and my eyes narrow.

"Bye." He climbs out of bed, dresses, and leaves.

I'm still staring after him when I say, "He was hot. At least, objectively. Though, he's prettier than a lot of the guys you've been with. Going to call him again?"

When Tripp doesn't answer, I turn my attention to him and find him wearing the odd look he gives me sometimes that I can never figure out.

"You're unbelievable," he says.

"Thank you."

Tripp sighs and gets comfortable again. "You okay?"

"I dunno."

"Go to sleep." His eyes drift closed. "We'll talk later."

"Tripp?"

"Yeah?"

"Can you hold me?" I wriggle closer to him.

"Fuck's sake, I'm naked under here."

"And? It's nothing I haven't seen before. Besides, the blanket is between us, so it's not like it's gay."

"Right. Because being gay would be terrible."

"You know that's not what I mean. It's just platonic snuggles."

Finally, the tension starts to leave him. "Yeah, I know."

When he finally pulls me to him, his arms are warm and comfortable. More dudes really should do this. People joke about us having a bromance all the time, but it's the best way to describe us. I love him. More than Jessica.

Tripp's my ride or die.

No one can come between a friendship like ours.

"Hey, Tripp?"
He acknowledges me with a sleepy grunt.
"It smells like sex in here."